Emily Oak's Little Black Book

LIZ DAVIES

CHAPTER 1

Ava grabbed a handful of Emily's popcorn and Emily slapped her away, little realising that she would want to slap her boyfriend – *hard* – before the evening was over. She wouldn't of course, but the temptation would be there...

'You've got your own,' Emily admonished, ignoring Ava's puppy-dog eyes.

'Yes, but yours is toffee,' Ava replied. 'Pleaeeese?'

Emily relented. She had fully expected to have to share her popcorn with her best friend, despite Ava insisting she would be perfectly happy with her salted version.

'Go on, but the next time you say you want salted, I'm going to ignore you.' She tilted the bowl towards her and Ava plunged her hand in.

'Yum,' Ava said, her mouth full. She crunched loudly.

'Shush.' Emily scowled at her. 'I can't hear the TV.'

'Sorry.' More crunching was followed by a slurp of wine.

Emily pointedly turned up the volume on the telly. She loved this film. It didn't matter that she'd watched it twenty times already. She would happily watch it another twenty – if someone would keep the noise down.

'You've hardly touched your wine,' Ava noticed. 'Don't you like it?' Her eyes widened and her mouth fell open. 'You're not pregnant, are you?'

'No, I'm not. I'm going to eat my popcorn first – *if* there's any left – then I'll drink my wine.'

'You're weird.'

'So you keep telling me.'

'I like weird.'

'That's good, considering you're my best friend and you're spending the night at my house.' Technically, it wasn't *her* house, it was Cole's, but she lived in it and they were a couple, so to all intents and purposes it *was* her house. Or as good as, and it would definitely be her house once they were married.

Which she was certain they would be, at some point. Cole would propose sooner or later, she was convinced of that. He was just taking time to get around to it.

They hadn't discussed marriage, but Emily assumed it would be the next step. After all, she had lived with him for nearly a year, which should be long enough to iron out the little niggles which living with someone else inevitably brought. No matter how much you loved a person, there was always something…

Cole had several somethings (as she herself probably did, she acknowledged) but lately the something she found most annoying was his determination to run a marathon.

It wasn't the running that irritated her, or his taking part in the event. It was the large amount of time he devoted to training, and the way he couldn't seem to talk about anything else. If he wasn't out pounding the streets, he was regaling her with how many minutes he had shaved off his time on a particular stretch of the road.

She hoped that once the marathon was over, he would have got it out of his system and would never again don a pair of running shorts – although she had to admit that he did look rather sexy in them: he had very nice legs. But her greatest fear was that he would become a serial marathon runner, and that she would become the runner's equivalent of a golf widow.

'I hope Ben doesn't get too drunk tonight,' Ava said. 'We're supposed to be going to his parents' house tomorrow. His mother won't be pleased if he doesn't eat his Sunday lunch.'

'Cole will keep him on the straight and narrow,' Emily told her confidently. 'He's planning on doing a final training run tomorrow, so he definitely won't be drinking much.'

'Oh yes, I forgot the race is next week.'

'I haven't. It's all he can ruddy well talk about.'

'Ben said he's lost a good few kilos.'

'He has.' Emily eyed the bowl of popcorn, then glared balefully at the rounded belly it was resting on. She wished *she* could lose a couple of kilos, but she didn't fancy doing the exercise to make that happen. Or cutting down on her food intake. It would be time enough to get into shape when Cole popped the question, she thought, as images of slinky wedding dresses with fishtail silhouettes floated into her mind.

'Who is leaving?' Emily asked, shovelling another handful of the distinctly moreish snack into her mouth. Cole and Ben worked for the same company and this evening they were having leaving drinks for one of their colleagues.

'One of the senior managers. He got headhunted apparently. Don't you two ever talk to each other?'

'Cole probably told me, but it must have gone in through one ear and out the other. He tends to start every conversation with marathon updates before he moves on to anything else, but by then I've stopped listening.'

'My mum used to do that with my dad.'

'Talk about marathons?'

'No, silly. Talk about stuff she knew Dad didn't have any interest in. When he switched off, she would slide in something she knew he wouldn't want to hear, and legitimately say that she had told him about it and it wasn't her fault if he hadn't been listening.'

Emily was fascinated. 'Such as?' She licked the last of the sticky toffee from her fingers and reached for her wine, taking a mouthful. Ava might think she was weird, but toffee and wine didn't mix. The intense sweetness made the wine taste funny. Even now it would take a couple more sips before the wine washed away the popcorn.

'Such as... booking a weekend away, spending a fortune on a dress, arranging for a man to cut the hedge because Dad had been promising to do it for weeks and hadn't got round to it yet. That kind of thing.'

'I don't think Cole is that devious,' Emily said. 'With him, what you see is what you get.'

'Yeah, I can't see Ben doing anything like that, either. Me, on the other hand... Let's just say I've popped that in my back pocket in case I ever need it.' Ava smirked, then fumbled for her mobile when it trilled. 'Talk of the devil, that's Ben now,' she said, staring at the screen. 'He's sent me a photo. God, he looks pissed.' She turned the phone around for Emily to take a look.

Ava was right – her boyfriend did look rather the worse for wear, and it wasn't even half-past nine yet. He would pay for that come the morning.

'Oh dear...' Emily laughed. 'So much for me saying that Cole would keep him sober.'

Ava's phone trilled again, then again. 'He's turned into a selfie addict,' she announced.

Sure enough, Ben was beaming blearily out of each photo. 'He looks like he's enjoying himself,' Emily said.

'Yeah, a bit too much. I'm so glad I'm staying here tonight – I don't think I could face putting him to bed. And what if he throws up like he did last time? Mrs Fortnum next door wasn't amused to find that her prize roses had been pebble-dashed by my boyfriend.'

Ava's phone trilled again. 'Bloody hell, he's sent me a video this time.' She scooted over to share the screen with Emily.

Emily watched in amusement as Ben's face loomed into view, then disappeared again, before coming into shot once more. The poor man was having trouble aiming the camera in the direction of his face, and looking at the state of him, Emily wasn't surprised. She hoped Cole wasn't in the same—

Emily froze.

'Play it from the beginning,' she demanded. Her heart was suddenly thumping madly and her mouth was cotton-dry.

'Do I have to? Once was bad enough. He's going to be a nightmare tomorrow.'

'Please just play it,' she begged.

Ava gave her a curious look but did as she was asked, and when Ben's face appeared for the second time, Emily swore and snatched the phone out of her friend's hand.

'I don't believe it,' she muttered.

'Believe what?'

Emily stared at the screen. Biting her lip, she went to the start of the video and played it yet again. 'There,' she said. 'What do you see?'

'Er, a load of people in a bar having a good time. *Oh…*' Ava breathed out. 'Is that who I think it is?'

'It had bloody well better not be,' Emily snarled. She played the video once more, pausing at the image of a man with a woman wrapped around him. He was snogging her face off, and although Emily could only see his forehead and his hair clearly, she knew without a shadow of a doubt that the man was Cole, because he was wearing the shirt she had bought him for his birthday. It was supposed to have been a jokey one, but he had loved it and wore it every chance he got. She would recognise those neon pink palm trees anywhere.

The woman had her back to the camera, and Emily could see Cole's hands ranging up and down the woman's spine, before cupping her pert backside with both hands.

Shaking her head and muttering, 'No, no, no,' Emily quickly scrolled through the photos Ben had sent, searching for any sign of Cole or the woman.

It didn't take her long to find one…

It was a group photo of half a dozen guys Emily didn't recognise, plus Cole, Ben and the woman. She was standing next to Cole, who was looking into the lens with a wide smile on his face, showing off his perfectly white teeth.

The woman wasn't looking at the camera, however, she was looking at Cole, and that look told Emily everything she needed to know, whether she wanted to know it or not. It was a proprietary look, not a predatory one. This woman wasn't out to get Cole – *she had already got him.*

The woman wasn't some random stranger he had met this evening who had thrown herself at him. This was someone he worked with, someone he already *knew.*

Blindly, Emily shoved Ava's mobile back at her, her eyes brimming with tears. Ava took it wordlessly and scrolled through the images again.

'Bastard,' Ava muttered. 'This isn't a drunken one-off.'

'I know,' Emily wailed. 'He's not even drunk.'

'What are you going to do?'

Emily pursed her lips to stop her chin wobbling, then said, 'I'm going to phone him.'

'And say what?' Ava's eyes were wide. 'I don't think that's a good idea. Why don't you wait until he comes home and speak to him then?'

'I want to see how deep he digs the hole. The more evidence I have, the better.' What she was going to do with it, she hadn't quite decided yet.

She dashed away the tears with the back of her hand and cleared her throat. Then taking a deep breath, she dialled his number.

'Hiya, love, just wanted to check you are having a good time,' she chirped, brightly. Her heart was thudding so hard she thought it might burst out of her chest and she could hear her pulse throbbing in her ears. But she sounded perfectly normal, as though she didn't have a care in the world. Cole would never guess she had just seen him in an amorous clinch with one of his colleagues.

'Yeah, it's good. Ben is off his face already.' Cole sniggered.

'I hope *you're* behaving yourself.'

'Of course I am – I always do, don't I? Anyway, I can't afford to get drunk, not when I've got the race next week. I want to get my final training run in tomorrow.

'Who's there altogether? Anyone I know – besides Ben?'

'Just some of the guys. No one important.'

Ava tapped her on the shoulder and pointed frantically at her phone. 'Ben's Facetiming me,' she mouthed. Careful to keep Emily out of shot, she showed her the screen. Ben's face was front and centre, but just behind him Emily could see Cole. He had his mobile to his ear and that woman sitting on his lap. Her arms were around him and she was nibbling his neck. From the way Cole was looking at her, he didn't seem to mind it one bit.

Abruptly, Emily hung up, and suddenly she was sobbing uncontrollably.

Ava's arms came around her and held her tight as she cried, smoothing her hair until eventually Emily managed to regain some composure.

And with it came the first twinges of anger.

Grasping it with both hands, she allowed it to build. How dare he do this to her! Cheating on her with someone at work? Was he so stupid that he thought she wouldn't find out?

Or maybe he didn't care!

Fresh heartache surged through her. Of course he didn't care. If he cared, he wouldn't have *looked* at another woman. But he had done more than look, and she suspected he had done more than kiss her.

Emily wanted to believe that this woman had been aware that he had a girlfriend, but she worked with him for goodness' sake, so she must know. Which meant she was nearly as much to blame as he was.

Well, she could bloody well have him! If she wanted him badly enough to steal him from under Emily's nose, then the woman was welcome to him – because if he could do it once, he could do it again. Let's see how the cow liked it when the tables were turned!

Ava was gazing at her, her expression full of sympathy. 'What are you going to do?'

'I don't know,' Emily wailed. 'But I can't stay here.'

'Of course you can't. You can stay at ours tonight, then we'll figure out what to do in the morning.'

The "we" set Emily off again. Her chin wobbled and her face crumpled. 'What about Ben?'

'He won't mind.' Ava paused. 'I wonder if he knows about Cole and this woman. I bloody hope not, because I'll skin him alive if he knew Cole was cheating on you and didn't say anything.'

'I hope he doesn't too, but even if he does, please don't give him a hard time. He probably didn't want to say anything for fear of upsetting me. And don't forget, he has to work with the cheating bastard.'

'How long do you think it's been going on?' Ava asked.

'I don't know, but she's welcome to him.' Emily blinked back tears. 'Can you help me pack?'

'You bet I can. What do you want to take?'

'Everything.'

CHAPTER 2

By "everything" Emily meant everything of hers, but it didn't take her long to realise that not much in the house actually belonged to her. She had moved in with Cole, bringing little in the way of furniture with her because she had been renting a room in a furnished house at the time and hadn't therefore owned any big items, such as a sofa or a fridge.

She'd brought some homely bits and bobs that she had bought over the years, but those had gradually been replaced by items that she had chosen to suit Cole's house. Gazing sadly at the cushions that picked out the exact same shade as the sofa, and the print above the fireplace that she'd bought because it reminded her of their first (and only) holiday together, she knew that she didn't want to take them with her. Every time she looked at them they would only remind her of Cole, their relationship, and this house. Besides, where would she put them? If she walked out now, she would be homeless, so there was little point in her taking the rag rug she had picked out for the bedroom, because she no longer had a bedroom to put it in.

She did have a suitcase though, and she climbed the ladder into the attic to fetch it. She would manage to get about a third of her clothes in it – everything else would have to be stuffed into bin bags, like so much garbage. It was an apt euphemism for her relationship.

Whilst Ava cleared Emily's side of the wardrobe, Emily tackled the dressing table and the chest of drawers, and once that was done and the case and the bags had been hauled downstairs, Emily searched the house for anything else that was hers that she wanted to take with her. There were some things stowed in the sideboard, and she added those to her workbox, and she grabbed the little collection of felted animals that she had made, which Cole despised and would probably throw in the bin if he had the chance. She made a point of taking the macramé plant pot holder because she had spent ages on it, even if it wasn't as neat as she would have liked.

Finally, hoping she hadn't forgotten anything – because she as sure as hell didn't want to come back to this house – she took a final look around.

'My jewellery box!' she cried. 'Did I pack it?'

'I put it in the case, wrapped in your cat onesie.'

Emily let out a sigh of relief. She would hate for that to go missing: it contained the pieces which had been left to her by her godmother. Lilian had left her some books too, and those were in a box in the attic. Unlike the jewellery, they didn't have any sentimental value, and although she felt a pang at leaving them behind, she hadn't taken them out of the box since she'd been given them, apart from a quick glance to check that they weren't anything personal like diaries or journals. After briefly wondering why Lilian had wanted her to have a pile of dusty old books, she had put them to the back of her mind and hadn't given them another thought.

With a lingering look at the print above the fireplace, she snatched up a last remaining felt animal which had been hiding behind her favourite photo of her and Cole, shoved it in her bulging shoulder bag, and was ready to go.

'Before we leave,' Ava said, as Emily opened the front door. 'Have you got your passport, driving licence, birth certificate…?'

Emily hefted one of the plastic bags. 'In here. I keep all my documents in one of those concertina wallet things.'

'OK, are we ready to go?'

Emily nodded. 'I'm ready.'

And with that, she lifted her chin and stalked out of Cole's house and out of his life. But not out of his heart, because she had a horrible suspicion that she'd never had a place in it to begin with.

***

An hour later Emily regarded the stuffed-to-the-brim back seat and boot of her hatchback with dismay. Where in the world amongst all these bags would she find a pair of pyjamas, never mind her toothbrush? She should have thought of that before she randomly shoved all her worldly possessions into the back of her car.

But to be fair, she hadn't been thinking straight and the last thing on her mind had been nightwear and teeth cleaning.

She still wasn't thinking straight, and she didn't expect to think straight for some time to come. So, she was taking it one teensy-weensy step at a time – and for this step she was concentrating on not going to bed naked (not in someone else's house) or sleeping in her clothes. She desperately wanted to brush her teeth too, and wash her face. She could manage the face washing part, but couldn't do much about her teeth without a toothbrush.

'Emily, what are you doing out here? Come back inside,' Ava called from the front door. Ben had only just arrived home, a taxi spilling him out onto the pavement in a drunken puddle, and Emily had slipped outside to give Ava some space to persuade her bladdered boyfriend that sleeping upstairs was better than crashing in the hall.

'You aren't thinking of going back to him, are you?' Ava demanded, picking her way down the short path in her bare feet, and wincing.

Emily hadn't, but now that Ava mentioned it, it was a possibility. She would bet her last penny that Cole wasn't home yet, and she guessed it would be at least another hour or longer before he was. She would have enough time to go home, unpack, and pretend nothing had happened.

Their relationship could carry on as it was and she would put this incident behind her, flush it from her mind. It had been a one-off, nothing more. The woman must have thrown herself at him and caught Cole in a moment of weakness. Was he home already? Had he realised that all her clothes had gone? He must be wondering what the hell was going on. She should have at least left a note...

'Um...' she began.

'Emily...' Ava trailed off, her voice loaded with pity.

Blinking back fresh tears, Emily straightened her shoulders. The last thing she wanted was pity — sympathy, yes — but she didn't want Ava to think that she was a doormat, that Cole could walk all over her heart and that she would take it.

She'd sleep on it tonight and think about it in the morning. And maybe, when Cole got home and realised that she had left him, he would beg her forgiveness.

In the meantime, she didn't have the slightest idea what she was going to do now that she was boyfriendless and homeless, so she did the only thing she could — she allowed Ava to lead her inside and dripfeed her wine so she could drown her sorrows.

***

Ben isn't the only one who is hungover this morning, Emily thought as she staggered downstairs to sit at the kitchen table and rest her poor aching head on her arms.

'Coffee?' Ava offered sympathetically.

Emily shuddered. 'Tea?' she asked. To her own ears she sounded pathetic and needy, and she vowed to pull herself together — after a cup of tea and some painkillers.

As though reading her mind, Ava placed a blister pack of tablets on the table, along with a mug of steaming tea and a glass of water. 'Did you get any sleep?' she asked.

'Not much. I think I dropped off just as the birds were waking up. Why do they have to be so bloody *chirpy*?'

A noise from above alerted them that Ben was up, and Emily listened to the slow plod of his footsteps as he made his way downstairs. She was momentarily cheered to see that he looked worse than she felt.

He did a double take on seeing them. 'Who was driving the steam roller?' he croaked. 'I think I've been run over and flattened.'

'You,' Ava replied. 'I take it you had a good time, or don't you remember?'

'I *was* having a good time, then things started to get fuzzy around the edges. I thought you were staying at Emily's last night?'

'I was, then Cole happened.' Ava pressed her lips together.

'Cole?' Ben gave Ava a grateful smile as she handed him a glass of orange juice and nudged the pack of tablets nearer. 'My head is killing me.'

'I'm not surprised,' Ava retorted. 'You were plastered. I've got the photos and the video—' she gave Emily a significant look '—to prove it.'

'Oh, heck, it's all a bit of a blur. I wasn't doing anything stupid, was I?' Ben groaned.

'Just looking gormless. Cole, on the other hand, was doing something very stupid indeed.'

'Is that why Emily is here?'

Ava nodded. 'Cole was seen kissing another woman, someone you work with.'

Ben's guilty expression told Emily that he knew all about it, and as he couldn't remember much about last night, she concluded that her suspicions were right and that Cole's behaviour wasn't an isolated incident.

'Why didn't you tell me?' she wailed.

Ava tutted, put her hands on her hips and glared at him. 'Well? Answer her.'

Looking pained, he said, 'I wasn't totally sure.'

'But you had your suspicions?' Ava was shaking her head in disbelief.

'That was all they were – suspicions. I didn't have anything concrete.'

'And even if you had, you wouldn't have said anything,' his girlfriend guessed.

'It's not that easy; I've got to work with the guy,' Ben protested.

'What about poor Emily? Can you imagine how she's feeling? She only found out because she could see him kissing this woman in that video you sent.'

'Oh, hell.' Ben winced and put his head in his hands.

Emily had been listening to the exchange with a surreal air of detachment, but she found her voice to ask quietly, 'How long has it been going on?'

Ben's gaze met hers. 'Sorry, Em. A while, I think… a couple of months. I'm not really sure. It's not as though they've been caught snogging by the water cooler.' He winced again, realising what he'd said, and repeated, 'Sorry.'

'What made you suspect he might be cheating on me?' Emily wanted to know every single detail, despite also *not* wanting to know any of them.

'They take their lunch together, and they often leave at the same time. They think they're being discrete, but I've caught them sending each other long lingering looks. Cole says they're just training buddies – she's a keen runner – but I always had a feeling there was more to it.'

Emily felt sick: *training buddies*? Is that what being unfaithful was called these days – *training*? Anger swept over her, and she wondered whether Cole had been training for a marathon at all, or whether the only marathon he had been training for was a marathon session in bed with his floozie.

'He's never mentioned a training buddy,' she said flatly.

'Sorry, Em,' Ben repeated. 'What does he have to say for himself?'

'I haven't spoken to him.' Emily could feel herself welling up again, her anger swinging back to heartache.

'And neither is she going to,' Ava snapped. 'Not after the way he's behaved. I told her she could stay here until she finds somewhere else to live. That's OK with you, isn't it?'

Ben's voice was gentle. 'Of course it is. You can stay as long as you like, Em; but don't you think you should at least talk to him?'

'And say what?' Ava demanded. 'Tell him that he's a cheating bastard, and she never wants to see him again? What good will that serve?'

'I might have got it wrong, and there hasn't been anything going on,' Ben argued.

'It's on camera,' Ava reminded him. 'They were all over each other.'

Emily flinched, and Ava said, 'Sorry hon, but it's true: they *were.*'

Ava was right, but maybe it had been a one-off. Maybe he was at home right now, staring at the empty hangers on her side of the wardrobe and regretting last night. Perhaps, despite his assurances to the contrary, he *had* actually drunk too much and had got carried away before he realised what he was doing.

Emily knew she was clutching at straws, but Ben was right. She had to talk to him: this not-knowing was killing her.

She wasn't going to make it easy for Cole, though. Cheating was cheating, no matter how much alcohol he'd had, but if he was suitably contrite and vowed never to do anything like that again, she might be prepared to forgive him. They were too good together to throw it all away because of one silly mistake.

Emily reached for her phone, ignoring Ava's disapproving glare.

Debating whether to speak to him in person, she sent him a message instead, not trusting herself not to cry. She wanted to have some semblance of control for now, although she guessed she would probably break down and ugly cry when she came face-to-face with him

Her message was brief and to the point. **We need to talk.**

His reply was immediate. **Be back later babe. No need 2 get mad. Took Ben home and crashed at his. Didn't want him to choke on his own vomit LOL x**

The lying, cheating bastard! He'd only gone and spent the night with that bloody woman!

'Arggh!' she yelled, then stamped her foot in a mixture of anger and dismay. 'Apparently, Cole spent the night *here*. He brought Ben home, and thought he'd better stay to keep an eye on him.'

'Is that so?' Ava pressed her lips together, her mouth a straight line. 'That was very considerate of him.'

'Keeping an eye on a mate because he might be sick in the night, is commendable.' Emily's voice dripped with sarcasm.

'Isn't it just.' Ava sighed and slung her arm around Emily's shoulders. 'I know you're hurting, but he's not worth it.'

'You're preaching to the choir,' Emily replied, and although she knew Ava was right, she couldn't help the awful pain in her chest. She felt as though her heart had been ripped out and replaced with a lump of red-hot lead.

Filled with outrage and disbelief, she read it again, and was wondering whether she should reply, when Ben's phone vibrated.

Ava snatched it up off the worktop, glanced at the screen and grimaced, but instead of giving it to its rightful owner, she handed it to Emily.

Emily gasped as she read the message. It was from *Cole*.

Do me a favour m8 if Emily asks I crashed at yours last night it said, followed by prayer hands and a winky face emoji.

That did it! She never, ever wanted to set eyes on that two-timing snake ever again.

If that woman wanted him, she could sodding well have him.

***

'Her name is Zelda,' Ben said sometime later, in answer to Emily's question.

After throwing her phone at the wall, sobbing through another crying fit, then checking that her phone still worked so she could block Cole's number, she had calmed down somewhat.

She was aware that knowing more about the other woman was just going to make her feel worse, but she simply couldn't help herself.

'How old is she?' she asked.

Ben shrugged. 'Dunno. Thirty, maybe?'

Around the same age as Emily herself. 'Is she single, or is she cheating on someone too?'

'Single, I think. She's never mentioned a husband or boyfriend.'

'Is she pretty? She *looked* pretty.'

'She's OK, I suppose.'

'Just OK? Cole has cast me aside for someone who is *just OK*?' Emily knew she was being unreasonable and that whatever answer Ben gave her would be wrong, but *damn it* she could understand if Cole had been taken in by a beautiful siren. *Just OK* was a hundred times worse.

Hysterically, she hummed a few bars of Dolly Parton's Jolene, before realising that Ava was giving her a worried look.

'I'm all right,' she insisted, despite it being blatantly obvious that she wasn't all right at all. 'Is she slimmer than me?' she demanded, and Ben's expression reminded her of the saying 'a deer in the headlights'. 'Never mind.'

The woman must be slim if she was running a marathon, and she had looked very slim indeed. Skinny, really. Not Cole's cup of tea…

Cole had insisted that he loved Emily's curves: 'more to grab on to,' he used to say.

Emily shoved the image of Cole's hands grabbing Zelda's peachy rounded buttocks firmly out of her mind, and took a deep breath.

That was it. She was done. She wasn't going to torture herself anymore. Besides, going over and over the events of the last few hours and the discovery she had made, wasn't going to help her going forward. She didn't have the luxury of being able to spend time licking her wounds and coming to terms with what had happened. She needed to sort herself out sharpish, because right now, despite Ava's very kind offer, Emily was homeless.

CHAPTER 3

The sun was shining directly into her eyes when Emily turned west off the A485. Forced to put the sun visor down, she squinted at the road ahead, hoping the traffic would be lighter now. Being blinded and having a crash would be the last straw in what had been the most horrid twenty-four hours of her life.

She was exhausted, but so far adrenaline had kept her going, but as she grew closer to the little village where her parents lived, weariness began to take hold. She had been on the road for five hours already, with nearly an hour still to go. The journey had been horrendous, road works at every turn, slow-moving tractors, caravans, and holiday-makers by the carload. Worcester to Glynafon in northwest Wales should only have taken four hours, and she should have been at her parents' farm by now. But at this rate she would be lucky to get there before nightfall.

Reaching the small seaside town of Criccieth, she decided to stop for a few minutes to stretch her legs. She could also do with a drink, so she pulled into a small carpark off the main street and clambered stiffly out. She had made a couple of stops so far, mainly to use the loo and stock up on water, but she had drunk the last of it a few miles back. Still dehydrated from her overindulgence last night, her mouth was dry and the headache that had been a constant companion since she had got up this morning was in danger of turning into a migraine if she didn't head it off at the pass now.

She'd spotted a convenience store further down the street, and she bought what she needed there, plus a coffee, then strolled down to the seafront to drink it.

Spotting a bench on a patch of grass on one side of a small sandy beach, she perched on it and caught her breath. Only yesterday she had been arguing with Ava over popcorn, and everything in her life was rosy.

Now look at her. She had dumped her boyfriend, made herself homeless, and was now running back to her mum and dad with her tail between her legs. The only thing she still had was her job. Thankfully her line manager was one of those approachable people who didn't mind being contacted outside of working hours. So when Emily had made the spur-of-the-moment decision to return to Glynafon, she had sent her a text asking if she could take two weeks holiday, starting tomorrow, as a matter of urgency, because something had come up.

Something had come up all right! Just not what her line manager might be envisaging. There was no death in the family (unless the death of her relationship with Cole could be classed as one) and neither was anyone ill or had been in an accident (although she felt sick to her core and her heart was in a million pieces). What had actually come up was a certain part of Cole's anatomy that she had mistakenly believed was reserved for her.

To her relief, permission had been granted, and Emily had left almost immediately she'd received it – although Ava had insisted that she eat two slices of toast before she went.

Emily checked her phone and saw that she had a couple of new messages – three from Ava and one from her mum. She dealt with the one from her mother first, because that was the easiest, telling her that she had got caught up in traffic and she'd be a while longer yet. She had called home this morning to say that she was coming to stay for a few days, but not the reason why. She'd share that nasty piece of news with her parents when she got there.

Then she phoned Ava. It would be quicker than messaging back and forth, because she wanted to get on the road as soon as she'd finished her coffee.

'Are you there yet?' Ava demanded before Emily had a chance to say a word.

'Not quite, but almost.'

'How are you?'

'Tired, stiff, headachy.'

'Not physically…'

'Heartsore. I still can't believe Cole would do that to me.'

'He's been on the phone to Ben. Ben told him that you knew, and how you found out, and Cole gave him a right earful.'

'He's unbelievable! He makes it sound as though it's Ben's fault. If Cole hadn't cheated on me in the first place… Grrr.'

'I know,' Ava soothed. 'He didn't deserve you. I hope this Zelda-woman takes him for a ride then dumps him.'

'So do I, but I bet it won't happen. He'll probably do the dirty on her with someone else.'

'Then *she'll* know what it feels like,' Ava replied loyally.

'I'd better get going. I only stopped for coffee.'

'Let me know when you arrive. I was getting worried.'

'Yes, Mum,' Emily joked. Her laugh sounded as forced as it felt.

She took a moment to finish her drink and gaze at the view. It wasn't quite six in the evening, and holidaymakers were still on the beach. The sun glittered on the rippled waters of Cardigan Bay, and in the distance was the purple sweep of the coastline. To her right, if she craned her neck, she could see the remains of once-proud Criccieth Castle. It was still impressive, she noticed absently; but she wasn't in the mood for appreciating it. All she wanted was for her mother to give her a cuddle and tell her everything would be all right.

***

If it feels like coming home, that's because it is, Emily thought, as she drove the last few miles along the peninsula which jutted out into the Irish Sea. This part of northwest Wales was relatively flat compared to the impressive mountain range further east, and the road she was on was surrounded by rolling farmland with glimpses of the sea between the low hills.

She knew this place like the back of her hand, especially the area above the village, because that was where her parents' farm was situated, and it was with a sigh of relief that she left the narrow road leading down to the village and the sea, and swung onto the rutted track that would take her to the farm and sanctuary.

She knew she was running away and that her problems would still be there when she returned to Worcester, but she just needed some breathing space and distance (and her mum's sage advice) in order to get her head together and figure out what she was going to do next.

Dina had heard the car pull up and hurried out of the house before Emily switched the engine off. Even before she had fully emerged from the passenger seat, her mum was dragging her into an embrace.

'Mum,' Emily mumbled into her mother's shoulder, as she tried to extricate one foot from the car whilst balancing on the other. She tapped her mum on the arm. 'Let go, I can't breathe.'

Her mum reluctantly released her and said, 'You won't fully understand until you have children of your own, but I always feel as though I'm holding my breath until I see you again.'

Mu-u-um, I try to come home as often as I can.' *Please don't guilt-trip me right now,* she thought.

'That's not what I mean. When you're here, where I can see you, I know you're safe.' She grasped Emily by the upper arms. 'Let me look at you. This is a lovely, lovely surprise. I wasn't expecting to see you for a good few weeks. I was over the moon when you called to tell me—'

The tears Emily had been holding back ever since she left Worcester, spilled over and her face crumpled.

Without a word, her mum gathered her into her arms and held her close, rocking slightly. 'What is it, my lovely? What's wrong? Whatever it is, we can sort it out. You're home now, that's all that matters.'

With deep hiccupping breaths, Emily fought to regain some control. She didn't want her mum to worry that something truly awful had happened (although a broken heart wasn't to be sneezed at), so she gulped back a sob and blurted, 'Me and Cole have split up.'

Emily sensed some of the tension leaving her mum as she asked, 'Is that why your car is jam-packed?'

She nodded and swiped at her face using her sleeve. Without the censure such an action would have normally invoked, her mum delved into her bra and pulled out a tissue.

'It's clean.'

Emily took it and dabbed at her face. 'I found out last night that he has been cheating on me.'

'I'm so sorry. Come on, let's go inside and you can tell me all about it.'

'I need to unpack the car.' Emily hesitated, then wailed, 'I don't know where my toothbrush is.'

'We'll find it,' her mum said, 'and if it doesn't turn up tonight, I'm sure there's a new one in the bathroom cabinet.' She scanned the farmyard, then called,

'Graham? Graham! Emily is here! Can you unpack the car?'

'Where is Dad?'

'In the shed. One of the cows has just calved and he wanted to check on her. Graham!' her mum bellowed again, making Emily jump.

'For God's sake woman, keep your hair on. I'm coming.' Her dad was striding across the yard, wellies clumping over the cobbles. 'Emily, love…' He held his arms out and Emily sank into his embrace.

As she inhaled the familiar smell of lavender washing powder, aftershave and faint whiff of cow, Emily knew that everything would be all right. Maybe not just yet, and she might have to work at it, but her mum and dad would move heaven and earth to make sure of it.

'Don't cry, my lovely,' he said, stepping back to examine her worriedly.

'Her and Cole have split up,' Dina told him. She lowered her voice to barely a whisper and added, 'She caught him cheating on her.'

Her dad drew in a sharp breath. 'Is that true? Cole cheated on you?'

'He did.' Emily's chin wobbled again.

'The little… If I get my hands on him, I'll…' He let the sentence hang. 'It's enough to make a man swear,' he added.

That was one of the things (one of many) that she adored about her dad; he never swore. Emily, on the other hand, could swear like a trooper, although she was careful not to when her dad was around.

'I take it you've left him. Or did the so-and-so throw you out?' The way he said that last sentence left Emily in no doubt that her dad would be more than happy to take Cole to task if her boyfriend had, in fact, kicked her onto the street.

'I left him,' she confirmed. 'I stayed at Ava's last night, and as soon as work told me I could take the next two weeks off, I came home.'

'Are you staying for the full two weeks?' her mother wanted to know, as they went into the house, her mum's arm slung around her shoulders.

The welcome smell of home brought fresh tears to her eyes, but she blinked them away. Her parents didn't need her wailing and gnashing her teeth every five minutes – she knew they worried about her as it was, without being forced to see how upset she was.

'Tea?' her mum asked. 'Or would you prefer something stronger? You look as though you could do with a stiff drink.'

Emily shuddered, the very idea of alcohol making her stomach roil. 'Tea, please.'

'What have you eaten today? I bet you didn't stop for lunch; you must be starving. I'm cooking your favourite, but it won't be ready for about forty-five minutes because I didn't want to start it until you got here. I thought you would be here sooner than this. Was the traffic bad?'

'Dina, let the poor girl get a word in edgeways,' her dad huffed, as he struggled into the kitchen with armfuls of bags. He dumped them down on the floor.

'Can you take them upstairs, otherwise they'll get in the way when I start tea.'

Her dad sighed, but he did as he was asked.

As soon as he was out of earshot, her mum said, 'I swear to God if it's not got four legs and a tail, he's clueless. We'll eat first and I'll help you unpack later. There are fresh towels in the bathroom and clean sheets on your bed.'

Emily smiled. It was a small smile, but a smile nevertheless. Just being at Glynafon Farm made her feel better, and it was a relief to let her mum take charge. Emily could revert to being a kid again for a few days, until she felt strong enough to deal with the problem of where she would live when she returned to Worcester. If push came to shove, she could stay with Ava and Ben for a while, but that wasn't a long-term option, and she wanted to at least have started the ball rolling on flat or house hunting.

She felt like she was going back to square one, and she wished she hadn't moved out of the shared house she had been living in when Cole suggested she move in with him.

But she had been convinced she was doing the right thing, and why wouldn't she have thought so? Cole had told her he loved her, he had claimed he wanted to be with her every minute of every day, and that they would be able to spend more time together if she moved in with him.

She had been thrilled, excited and nervous all rolled into one. Having never lived with a man before (not in the romantic sense – there had been two guys living in her shared student accommodation, but they had just been friends), she hadn't known what to expect.

And at first, it had been everything she could have wished for: evenings spent cuddling in front of the telly, early morning escapades in the shower before they both had to dash off to work, cooking together in Cole's small kitchen, chats on the little patio with glasses of wine on the weekends…

Then, as she supposed happened to all relationships, life got in the way, and they weren't as lovey-dovey as they had been in the first few months. Emily found she preferred an extra fifteen minutes in bed in the morning to a quick fumble in the shower, and Cole often had to work late, meaning that Emily usually did the cooking on her own, presenting a meal to him with a flourish when he eventually arrived home, tired and distracted. As for the telly, he liked sport and she didn't; and summer turned into winter, and it grew too cold to sit outside. This year, she had been hoping to resurrect the wine and chat, but Cole had taken up running just after Christmas, and the training for the marathon he had decided to enter took up large swathes of his time.

Emily had been forced to content herself with girly nights out with friends, crafting, and shopping. She never bought a great deal because she was saving hard for the wedding she was hoping to play a starring role in (when Cole finally got around to popping the question), but it didn't stop her from strolling along Friar Street and gazing into the artisan shop windows as she planned what her dress would look like, and wondering how much it would cost to hold the ceremony in Worcester Cathedral, or whether that was even allowed.

She had been such a fool, and she wanted to kick herself. But hindsight was a wonderful thing and how could she have known that Cole would cheat on her?

What was he doing now, she wondered. Was he missing her, or was he out with Zelda? Or worse, was he *in* with Zelda?

Emily felt sick at the thought that Cole might have slept with her in *their* bed. Technically, it was Cole's bed... but that wasn't the point.

She was brought out of her dismal thoughts by her mum placing a hand over hers. 'It'll be all right, love, you see if it isn't. Before you know it, this will all be behind you, and you'll be struggling to remember Cole's name.'

She liked to think that her mum was right, but Emily knew it would be easier said than done to get over the heartache he'd caused her. At least Worcester, although not a large city, was big enough so that she wouldn't bump into him every five minutes.

And if she had her way, she hoped she would never set eyes on him again.

CHAPTER 4

The Smuggler's Rest had probably never seen a smuggler in its life, but it had seen plenty of locals and tourists alike, and Tuesday evening was no exception. Having spent yesterday sorting out her hastily packed belongings, a job that consisted of emptying everything out of the case and the bags, deciding which items she needed for now, and repacking everything else ready for when she returned to Worcester and storing it in the spare bedroom, Emily had then reacquainted herself with farm life.

She had missed this, she realised, as she always did when she came back for a visit. The peace, the smell of the sea (unless it was overpowered by the acrid aroma of cow or sheep dung when the wind was blowing in the wrong direction), the slower pace of life, and being fussed over by her mum. No matter how old she was, she always loved having her mum fuss over her, and she particularly welcomed it right now.

Earlier today, as Emily had piled onto the quad bike with her dad and two dogs to round up the sheep, she thought back to the one and only time she had brought Cole to Glynafon. Despite her hopes that he would fall in love with both the farm and the village, the visit hadn't gone as well as she would have liked.

Although he had been polite and friendly to her parents on the surface, beneath his civility she sensed that Cole had been disgusted with the farm's muckiness. It was the middle of winter, just after Christmas, and it had rained incessantly for days, so of course the farmyard had been muddy. But he needn't have curled his lip when he saw the *inside* of the house. His expression had been fleeting, but she had noticed it as soon as he'd entered the kitchen through the messy boot room. But that was what boot rooms were for – a place to leave muddy boots and all those things that you had to have close at hand but didn't want to bring into the rest of the house.

It had upset her (although she hadn't shown it) and had cast a shadow over the visit.

He was casting more than a shadow over *this* visit – it was more like a ruddy great big black cloud – and Emily's mind was still on Cole as she pushed open the pub's door and went inside.

Greeted by the smell of beer and the sound of many voices, she scanned the tables until she spotted her friends and hurried over.

Lucy and Jo rose to give her a hug, and she embraced them warmly. When she had let them know that she was back in Glynafon for a few days and had asked whether they fancied going out for a drink this evening, she hadn't told them she had split with her boyfriend, preferring to tell them in person, so when Lucy asked, 'Did Cole come with you?' Emily flinched.

'What?' Lucy looked worried. 'Did I say something wrong?'

'We've split up,' Emily replied, feeling the far too familiar sting of tears. She wouldn't cry. She *wouldn't!* She had already cried bucket loads, and she refused to shed any more tears over the man.

Lucy and Jo exchanged a look, then Jo said, 'That's rough. I'm sorry.'

'Me, too,' Lucy added, but Emily could tell that neither of them meant it.

They'd only met Cole the once, before Emily had moved in with him, but it had been clear that he hadn't been their type of people, and vice versa.

'Here.' Lucy nudged a glass towards her. 'I got you a Peroni.'

'Thanks.' Emily took a sip. 'I'll get the next round.'

'I feel incredibly naughty, drinking on a school night.' Lucy glanced around and smiled at a couple of people.

'I don't.' Jo smirked. 'Any excuse not to have to put Oliver to bed. Let his dad wrestle him into his pyjamas for once. Cheers!' She took a large mouthful.

'How is Oliver? Growing fast, I bet.' The last time Emily had seen the baby, he had been pulling himself up on the furniture and trying to walk.

'A menace,' Jo said, but her face glowed with love and pride. 'You'll have to pop round to see him. How long are you here?'

'A week, probably longer. I needed to get away for a bit,' Emily replied, and she told them all about how she had discovered that Cole was cheating, and that she was now technically homeless.

'Aw, my lovely, that's awful,' Lucy said, when Emily came to the end of her sorry tale, finishing with, 'So, I'm hoping to have some viewings lined up for next week. I'll have to start looking tomorrow.' She sighed. 'I thought he was special, you know? That we'd get married, have kids...'

Lucy and Jo exchanged looks again.

'What?' Emily asked. They may as well get it out in the open. These girls knew her darkest secrets (or had until she'd left Glynafon to live in Worcester) so they may as well be honest with her.

Jo began, 'I know you love him, but we never thought he was right for you.'

Lucy picked up the baton. 'He was a bit too… reserved? Is that the right word?'

'I don't know; you tell me.' Emily's voice was tight.

'What Lucy means, is that he wasn't very friendly,' Jo said. 'And you didn't seem yourself around him.' She glanced at Lucy again. 'We were surprised when you said you were moving in with him.'

'What's that supposed to mean, *I didn't seem myself?*' Emily was confused and rather hurt. Although *she* was more than happy to slag Cole off, she wasn't too keen on her friends doing it. Ava was different; Emily felt closer to Ava these days and Ava knew Cole well. The four of them had been on numerous nights out together, and had been to each other's houses for meals. Heck, they had even discussed the idea of going on holiday together.

Jo shrugged. 'I don't know how to explain it, but you weren't you when you were with him.'

Emily was beginning to regret coming out this evening (it was her mum's fault – she had nagged her, claiming that Emily would feel better if she went to the pub, instead of moping around with her knitting) and she was about to gear herself up to defend Cole, when she subsided. Her friends were right, she realised: she *hadn't* been wholly herself around Cole. She had been trying to be what she thought he wanted her to be — but that hadn't worked, had it?

Lucy reached out and gave her hand a squeeze. 'Sorry, we shouldn't have said anything.' Out of her and Jo, Lucy was the one who had always been scared of hurting anyone's feelings, and she bit her lip, worry in her eyes.

'No, you're right,' Emily admitted. She upended her glass, the alcohol sliding easily down her throat. 'I believe it's my round. Same again?'

Gathering the empty glasses, she made her way to the bar and propped herself up against it whilst she waited to be served. It had changed hands since the last time she was here, and the new owners had spruced it up. During one of her mum's gossipy phone calls, she had learnt that Ted and Jean, who had owned it for years, had retired and had moved to Harrogate to be nearer their son and his family.

'Nuts! How the devil are you!'

Emily turned around to see a rather handsome guy standing behind her, and it took her a moment to realise who it was. The floppy hair had gone, and his formerly pale, clean-shaven chin now sported a neatly trimmed beard. Instead of the devilishly handsome teenager she remembered from her school days, he was now a devilishly handsome and very sexy man.

'Macsen Rogers,' she said with a smile.

She'd had a serious crush on him once, and she blushed, remembering. Thankfully he had never realised how she had felt, and her infatuation had faded when she'd left for university.

'How long are you in Glynafon?' she asked.

'Permanently. I moved back about six months ago.'

Emily was surprised. Like her, he had been eager to leave the village. But he hadn't headed for the bright lights of a city, though. The last she'd heard, he was in the Lake District.

'Are you living in Lilian's house?' she asked. Lilian had been his aunt, and she had left him her house when she'd died. She'd never married and hadn't had any children of her own, so she had doted on Mac. Emily suspected that her mum had asked Lilian to be Emily's godmother because she knew Lilian would have loved a family of her own.

'I am,' he confirmed.

'I bet your mum and dad are pleased you're back in Glynafon,' she said. She knew how much her parents missed her, and she guessed Mac's must have felt the same.

'Huh, they couldn't give a monkey's uncle,' he huffed. 'They're in Sweden right now. Last month it was Norway. Who knows where they'll be next month, or even next week? They've bought a camper van,' he explained, 'and they're renting out their house as an

Airbnb to fund their nomadic lifestyle, so I've been tasked with keeping an eye on Gran.' He grinned and patted his flat stomach. 'She's loving it, but if she keeps feeding me these huge meals she's going to have more of me than she bargained for. I might have to take up jogging to burn off all the excess calories.'

Emily winced. Anything to do with running was a sore point. 'I'd better get back; Lucy and Jo are waiting.' She spanned her fingers around the three glasses. 'I might see you around before I go.'

'I hope so. Take care, Nuts.'

Emily rolled her eyes. 'You do realise no one else calls me that?'

His gaze dropped to her left hand, before returning to her face. 'You haven't changed your surname, have you?'

'No, it's still Oak.'

Macsen beamed at her. 'Good; there's a chance for me yet. Bye, Nuts.'

Emily turned to walk away and nearly bumped into Lucy.

Lucy jumped back. 'Whoops, sorry, I came to see if you needed any help.'

'I'll be OK, if no one jostles me.' Emily negotiated her way carefully between the tables, Lucy hot on her heels.

'Did I just hear Mac call you nuts?' Lucy asked.

Concentrating on not spilling them, Emily put the drinks down. 'Yeah, but he's not commenting on my state of mind. It's his nickname for me.'

'Since when?' Jo asked, grabbing her drink. 'Thanks. I'm going to make the most of this. It's a rare treat to be out on my own.'

'Since we were at school,' Emily said. It was quite sweet, and she was touched that Mac had remembered.

'Why Nuts? Was he being ironic, because if he was, you weren't any nuttier than the rest of us. In fact, you were quite sensible.' Lucy said, sounding put out. If Emily remembered rightly, Lucy had been the most sensible of all of them.

'Oak,' Emily said, then when faced with two pairs of baffled eyes, she went on, 'Acorn... nut... Nuts. He thought he was being clever.' She glanced over her shoulder and caught Mac's eye. He was gazing at her thoughtfully, and she smiled at him, feeling awkward.

'He *was* clever,' Lucy said. 'He got good grades at A-level, remember? He works in conservation now.'

'He can conserve me any time,' Jo said dreamily, and Emily wriggled around in her seat, ostensibly to adjust the lightweight jacket she had slung over the back of it, but in reality she wanted to take another gander at him. He was leaning against the bar and was now chatting to the woman behind it. Emily thought his rear view was just as sexy as the front of him.

'Jo, behave yourself!' Lucy cried. 'You're a married woman. And you'd better stop ogling him too, Em, if you know what's good for you. He's got a reputation, and you don't want to get involved with him, or else you'll end up being just a number in his little black book.'

Jo sucked on her straw, her eyes studying him over the rim of her glass. 'Isn't it supposed to be a little *red* book? You know, that song by The Drifters…?'

She started singing and Emily frowned. 'Can't say I've heard of it.'

'La, la, something, something,' Jo warbled. 'More than a number… written in my little *black* book.' She emphasised the word 'black'. 'Yeah, black does sound better,' she agreed. 'More bad-boy. Red reminds me of Chairman Mao.' Jo had studied philosophy and politics at A-level.

'Who are The Drifters anyway?' Lucy asked.

'Some group from the seventies. My nana and grandad used to love them. Nana had a thing for one of the band members. She used to call it her secret crush, but we all knew about it and whenever one of their songs came on the radio she used to go all gooey-eyed. She still does. And she used to like The Osmonds. And Cary Grant.'

Emily didn't know who The Osmonds were, although she thought she might have heard of Cary Grant.

Giggling, Jo leant forward and lowered her voice. 'I used to have a crush on Mac when we were in school.'

Lucy snorted. 'Didn't we all.' She narrowed her eyes and stared at him. 'I actually dated him.'

Emily felt envious. She would have given her right arm to go on a date with Macsen, but apart from teasing her occasionally and giving her a daft nickname, he hadn't been interested in her in the slightest. Not like that. To him she had just been one of a loose gang of mates who all hung out together.

'You kept that quiet,' Jo said. 'What was it like?'

Lucy examined the contents of her glass. 'He's a damn good kisser, but so he should be with all the practice he's had. I've heard that he's dated every woman within a fifty-mile radius. I wouldn't touch him now with a ten-foot barge pole.'

Jo said, 'I kissed Nathan Evans once. And it *was* only once. I worshipped that boy for months, but when I eventually went out with him it was a huge let-down. Being kissed by him was like being attacked by a sink plunger.' She shuddered.

Emily and Lucy began to giggle, and after glaring at them Jo joined in, spluttering, 'I hope he's got better at it, otherwise I feel sorry for his wife.'

'He must have!' Lucy exclaimed. 'He's got two kids and another on the way.'

Suddenly, Emily was so pleased that her mum had talked her into a night out down the pub. It was great to catch up, and she felt better for having a giggle.

For the next couple of hours, she hardly thought about Cole, too busy listening to gossip and reminiscing on their schooldays. And later, as she lay in bed, ever so slightly tipsy, when she did think about her ex it was with considerably more anger than sadness; which made her wonder if she loved him as much as she thought she did, or whether she had been more in love with the idea of being in love... Rather like Jo and her experience with Nathan – in hindsight, maybe the reality of living with Cole hadn't been quite as good as her perception of it.

CHAPTER 5

'Any luck, love?' her mum asked, and Emily looked up from the computer and wrinkled her nose.

'Not a great deal. Most of the shared accommodation is aimed at students. Been there, done that, and I don't want to do it again. I'm trying to find a house or a flat with someone my own age or a bit older.' She had spent all of Wednesday morning on the internet, without any success.

Her mum came to stand next to her and peered over her shoulder. 'That one looks nice.'

The screen depicted a whole house for rent, not the shared accommodation Emily was looking for. 'It does, but it's way out of my price range.'

'It's a pity you can't find someone to share it with you.'

'I know, but all my friends are happy where they are.'

'It doesn't have to be a friend. You could rent somewhere with two bedrooms, then advertise for a lodger.'

It was an idea, Emily admitted. 'I could, but that will take a while. I was hoping to sort something out a bit sooner.'

Dina put a hand on her shoulder. 'I do worry about you, you know.'

Emily swivelled around and saw the concern on her mum's face. 'I'll be fine, Mum, really I will. It'll be OK.' She turned back to the screen, praying she was right, but swamped by the awful feeling that she mightn't be.

Her mother said, 'You could always stay here, in Glynafon.'

Emily frowned. 'I *am* staying here.'

'I mean permanently.'

'What about my job?'

'I'm sure you could get another job, although it might take a while. And in the meantime, you can help on the farm.'

'But my friends are in Worcester.'

'You've got friends here.'

'My life is *there*, not in Glynafon.'

'Your life is wherever you want it to be,' her mum stated. 'Be honest, Emily, you haven't been happy in Worcester for a while.'

'I have!' Emily objected. 'Or I was until I found out Cole was cheating on me.'

Dina gave her a shrewd look. 'Were you? Hmm… Just think about it, eh?'

Emily listened to her mother's footsteps as she walked across the old flagstones in the hall and on into the kitchen. and she thought about what her mother had said. *Could* she stay in Glynafon? Did she *want* to? Her job aside, she didn't have much else to go back for. She had brought all her worldly possessions with her, apart from the box of books Lilian had given her – which she now regretted leaving behind but had no intention of asking Cole for. And as for Ava, she and Ben were getting married next summer and Emily had already noticed that Ava had less free time to spend with her – and that the situation was only going to get worse as Ava and Ben became more deeply entrenched as a couple.

But, as she had said to her mum, her life was there. She loved the little city with its mix of modern and old buildings, the pedestrian shopping centre which sat alongside a medieval cobbled street, and the ancient cathedral which dominated the landscape. She loved walking down to the river on warm summer days, and watching the swans paddling lazily whilst children played in the fountains, and there were loads of cafes and bistros, as well as traditional pubs, and lots of lovely shops.

Nah, Worcester was her home now, just as much as Glynafon was. More so, in a way, because she had *chosen* to live there. Out of all the universities in the country, she had decided to go to Worcester, and had enjoyed living there so much that she had stayed after she'd graduated. She had a job she liked and good friends – why would she want to leave?

Restless, she turned off the computer, deciding to go for a walk to clear her head. Maybe a bit of alone time would give her a chance to think, because, despite her protestations, her mother's suggestion had thrown a spanner in the works.

Stuffing her phone into the back pocket of her jeans, Emily slung a hoodie around her shoulders and shouted to her mum that she was going out for a bit.

The sea was calling…

***

A graveyard wasn't usually the first thing to pop into someone's mind when they thought of the beach, but this particular graveyard was perched above the sweeping sands of Glynafon bay, with a wonderful view out to sea. It was a grand spot in which to be buried, and Emily picked her way through the headstones, some of them two or three hundred years old, until she came to a much newer one.

Sinking down into the grass beside it, she ran her hand across its smooth marble face, the stone not yet pitted by the wind or salt spray.

She read the words carved into it and smiled sadly, her gaze resting on the name: Lilian Jenkins.

It was Lilian's box of books that Emily had left behind in Cole's attic, but at least she'd brought the jewellery with her.

'Sorry, Lilian,' she muttered, thinking that the dusty old tomes must have meant something to her godmother, else she wouldn't have given them to Emily in the first place.

But they didn't have any sentimental value for Emily whatsoever. She couldn't even remember seeing them in Lilian's house.

Tilting her face up to the sun, she closed her eyes, the heat warming her skin. It was blissfully peaceful: the only sounds were the cries of the ever-present gulls and the pounding of the waves, along with the distant shout of children playing on the sand.

Glynafon had its fair share of tourists, but it was far smaller than Pwllheli, its more raucous cousin further east, and Emily loved the lack of amusement arcades and the absence of tacky gift shops. Neither was there a pier or a funfair to spoil its beauty, and it didn't even have a harbour, although several small boats were anchored in the bay.

She loved the way it had hardly changed over the years. It was still the same as when she was a child, and until now she hadn't realised how much she relied on that. The village and the farm were anchors in the sea of *her* life.

Some changes were inevitable though, such as Lilian no longer being with them, and Mac's parents renting their house out to tourists while they toured Europe in a camper van. But for the most part it stayed the same, which had always brought Emily immense comfort.

A dog barked close by, and she opened her eyes. A golden retriever was bounding across the beach, chasing a ball, and she smiled at the animal's exuberance.

She followed their progress, the dog and its owner heading away from the village towards the small headland, but before they reached it they turned inland and disappeared from sight, leaving her alone with her thoughts once more.

Whenever she came back to Glynafon, it seemed to Emily that she had never left (apart from that time she had been accompanied by Cole, but the least said about that the better). Right now, it felt as though Worcester had been nothing more than a long weekend away, spent in a place she liked and knew well, but one she had no real emotional ties to. And she recalled how sometimes she used to feel so desperately homesick. The Welsh had a word for it – *hiraeth*, a deep, visceral longing for home, tinged with sadness and yearning. It was odd that when she wasn't in Glynafon, she felt the pull of the place where she had been born and bred, yet when she had been a teenager, she couldn't wait to leave it.

But that was when she was younger, eager for everything a city had to offer. Now, though, she realised she didn't feel quite the same urge to leave, and she guessed that was probably because of Cole: Worcester held so many memories of him. Then there was her mother's suggestion that she should come back here to live. In some ways it was an appealing idea. She wouldn't have to worry about finding somewhere to live or bumping into Cole. She could slot back into her old life on the farm…

Emily had never felt so torn.

'You're no help,' she said to the headstone, but Lilian remained silent. Yet, she knew what her godmother would have said – she would have told Emily to listen to her heart.

The problem was, Emily's heart didn't know what it wanted. Less than a week ago, it thought it did. But a week ago, Emily had been in a relationship with a man she loved (or thought she loved), and whom she had hoped to marry one day. Her life had been settled, and she had believed she knew the path the rest of it would take. But now she was adrift, her only anchor being her parents, the farm, and this village on the far tip of a peninsula jutting out into the wild Irish sea.

Should she stay, or should she go?

Staying would be the easy option, but was it the *right* one?

She sighed and clambered to her feet, dusting her jeans off with vigorous slaps. Even up here, the sand got everywhere.

It was time to get back; her dad was expecting her to help move the cows to the top field. It was a job he must have done a hundred times and could easily manage by himself, but he had asked and she had said she would help. Emily suspected that her dad was trying to make her feel useful, and to take her mind off things.

She made her way back up the hill and found her dad in the big barn, tinkering with the ancient tractor. He seemed distracted.

'Hiya, love. Do you mind shifting the cows by yourself? I want to try to get this going.'

Emily moved closer and peered at the exposed engine. 'What's wrong with it?'

'It's old, like me.'

'You're not old,' Emily admonished.

'I'll be sixty-three come September.'

'That's not old,' she repeated.

'Try telling that to my knees,' her dad grumbled. 'I should have gone into insurance, not farming. Farming is damned hard on the joints.'

'You would have hated it,' Emily pointed out. 'You love farming.'

'If I'd gone into insurance, I could be retired by now,' he retorted.

'I can't see you playing golf, or lawn bowls, or whatever it is that retired men do with their time,' she joked. 'You'd be bored stiff in a week.'

'Aye, you might be right,' he conceded. He didn't look convinced though, and Emily felt a sudden pang.

Her dad *was* getting older – there was no denying it. What would happen when the farm became too much for him? Would her parents sell it? And where was Ianto?

'Is Ianto on holiday?' she asked. 'I haven't seen him since I got here.' She glanced around the barn as though expecting the chap who had worked on the farm for the past twenty or so years, to suddenly pop up from behind a bale of silage.

'He doesn't work here anymore,' her dad said, wiping his hands on an oily rag.

'Why ever not?'

'He's older than me,' Graham said. 'It was about time he hung up his pitchfork, so to speak.'

Emily hadn't realised. Ianto had looked pretty good for his age. 'So, who have you got instead?'

'No one.' Her dad blew out his cheeks and threw the rag at the tractor, where it landed on the bonnet.

No wonder her father was griping about wanting to retire if he and Mum were doing everything themselves. It had been a stretch, even with Ianto's help... without it, it must be nigh on impossible.

'Have you got anyone lined up?' she asked.

'Not at the moment.'

'Do you need help writing an advert? I could put it online for you.'

'There's no point.'

'Yes, there is, Dad. You and mum can't manage the farm by yourselves.'

He shook his head. 'I know, but...' He hesitated. 'People don't want to work the land like they used to. It's not easy to hire farm workers.'

'Have you tried?'

He shot her an irritated look. 'Are you going to take those cows up to the top field or shall I do it myself?'

'I'll take them,' she said hastily, and hurried away, vowing to do more to help, at least while she was here. And maybe she could look into the problem of hiring someone at the same time... Because it made her blood run cold to think that the farm her parents had devoted their lives to, would one day have to be sold.

***

'Pass the salt, Em,' Dina said, holding out her hand.

Emily placed the saltshaker into her mum's palm, then picked up her knife and fork. 'I didn't realise Ianto had retired,' she said. 'You never mentioned it.'

'Didn't I? It must have slipped my mind.' Dina turned to Graham. 'Did you get the tractor fixed?'

Graham shook his head. 'I'll have another go at it tomorrow, but if I can't mend it, I'll ask if someone from Potters can come out and take a look.'

Emily had noticed earlier in the week that Potters Motors was still going strong. The garage had serviced the farm vehicles for as long as she could remember. If they couldn't get the old tractor running, no one could.

Her mum was giving her dad a meaningful look, as she said, 'Fingers crossed that you can work your magic, eh?'

Her dad grunted. 'It'll take a fairy godmother to get that thing going.'

'It's not that bad, is it? I was hoping we could keep it ticking along for a few more months.' Dina sighed.

'Ignore me. I'm just being grumpy. Tired, that's all.'

'Anything I can help with, Dad?' Emily offered.

Her father summoned up a smile. 'You might regret saying that: I've got a list as long as your arm.'

'Hit me with it,' Emily said. 'I'll do what I can while I'm here.'

'You're not here to work,' Dina pointed out. 'You've got other things to be getting on with, like sorting out somewhere to live.'

Emily said, 'I can do both. There's only so much internet trawling I can take in any one go. Helping you will give me something to do. I mightn't want to be a full-time farmer, but I don't mind mucking in while I'm here.'

Her dad looked regretful. 'I don't blame you for not wanting to go into farming. It's a tough life.'

As she so often did, Emily felt guilty for not wanting to take over the farm from her parents. This was their life's work, but she had run away from it as soon as she had been old enough.

Coming back was wonderful, but only for a holiday. She wouldn't want to move back to the farm permanently, although these past few days she couldn't help feeling tempted. Finding somewhere to live was proving difficult, and she knew she wasn't likely to secure anywhere before she had to go back to work. So, it looked like she would be forced to doss in Ava and Ben's spare room for a few weeks after all.

Not only that, even if she found furnished accommodation, she would still have to start from scratch as she didn't even have a sheet or a towel to her name. Once again, she had the impression that she hadn't moved on from when she was a student. Actually, she was worse off when it came to household stuff, and she was beginning to seriously regret leaving behind all those items she had bought for Cole's house when she had walked out. She'd not been thinking straight, just wanting to get out of there, and she'd had a vague notion that if she had taken them with her she would have been reminded of Cole and his infidelity every time she looked at them.

But, strangely enough, that didn't seem to matter so much now.

Maybe she *should* pick them up. After all, she still had a key...

***

Emily thumped her pillow and propped it up behind her head, before settling back and making herself comfortable. She was on the phone to Ava, and whenever the two of them got chatting it was rarely a two-minute thing.

'What are you doing?' Ava asked. 'You sound as though you're punching someone.'

'Just my pillow, although I am pretending it's Cole's face. Any news on that front? I've blocked him and he's not on social media much, so I feel out of touch. Do you think he's missing me?' She barked out a bitter laugh. 'If he is, it'll only be because he doesn't have someone to iron his shirts for him.'

Ava said, 'Actually, I do have something to tell you. I hate to be the bearer of bad news, but I can't keep this from you… Cole told Ben that Zelda is moving in with him.'

'What? *The bastard!* My side of the bed isn't even cold!' Emily was flabbergasted.

'I know. I'm sorry, Emily.'

Tears gathered in Emily's eyes and spilled over to trickle down her face as a thought occurred to her. It wasn't a pleasant one. 'Do you know what I think?' she said, a wobble in her voice. 'I think he's been planning this all along, and I've played right into his hands. I reckon I've saved him the bother of kicking me out.'

'I'm not so sure.' Ava sounded thoughtful. 'He was on to a good thing with you, and he knew it. His problem was that he wanted his cake and wanted to eat it, too.'

'He's certainly eating it now,' Emily wailed. She dabbed at her eyes with the hem of her T-shirt. How could he be so mean! She'd thought he loved her…

Gulping back tears, she swallowed hard and took a steadying breath.

She'd be OK. Cole had hurt her, but not broken her. She would survive this.

After taking a few moments to compose herself and recover from the shock of hearing that Cole was moving Zelda in, Emily knew that what she was feeling was betrayal and disappointment, along with a heavy dose of lack-of-self-worth. She wasn't as devastated as she should be: she didn't feel that her world had come to an end, or that she didn't know how she was going to carry on without him.

She would get over this, and she didn't think it would take as long as she initially feared. She had found out on Saturday what a rat he was, and today was only Wednesday, but she was coming to terms with it already.

Ava said, 'Sorry, Em, I thought long and hard about telling you, but you would have found out eventually anyway. Besides, Ben is bound to slip up sooner or later, especially if you are going to live with us for a while…'

'Is it still OK? I've been looking for somewhere, but I haven't found anything yet. I hate putting you out.'

'Of course it's OK. You're not putting us out at all. We'd love to have you.'

'My mum suggested I come back to Glynafon to live permanently.'

'Is that something you'd want to do?'

'Not really. It's lovely being back, but I don't think I want to stay here for good.'

'Thank God for that! I'd miss you.'

'I would miss you, too.' Emily heard Ben's voice in the background calling for Ava. 'I'll let you go – speak soon, yeah?'

'Keep your chin up, hon,' was Ava's parting advice. 'It'll all turn out OK.'

Emily wished she had her friend's confidence. Although she knew she had absolutely done the right thing in leaving Cole, she wished she had thought it through more carefully. In hindsight, it would have been better to remain in the house while looking for somewhere else to live, but she had been so hurt and had felt so betrayed that she hadn't been thinking straight.

She'd just upped and left, and now she found herself wishing she had kept her head and not stormed out. Despite Zelda moving in the minute Emily's back was turned, Emily suspected that if she had confronted Cole on Sunday, he would have insisted that it was a one-off, that he had drunk too much despite his marathon training, and he would have promised her that he would never do anything like that again, if only she would forgive him.

She wouldn't have believed a word of it, of course, but if she'd had any sense she would have pretended to. She suspected that he had only asked Zelda to move in with him so he could get his laundry, cooking and cleaning done, whilst having sex on tap.

Once again, she thought it was telling that she could think so logically now, after just a few days, and that she wasn't as heartbroken as she should be, considering she was supposed to be in love with him.

As she lay in bed, Emily examined her feelings, and was rather ashamed to discover that she was mourning the loss of being part of a couple more than she was mourning the loss of the man himself. Perhaps the idea of getting engaged, then married, had blinded her to the fact that she didn't love Cole as much as she had thought she did. It had taken him cheating on her for her to see the light.

Guiltily, she wondered whether he had subconsciously picked up on that. Maybe she had contributed to his roving eye and—

Stop that, she told herself. She refused to take the blame for his appalling behaviour. If he had suspected that things weren't right between them, he should have said something. Maybe they would have worked it out, and maybe not… but cheating wasn't the answer.

She turned her pillow over again and thumped it into submission, cross with herself.

There had been no drama as far as Cole was concerned. She had made the break-up incredibly easy for him. She hadn't even confronted him. She'd just upped and left, taking only her personal possessions with her.

What an idiot she had been.

Making a vow to grab what was rightfully hers as soon as she returned to Worcester, Emily gave her pillow another wallop, imagining it was Cole's sneaky, lying, cheating face, then snuggled down. Ava was right – everything *would* be OK.

CHAPTER 6

These last few days have flown by, Emily thought on Friday morning, as she consulted the shopping list, her gaze quickly scanning down it and mentally checking each item off. Yep, that was everything. The little convenience store in the village even had a supply of herbs and spices, so she had managed to add cinnamon to her basket.

She had paid for her shopping and was about to return to the car when she felt a tap on her arm.

'Bea!' she cried in delight, when she saw Lilian's sister. She gave the old lady a one-armed hug. 'How are you? You're looking well.'

Bea had hardly changed since Emily saw her last. She wore her grey hair in its customary bun, and maybe there was more white in it than previously, but she still had the same twinkle in her eye, and ready smile.

'Can't complain,' Bea said. 'Have you got time to pop in for a cup of tea?'

'Absolutely. Let me put this in the car.' She indicated the shopping bag, then noticed that Bea was similarly laden. 'I'll carry that for you,' she offered, holding out her free hand.

'I can manage,' Bea protested, but it was evident that the bag was heavy, and after Emily glared at her, Bea allowed her to take it.

'Crumbs, what have you got in here?' Emily exclaimed. 'Bricks?'

'Potatoes, bird seed, cat food, and two cartons of orange juice.'

'What you need is one of those trolleys,' Emily suggested. 'It would save you carrying everything.'

'Over my dead body. Shopping bags on wheels are for old people.'

Emily bit her lip as she stowed her own shopping in the car. Bea *was* old. She must be north of eighty. She was the younger of the two sisters, Lilian having been six years older.

As they strolled towards Bea's house, Emily said, 'I visited Lilian's grave yesterday. I bet you miss her.'

'Like crazy,' Bea said, 'especially now that John and Ivy are off on their travels.'

Emily chuckled. 'Mac told me that his mum and dad had bought a motor home and he doesn't know which country they're in from one month to the next.'

'I don't think they would have gone if Macsen hadn't been here to keep an eye on me.' Bea came to a halt outside a neat little house that had once been a fisherman's cottage, and withdrew a set of keys from her pocket as she led Emily through the wooden gate and into the pretty low-walled area to the front of the house. It was a typical English cottage garden, filled to bursting with hollyhocks, lupins, foxgloves and sweet peas. The scent was amazing, as were the colours, and the whole garden was alive with bees and butterflies.

Bea unlocked the front door and Emily followed her inside. 'Where do you want this?' She lifted the bag of shopping.

'On the table will do. Tea or coffee?'

'Tea, please.'

'How about a piece of cake to go with it? Your mum made it. She makes me something every Sunday, bless her. I tell her not to bother, but she insists.' Bea shrugged off her jacket and hung it on the back of a chair before flicking the switch on the kettle.

'I'd love a slice, thanks. I think she's planning on baking Welsh cakes and bara brith later. She sent me down for spices and currants, along with a few other bits and pieces.'

'She didn't tell me you were coming home,' Bea said, as she made the tea.

'It was a spur-of-the-moment thing.'

'How lovely. When do you go back?'

'Next Sunday.'

'Have you got your young man with you?'

'Er... no, Cole and I have split up.'

'Oh, dear,' Bea said, turning to give her a sympathetic look. 'I hope he didn't hurt you too badly?'

'You sound like Lilian! That's the kind of thing she would have said.'

'She used to warn me off men. Reckoned they were heartbreakers, the lot of them. She may have been right.'

'I always thought you and Victor had a happy marriage.'

'We did. But he left me in the end,' Bea said, putting a plate containing a slice of sponge cake on the table.

'Bea, he *died*,' Emily pointed out gently. 'He didn't exactly *leave* you.'

'I'm on my own, aren't I? And the heartache is the same, so in a way she was right. And now my John is traipsing all over Europe, so God knows when I'll see *him* again.'

'At least you've got Mac,' Emily soothed.

Bea's face lit up. 'He's been a godsend. I never thought I'd live to see the day he came back to

Glynafon. At one point I feared he was going to sell Lilian's house.'

'I bumped into him on Tuesday evening in the pub. I didn't know he's been home six months – Mum never said.'

'She probably did tell you, but you weren't listening,' Bea quipped. 'Far too busy for your own good, that's what you young people are. You need to slow down and smell the roses.' She returned to the subject of Mac. 'Yes, it must be coming up to six months now. He's a conservation officer, working on the Peatland Restoration Project.' The pride in her voice was evident. 'It's lovely having him back. And I bet your mum and dad are thrilled to see you, too.'

'They are, but I think my dad is pleased because he can shunt some of his to-do list onto me,' Emily joked. 'I've been mucking out the cow shed this morning. Yuck! And this afternoon he plans on repairing one of the dry stone walls. This visit is anything but relaxing,' she added. 'Last night I was so tired that I fell asleep in the chair. Not exactly living the high life, is it?' She hadn't even managed to stay awake long enough to get her latest knitting project out of the box, let alone do any actual knitting.

But being kept busy was serving its purpose in stopping her fretting about how badly her ex-boyfriend had behaved, or where she was going to live for the foreseeable future. But she had offered to help, so she could hardly complain if her dad had taken her up on it...

'What would you be doing today if you were at home – in Worcester, I mean,' Bea clarified.

'I'd be at work.'

'What about this evening?'

'Out with friends probably. Or maybe cocktails in a bar if I could persuade Cole to—' She stopped abruptly as the sound of the front door closing reached them, followed by footsteps in the hall.

Mac appeared in the doorway. He was holding a box of bedding plants. 'Hiya, Gran, I've brought you— Oh, hello, Nuts.'

'Hi.' Emily gave him a little wave.

'Cake?' Bea asked.

'Not for me, thanks.'

'Go on, a little slice won't hurt, and you need feeding up. You used to be such a skinny little thing.'

Emily smiled when Mac's eyes met hers. She could remember him being slim, but she would never have described him as skinny. He had been rather fit, she recalled. He still was. More so...

She saw the way the muscles in his arms bunched, and as he took the box into the garden her attention was caught by how well his behind fitted his jeans and how broad his shoulders were.

Bea caught her looking and Emily blushed. Lowering her head, she concentrated on the cake in front of her.

Mac came back inside and swilled his hands under the tap.

'What are your plans for this evening?' Bea asked him 'It's Friday – I always loved a Friday night on the town. That was when I was young, of course. A bunch of us would catch the bus into Pwllheli after work and go live it up. Dolled up to the nines we'd be.' She smiled fondly. 'That was before I met your grandad, of course. But even after we were wed, we'd go to Pwllheli a couple of times a month, either to the cinema or for a meal.' She gave Mac an arched look. 'I hear they do nice meals in the Smuggler's Rest now.' She turned to Emily. 'It went downhill for a bit, then new people took it over.'

'I know they do food, I go there regularly,' Mac reminded his grandmother. 'It is my local, after all.'

'Yes, but you don't eat there, do you? You eat *here*.'

'I thought you wanted me to eat with you?' Mac looked surprised. 'You cook enough for six!'

'That's only because I know you're coming.'

'Are you saying you don't want me to come for tea anymore?'

'I'm not saying that at all. I just thought you might fancy a change now and again. I'm not cooking tonight, by the way.'

Macsen's face was filled with concern. 'Why not? Are you ill?'

'I'm fine.'

'Why don't I cook instead?' he suggested.

'I can manage to warm up some soup by myself,' she said.

'Is that all you're having?'

'It's what I fancy,' she retorted. 'I don't always want a big meal, but I know you do. You're younger than me and you're always on the go. Why don't you try the food in the Smuggler's Rest? I'm curious to know if it's as nice as they say it is.' Suddenly Bea clapped her hands. 'I've got an idea!' she cried. 'The two of you can go together and report back to me.' She turned to Emily, who was rather gobsmacked at the suggestion, and said to her, 'I dare say Macsen would enjoy some company.' Then she said to Mac, 'You don't want to be eating on your own in a pub, Mac, and Emily will only fall asleep in the chair if she doesn't go out, and that's a criminal waste of a Friday night at her age.'

Mac's face was a picture, but it was nothing compared to Emily's shock. Was Bea trying to set them up, or was this a genuinely innocent suggestion?

'I don't think Mac needs his hand holding,' Emily said. 'Anyway, Mum and Dad will be expecting me to eat with them.'

Bea snorted. 'It's ages until teatime, so you can't use that as an excuse. If you let Dina know now, she can plan accordingly. Go on, give your mum a call.'

Emily didn't want to upset the old lady, but neither did she want to be railroaded into going to dinner with Mac – although she wouldn't mind going out this evening. She had been toying with the idea of asking Lucy or Jo whether they fancied a drink, but she didn't want to monopolise them for the short amount of time she was in Glynafon, then bugger off back to Worcester and not see them again for ages. It would be a kind of love them and leave them scenario.

Bea wasn't going to let this go. '*I'll* ring your mum, shall I? She can't expect to keep you all to herself, even if she doesn't see you as often as she would like. It's not as though you're only here for the weekend. When *did* you get here?'

Great, now Emily was feeling guilty as well as cornered. 'Sunday,' she muttered.

She was aware of Macsen grinning, and she sent him a sour look.

'In that case, I'm sure Dina won't mind you having a bit of fun,' Bea said. 'She can spare you for one evening. I hate to think of Macsen tucking into pie and chips on his own.'

'I won't be on my own,' Macsen argued. 'Everyone knows everyone else in Glynafon. But I wouldn't say no to sharing my table with Emily.'

Emily narrowed her eyes. She couldn't tell whether Mac was pulling her leg or not.

'Go on, have dinner with me,' he urged. 'Although calling pie and chips *dinner* may be a bit of a stretch.'

'I'll have you know I like pie and chips,' Emily said. 'But it's got to be steak and ale with a fluffy pastry top.'

'Steak and mushroom. Or chicken,' Mac replied.

'You can argue over what you're going to have when you get there,' Bea said firmly. 'Now, Emily, finish your cake, then you had better get off to help your dad with that wall. And you, Macsen, can put my bedding plants in for me, if you've got time. I'll show you where I want them to go.' She turned back to Emily. 'He'll pick you up at seven, if that's all right?'

'It's easier if I meet him there—' Emily began, but Bea was having none of it.

'Nonsense! He can pick you up from the door like a proper gentleman. Take my advice, Emily, and make him treat you properly right from the off.'

Bemused and feeling as though she had been run over by her dad's old tractor, Emily made her way back to the car. Macsen had looked just as stunned, but he had soon rallied – far quicker than she had – and she recalled Lucy and Jo's comments about Macsen having a reputation. There was no way *she* intended to become a notch on his bedpost, or a booty-call contact on his phone.

But this was only dinner, and she had (mostly) grown out of the crush she'd once had on him. Anyway, he had never been into her; she was just one of the gang to him. She seemed to recall him going out with the more popular girls, the ones with street cred, and she doubted whether anything had changed. The fact that he still called her 'Nuts' made his feelings about her perfectly clear. Even if she had been interested in him in that way (which she most assuredly wasn't – it would be a long time before she dated again), he didn't consider her anything other than a friend.

When she put it like that, there was no harm in going out for a meal with a friend. Besides, anything was better than watching documentaries on the telly with her parents or trying to watch a movie in her bedroom on her phone.

CHAPTER 7

'Emily, your date is here!' Dina called.

Emily, who was holding up the floaty skirt of her maxi dress so she didn't trip on it, trotted down the stairs and glared at her mother. 'It's *not* a date.'

Her mum smiled knowingly. 'You look nice.'

'Thanks. It's still not a date.'

'What do you call it, then?'

'A meal with an... um... friend.' Emily glanced out of the window to see an unfamiliar vehicle on the yard and Mac walking towards the rarely used front door. 'Gotta go. Won't be late.' She planted a swift kiss on her mum's cheek, grabbed her bag and dashed outside via the back door.

Mac did a double take when she appeared around the side of the house, but rallied quickly. 'Hi, Nuts.'

'You need to stop calling me that,' she retorted irritably.

'Sorry.' He gestured to the jeep. 'Shall we?'

'We'd better had. I'm not walking into the village in these.' Emily glanced down at her feet and the high-heeled sandals she was wearing, and wondered why she was being so unfriendly.

Mac was probably wondering the same thing, because he said, 'We don't have to do this, you know.'

Immediately contrite, it was her turn to apologise. 'Sorry. I'm not normally this grumpy. I've got a lot on my mind.'

'Would you like to tell me about it? A problem shared is a problem halved.'

Emily sighed dramatically as she got into the jeep. 'Only if the person you're sharing it with can do something about it.'

'It sounds serious.' He started the engine.

'Not really, not in the grand scheme of things. I'm trying to tell myself that it's nothing more than a minor inconvenience.' Realising it was unfair to leave him hanging, and guessing that Bea would probably tell him anyway, Emily went on to explain. 'Long story short, I caught my boyfriend cheating on me and now I'm homeless.'

'Bummer.'

'Yep.' She stole a glance at him.

Mac was still handsome. In fact, he had become even *more* attractive, if anything, and she had the feeling he knew it.

'What are you going to do?' he asked. 'Are you going to stay here, in Glynafon?'

'I'm going back to Worcester. I've got a job there, and friends. I just need to find a place to live.'

Mac steered the jeep into the parking area at the side of the pub.

As they got out, she said, 'What about you? I thought you were in the Lake District.'

'I was, but a job came up here.' He opened the pub's door for her.

The Smuggler's Rest was busy, but they found a free table at the back, and she wasn't surprised when he pulled out a chair for her. Hmm, she thought, some women might be impressed by his charm, but she wasn't.

It was rather nice, though. Cole had never opened a door for her or pulled out a chair. Oh… hang on. Yes, he had pulled a chair out for her once – he had deliberately pulled it out so far that she had fallen on her backside. He had laughed like a drain: Emily hadn't seen the funny side.

The table was next to the window with a view across the beach and the bay, and Emily drank it in. It was gorgeous: the sun was going down over the headland

and there was an orange glow on the water and in the sky. Staring at it also prevented her from gazing at Mac too much.

He didn't seem to have any such qualms and she was conscious of his eyes on her face. 'You haven't changed a bit, Nut— er, Emily.'

She seized a menu from the holder and opened it. 'Is that good or bad?' she asked, peeping over the top of it.

'I'm not being strictly truthful. If anything, you're cuter.'

Emily sucked in a breath. He didn't waste any time, did he? Well, she had been warned, so it was her fault if she fell for his cheesy lines and old-fashioned courtesy.

Talking of cheese, there was baked camembert with toasted pitta sticks served with a rocket and sun-dried tomato salad on the menu, so she decided to go for that.

Mac chose steak, medium rare. Why didn't that surprise her?

With drinks in front of them and whilst they waited for their food to arrive, they talked about school and people they once knew. Mac, having been living in Glynafon for several months, was more up-to-date than her, and was able to fill her in on some shared acquaintances and old friends.

'Remember old Moggy Maths?' he asked, chuckling. He was referring to one of their high school teachers.

'Gosh, yes! I haven't thought about him in years. Why did he have to bring cats into every equation?' Emily put on a deep voice. 'If y is a ginger cat and x is a tabby cat, what is $3y$ times $5x$?' She reverted to her normal voice and continued, 'You'd have thought all the sniggers and comments would have made him see sense. I wonder whether he's still teaching?'

'He retired years ago. I think the new curriculum before the even *newer* curriculum, saw him off. He really was old-school, wasn't he – pardon the pun. I think he struggled with modern teaching methods.'

'So did I!' Emily joked. 'Still, even though we all grizzled about school at the time, it beats adulting.'

'Oh? I quite like being an adult. Work aside, I enjoy being able to do what I want, when I want. Within reason, of course.'

'And what is it you enjoy doing?' she asked, after their meals had been delivered to their table. She immediately wished she could take the question back, so she busied herself by tucking into her cheese.

'Aside from taking a beautiful woman out to dinner?' He crinkled his eyes at her and picked up his knife and fork. 'Let's see: I like hiking, paddleboarding, windsurfing. Anything outdoorsy…'

'How about standing around in a field, waving your arms at a herd of cows which refuse to move?'

'Is that what you've been doing?'

Emily nodded. 'It's only fair I help out while I'm here. Dad's old stockman has retired, and they've yet to replace him. Dad seems to think it's going to be difficult to find someone. I dread to think how they'll cope if he doesn't. He's not getting any younger.'

'Do you think they'll sell up if it becomes too much?'

'I suppose they'll have to.' She stopped eating for a moment. 'I'm not sure how I feel about Glynafon Farm not being in the family.'

'Would you ever consider taking it on?'

'Gosh, no! Farming is blimmin' hard work. It's not like you can do a nine to five stint and switch off at the end of it.'

'True…'

'How are you finding living in the village? To be honest, I assumed you would sell Lilian's house.'

'I did think about it, but when I saw a job with Conservation Cymru, doing what I was already doing in the Lake District, I jumped at it.'

'Bea said you are working on a peatland restoration project?'

'I am. It's valuable and worthwhile, but I won't bore you with the details.'

'I don't mind,' Emily said, thinking that at least if Mac was talking about conservation, he wouldn't be flirting with her.

They chatted about that while they ate, Emily finding the subject more interesting than she would have thought. Mac was passionate about his work and she got the impression it wasn't just a job.

He said, 'We've just started trialling the use of logs made out of compacted sheep wool to shore up degraded peatland, instead of using the coir mats made out of imported coconut husk that we have been using up to now. Wool has a much lower carbon footprint and when it degrades it releases nitrogen and trace chemicals into the soil, which is good for the environment. So far, the experiment is a success.' He speared a chip. 'Sorry, I've just realised that I've been hogging the conversation. Tell me about *your* job.'

'It's not nearly as interesting as yours. I work for a company that makes insulation boards, panels, and fabric. I source and buy in the raw materials – it's not just me, there are two of us buyers.'

'Do you enjoy it?'

'Most of the time. I have days when I'm not so keen,' she laughed. 'I work with a good bunch of people, though.'

'That can make all the difference,' he agreed. His expression clouded for a second and she wondered why that might be.

By the time they had finished their meal, having given in to temptation and scoffed a dessert each, they had chatted about anything and everything, and she was surprised how easy he was to talk to. Back in the day she had been tongue-tied and giggly whenever he had looked in her direction, but she was pleased to discover she had grown out of that.

'I'm so full I could pop,' Emily declared, leaning back to ease the pressure on her waistband. She would have to work extra hard tomorrow to compensate for the amount of food she had consumed this evening. And the drinks; although to be fair, she'd only had two glasses of wine. Mac, she had been relieved to see, had drunk sparkling apple juice, considering he was driving.

'Me, too.' He called for the bill. 'Gran was right about the food. It is good. I can't believe I haven't eaten here before now.'

'Where do you usually take your dates?' she asked, without thinking. But when Macsen cocked an eyebrow, she realised how it had sounded. 'I know *this* isn't a date,' she said hurriedly. 'I was just wondering, that's all.' *Stop talking*, she told herself, hoping he didn't think she was asking him about his relationship status.

She was curious though, remembering what Lucy had told her.

'Pity,' he said, a smirk playing around his mouth. 'I was kind of hoping it was, what with Gran going to all that trouble to set us up.'

'Does she normally set you up with dates? Can't you find any on your own?'

'No, she doesn't, and yes, I can. And in answer to your question, I don't have a girlfriend at the moment.'

'I didn't ask any such thing!' Emily was outraged.

The smirk became a full-blown grin, as he said, 'My mistake.'

Thankfully, they were interrupted by the arrival of the bill and the ensuing verbal scuffle over who was going to pay. Macsen tried to insist that he should pay, but to Emily, letting him settle the bill would feel as though they *were* on a date, so she insisted they split it.

Once outside, she headed for the car, but Mac stopped her in her tracks when he said, 'It's still early and it's a lovely night. Fancy a stroll across the beach?'

Emily glanced at her feet. The heels of her strappy sandals hadn't got any lower over the course of the evening.

Mac followed her gaze. 'Take them off,' he suggested. 'I'll go barefoot too, if you like.' He slipped his feet out of the canvas deck shoes he was wearing and wiggled his toes. 'I might even go for a paddle.'

'In the dark?'

'It's no different to paddling in the day. Or are you too chicken?'

Emily's eyes narrowed as the challenge sunk in. Too chicken indeed? She'd show him!

She bent to undo the buckles on her sandals. Barefoot, she grasped them in one hand, grabbed the hem of her dress with the other, and scarpered across the road, her feet slapping on the tarmac.

There was a second of silence, then the sound of Mac chasing after her.

She reached the sand first and flew down the beach, but she could hear him close behind, so close that she imagined she could feel his breath on her neck. With a squeal, she flung her sandals over her shoulder, letting go of her dress as she did so.

It was her undoing.

The fabric twisted around her pistoning legs, tangling her ankles, and she fell, hands outstretched to break her fall as the beach rose to meet her.

'Oomph!' Two strong arms grabbed her around the waist, catching her before she face-planted the sand, and driving the air from her lungs. Yanked backwards, she stumbled before regaining her balance, and found herself with her bottom pressed firmly against Macsen's body.

Breathing hard, her heart pounding from the unaccustomed running, she relaxed against him for a second, relishing the feel of being held by him.

Before she could say anything, Mac steadied her, then let go. 'I won,' he declared, stepping away a pace.

Emily whirled around to face him. 'You did not! I was miles ahead of you.'

'So far ahead that when you fell, I was able to catch you? In your dreams, Nuts! Perhaps I should have let you fall, then it would have been clear who won.'

Emily gritted her teeth. 'I didn't realise it was a competition.'

'No?'

'No.'

'Do you still want to go for that paddle, or…?'

Or *what*? Did he have something else in mind, such as kissing her? 'Paddle.' Her tone was firm.

Mac shrugged and fell into step beside her. The tide was out, and there was still a little way to go to reach the water. 'Thanks for throwing your shoes at me. You missed, by the way.'

'I didn't throw them *at* you. I jettisoned them.'

'To run faster?'

'Uh huh.'

'I thought you said it wasn't a competition?'

'I lied. *Of course* it was a competition.'

'In that case, I *did* win,' he chortled. Even in the darkness, she could see his smug expression.

'Grr.' She couldn't help the growl, but at least she didn't stamp her foot. She had thankfully grown out of that. The growl turned to 'Brr,' when a tiny wavelet washed over her toes. 'Chilly!' she squealed.

'It's not that cold.'

'It *is*,' she insisted. But she took another step so the water was up to her ankles, and hoiked up the hem of the dress once more.

'Do you need warming up?' he asked.

Emily glared at him, hoping the lights from the village were bright enough to reflect her displeasure. 'No.'

He was just a silhouette, but she saw his shoulders move in a shrug.

She was tempted. There was a stiff onshore breeze that wasn't helping, but as a matter of principle she refused to get out just yet. The waves were lapping around her knees now, and she couldn't feel her feet. But being warmed up by Macsen would give him the wrong idea and she didn't want to risk that, no matter how nice it had felt when his arms had been around her (her teenage self was shrieking at her, but she elbowed it away – once upon a time she would have sold her soul and the souls of the rest of her family for an offer like that from hunky Macsen).

He said, 'If you don't want my jacket, that's fine, but if you change your mind....'

Damn it, *that's* what he'd meant. If she changed her mind now, he would think she'd taken his offer the wrong way. Which she had.

She felt a wavelet of disappointment wash over her but ignored it, feeling ashamed. It was barely a week since she had stormed out of Cole's house and here she was relishing being in another man's arms, however briefly.

Her reaction to Macsen was interesting though, because once again it reinforced her suspicion that she wasn't as heartbroken as she'd thought. Her feelings for Cole were less heartache and more anger. And if she was cross with *him*, then she was absolutely furious with *herself*.

Now that she had some distance from the relationship, she realised she had been looking at it through rose-tinted glasses. How had she failed to see Cole's true personality? He hadn't been averse to flirting with other women when she had been present, but she had stupidly put it down to him being friendly.

Friendly, for Pete's sake! What an idiot she had been!

'Have you paddled enough?' Mac asked.

Emily most definitely had. Everything below the knees was numb, the bottom of her dress was wet, and the tide was coming in.

She splashed her way onto the damp sand and stared up the beach towards the village. It looked even prettier from this angle.

Mac followed her gaze, and said, 'Sometimes I wonder why I ever left.'

'Me, too!' Emily's reply was heartfelt, but when she was younger she had craved bright lights and excitement, although the small cathedral city of Worcester was as exciting as she could cope with. On the few occasions she had been to London, it had scared the crap out of her. Way too big, way too many people, and travelling on the tube had almost given her a panic attack. No, Worcester was big enough, thank you!

But there was something magical about this wild Welsh peninsular and the pretty village at the tip of it. And whenever she visited her parents she invariably felt as though she was coming home, despite having made a life for herself elsewhere.

In companionable silence, Emily and Mac strolled up the beach, retracing their steps as Emily hunted for her discarded sandals.

After a couple of false starts, where she had mistaken a rock or a sandcastle for her shoes in the darkness, she finally found them.

'Good!' she exclaimed. 'These are my favourite sandals.'

She waited until she had stepped onto the pavement before she put them on, balancing awkwardly on one leg as she tried to brush stubborn sand grains from her feet. Helpfully, Mac offered her his arm, and she clung to him for a couple of wobbly minutes.

He seemed preoccupied on the drive back to the farm, and Emily wondered whether he was disappointed that the closest he'd got to getting into her knickers, was stopping her from falling on her nose. He must be worried that he was losing his touch.

And when the car pulled into the farmyard and she opened the door as soon as the vehicle came to a stop, she noticed the wry smile on his lips.

Ha! She'd scuppered his plans, all right!

But it would be churlish not to at least thank him for the lift.

However, Mac got in first. 'I enjoyed this evening. We should do it again before you leave.'

'I'd like that,' she replied, and was surprised to find she meant it. She had enjoyed the evening, despite knowing it wouldn't go anywhere. Even if she hadn't been leaving Glynafon in nine days, she would never contemplate having a relationship with Macsen Rogers. Once bitten, twice shy, and all that. She'd had enough of men who couldn't keep it in their trousers to last her a lifetime.

***

Emily rearranged the pillows behind her head, then settled back and continued to scroll on her phone.

It was late, but she couldn't sleep, despite knowing that she had to be up in a few hours. She kept replaying the events of the evening in her head, especially the part where Mac had caught her around the waist. The only man in the past two years who had held her like that, was Cole. And although the contact with Mac had been unintentional, it had made her restless, and a little sad. How long would it be before she felt another man's embrace?

Although why she was concerning herself with that when she had far more important things to worry about, was beyond her.

Emily silently told herself off and carried on with her midnight property search. She had been at it for about an hour, with no luck, but when she clicked on a site she hadn't visited before, an advert immediately caught her attention and she read it eagerly.

Someone called Frankie wanted a female housemate to share a two-bed terraced house in the Diglis area of the city. The rent would include all bills, and there were several photos, including one of a bedroom which Emily assumed must be the room on offer, which she studied with interest. There was a pale-coloured wardrobe, a matching chest of drawers, a lamp with a pretty shade, and cushions and a throw on the bed, which appeared to be a double. The bathroom was shared, unfortunately, but it looked clean, modern, and very tidy, as did the rest of the house. The location was good too, and the rent was doable.

Emily decided to email Frankie immediately. There was no time to lose – a room like that would be quickly snapped up.

She took her time composing it, but was eventually happy and sent it off, keeping her fingers crossed that Frankie would like the sound of her.

Even though it was impossible to tell whether someone was nice until you met them, Emily had a feeling the two of them would get on: a premise based solely on the fact that she had a similar taste in soft furnishings as this woman.

Putting her phone on the nightstand, Emily switched off the bedside light and snuggled under the covers. With the prospect of a place to live on the horizon, she felt a little more optimistic about her immediate future.

But it wasn't her *future* that filled her thoughts as she finally drifted off to sleep. It was her *past* – in the form of sexy, handsome Macsen, and the torch she had once held for him.

CHAPTER 8

There was always something that needed doing on a farm, and Emily's dad was making full use of her services. Despite feeling groggy from lack of sleep last night, Emily was currently holding a wooden post in place, while he hammered it home. Each blow sent a reverberation up her arms and through her body, and she flinched. This wasn't how she liked to spend a Saturday. Saturdays were for lie-ins, shopping, and brunch in a trendy bistro.

'Are you OK?' her dad asked.

Emily gritted her teeth. 'I'm fine.'

'Only a couple more and we're done.'

'A couple more *posts*?' Her dismay was reflected in her voice.

Her father chuckled. 'A couple more strikes. Two.' Thud. 'One.' Thud. 'There, all done. Now for the wire.'

Emily was already wearing thick workmen's gloves, and Graham also donned a pair before he began to unwind the wire fencing. Positioning the end against one of the posts, he indicated for Emily to hold it in place as he stapled it firmly to the wood.

Forty-five minutes later and the fence was once again secure.

'Good job,' he said, standing back and nodding as he gazed at the repair.

'What's next?' she asked, dreading the reply.

'A cup of tea and a slice of your mother's bara brith.'

'Sounds good. She hadn't had any delicious bready, cakey bara brith in ages, and she was more than ready for a break. As well as being physically tired, she felt drained mentally. When she had woken this morning, an alert on her phone had reminded her that today was the day Cole was running the marathon he had supposedly been training for. She wondered whether he had bothered to turn up. She might have suspected that the training had been merely an excuse to be out of the house for hours on end, if it wasn't for the fact that he came home all sweaty and out of breath. But then again, running wasn't the only activity to cause that!

'All done?' her mum asked as Emily and Graham trooped in, leaving their boots in the appropriately named boot room. Moss, the farm's most experienced sheepdog, followed them inside. Dina glared at him but allowed him to stay.

Emily estimated that the Border collie was about eleven, so was getting on a bit and deserved a few creature comforts.

'All done,' Graham confirmed. 'Emily has been a great help. Mending a fence is a two-man job.'

'Do you need her for anything in the next hour?' her mum asked.

'I can manage, if there's something you want her to do,' her dad replied.

Emily had been half-listening to the conversation while she checked the notifications on her phone, but she tuned back in to find out what task she was about to be given next.

Dina said, 'Emily, my lovely, can you dig up some potatoes for me? There's a tub by the runner beans, and if you can pick some peas that will be a great help.'

Feeling that she'd got off lightly, as soon as Emily finished her cake she scampered outside before anyone changed their minds and found something more arduous for her to do instead.

Hearing the ping of an email notification, she took her phone with her, slipping it into her pocket. She would pick the peas, then sit in the sun and shell a few pods – peas eaten within minutes of being picked were simply delicious – and while she ate her sneaky snack, she would check her emails.

It didn't take long to fill a small trug with pea pods (her mum had a bumper crop this year), and as soon as she was done Emily found a rock on the edge of the veggie patch and plonked her backside on it.

Taking one of the pods, she used her thumb to slice it open and popped the peas into her mouth. Only then did she take out her mobile and check the notification.

Her squeal of excitement when she read it disturbed a free-roaming chicken, who had been scratching about in the dirt. It let out a squawk and fluttered off.

Giving it an apologetic glance, Emily turned her attention back to the email.

Frankie had replied to Emily's enquiry and wanted to know if she'd like to view the room on Monday evening.

'Yes! Yes! Yes!' she cried, leaping to her feet and doing an on-the-spot victory dance, before sitting down again, peas forgotten, to confirm that she would love to view the room and was looking forward to meeting Frankie herself.

She sent it, then realised that she had a decision to make. Should she take everything with her when she returned to Worcester and move into Ava and Ben's spare room earlier than planned? Or should she pay the city a flying visit and drive back to Glynafon the same evening?

After debating the issue for a few moments, the deciding factor was that she didn't want to impose on Ava any longer than necessary. She would drive back to North Wales after she'd viewed the property, and spend the remainder of the week at the farm.

There was one thing she wanted to do though, and that was to collect the rest of her stuff from Cole's house – the stuff that she had bought for the house and had originally decided not to bring with her. She now realised how short-sighted that decision had been. She might need those things for her new place, and she was damned sure she wasn't going to dip into her own pocket when she had left perfectly good cushions, curtains, and bed linen behind.

The ideal opportunity to collect everything would be before going to view Frankie's house, because Cole should be at work. She still had a key, and although she wasn't sure whether she should use it (considering she didn't officially live there anymore), she also didn't want to see Cole again if she could help it.

The only things she would take from the house were the items she had bought with her own money, and any of her possessions she might have forgotten – such as the box of books Lilian had left her. Cole shouldn't have an issue with that, but in case he decided to make things awkward, she thought it best to avoid him completely.

She suspected that he would happily hang on to things such as the cushions, the retro lava lamp, the pale pink mixing bowl (even though he would never use it), the rug in the sitting room, and the print above the fireplace (which would also be coming with her), but at some point he would throw the books out, along with the files and folders that Emily had kept from her university course. They were in the attic too, gathering dust. Emily didn't particularly want them, but she preferred to dispose of them herself rather than have Cole sling them in the bin.

And when she had removed everything of hers, she would leave the house key in a prominent position, so Cole didn't think he had been burgled.

Emily was grinning as she went to tell her mum the news. She stepped inside, chuckling to herself as she imagined the look on Cole's face when he came home from work on Monday. Her parents were chatting in the kitchen, and she was shucking her boots off when she heard her name mentioned. She wasn't sure what made her pause and listen, but for some reason she froze and her ears pricked up.

'Of course she won't stay,' her mother was saying. 'There's nothing for her in Glynafon.'

Emily heard her dad huff out a breath. 'She's got a roof over her head, which is more than she's got in Worcester. I could throttle that damned man. How dare he cheat on my daughter!'

'I could too, but throttling him won't get us anywhere.'

'It might persuade her to stay if she has to hide from the press because they want to interview her about her father murdering her ex-boyfriend,' he grumbled.

Emily stifled a laugh. Dad sounded seriously peeved.

He carried on, his voice sombre. 'I worry about her being so far away, and I'm going to worry even more now that she doesn't have anywhere to live. I wish we were in a position to help…'

'I know, but everything is tied up in the farm.' Her mother sighed deeply. 'Land rich, cash poor, isn't that how the saying goes?'

'Talking about cash poor, have we got enough to pay Potters if I can't fix the tractor myself?'

'It depends. I might have to do some creative accounting, like not paying the gas bill for a month or two.'

Emily strained to listen, a lump forming in her chest as her dad said, 'When do you think we should tell her about the farm?'

'Not yet,' her mother said, firmly. 'She's got enough on her plate without worrying about that.'

What would I be worried about? Emily fretted. *What aren't they telling me?*

'We'll have to tell her at some point,' her dad retorted. 'Sooner might be better, then it won't come as so much of a shock.'

'We can't tell her *right now*,' her mother insisted. 'The poor girl has enough problems of her own, without worrying about ours, and I want to make sure she's got over that toerag she was with and is settled in a place of her own first. I must admit though, I'm not looking forward to telling her. She loves it here and this is her childhood home after all. She'll be devastated.'

Her dad said, 'We've been over this. It'll be a wrench for all of us, but we can't go on robbing Peter to pay Paul. She'll understand. Anyway, you heard what she said – farming isn't for her. If it were, things would be different.'

'She might change her mind. She seems to be enjoying helping you,' her mum pointed out.

'And I'm grateful for it. I wish we hadn't had to let Ianto go… There's so much to do and I can't manage it all by myself. There's the shearing to be done soon, and—' Her father broke off with a loud sigh.

Wait…*what?* Her parents let Ianto *go?* Emily distinctly remembered her father telling her that Ianto had retired. And what was that about not being able to afford to get the tractor repaired, and robbing someone to pay someone else… *What was going on?*

The realisation, when it came, was like a punch to the gut. The farm was in financial difficulty and her parents were struggling to make ends meet. That was what they'd meant, and that was why her dad had lied and told her Ianto had retired, when the problem was that they couldn't afford to keep him on. No wonder her dad looked so tired, and no wonder he was so grateful for her help.

Emily had heard enough. Too much.

Lilian used to say that nothing good ever came of listening at keyholes, and her godmother had been right. But the damage was done. Emily couldn't unhear the news that the farm was struggling financially.

She quietly picked up her boots and crept back outside, not knowing what to think. On the one hand, she was cross with her parents for not telling her, but on the other she felt like crying because they didn't want to burden her with their problems.

She made her way back to the veggie patch and stared forlornly at the trug of peas, her thoughts whirling. But one was uppermost – if she moved back home and got a job in Glynafon, would her wages help her parents hang onto the farm? As well as ploughing everything she earned back into it, she would also be able to take some of the burden of running it off her dad's shoulders. She was young and strong, and she could help out before work, after work, and on the weekends, the way she used to when she was growing up.

As she saw it, she didn't have any choice, because how could she *not* stay after hearing what she had just heard?

Bless her, Mum had given her a way out by not wanting her to know, and someone else (someone like Cole, perhaps?) might pretend they'd never eavesdropped in the first place.

But not Emily.

She couldn't do that to them. As far as she was concerned, she had no option other than to move back to Glynafon Farm permanently. She would tell them she'd had a change of heart, that she couldn't face going back to Worcester and that she wanted to make a new life for herself in her old home.

Disconsolately, she began rooting through the tub of potatoes, hoping she would find enough for their evening meal, even though she felt sick and didn't think she would be able to manage a single bite. She would just have to pretend – because there was no way she would ever let her mum and dad know the real reason she wasn't going back to Worcester.

***

Peas, new potatoes, bacon and a fried egg... Emily eyed the food on her plate and tried not to wince. She still felt sick and suspected it might take a while for her appetite to reassert itself. The thought of having to inform her employer that she wouldn't be returning to work after her two-week leave of absence filled her with dread, and imagining how Ava would react when she heard the news was even more distressing.

Emily could only imagine what her dad must be going through. The farm had been in her father's family for five generations. It was part of him. Farming was in his blood and it was the only thing he had ever known.

She would do anything and everything she possibly could if it meant he didn't lose it.

The thought of strangers living in the house she had grown up in, tore at her heart. Her mum was right — she would be devastated. Glynafon Farm was her rock, the one constant and reliable thing in her life. It was her *home*.

'Are you all right, love? You've hardly touched your tea.' The concern in her mum's eyes almost made Emily cry. With all that was going on in her mother's life, she still worried about her.

'I'm fine. Just tired. I think I'll have an early night.'

'Good idea. Graham, you've been working that poor girl too hard. She's here for a bit of TLC, and you are wearing her out.'

'He's not, honestly,' Emily was quick to reply. 'I, er, think the events of the past few days might have finally sunk in.'

'Oh, my poor sweetheart. I could murder that man.'

'Get in line,' her dad muttered.

Emily smiled sadly. 'My turn first,' she joked. Oh well, one good thing about not going back to Worcester was never having to see Cole again. There would be little chance of her bumping into him in the biscuit aisle of her local supermarket.

She was just about to open her mouth to tell them that she had decided to stay on the farm if they'd have her, but she closed it again. She knew she was doing the right thing, but just to make sure, she would take a day or so to mull it over, to see if she could come up with any alternatives, but she strongly suspected she wouldn't. Her mum was the savvy one when it came to the farm's finances, and Emily guessed she would have already explored every possibility.

It wasn't just finances that her mum was savvy about: she might well be suspicious if Emily told her that she intended to say in Glynafon less than half an hour after her parents had been discussing it. Her mum would probably smell a rat, so Emily decided to leave it for a couple of days. She would talk to them on Monday, then hand in her resignation. She might have to work her notice, but she'd cross that bridge when she came to it.

Emily helped her mum wash up, then headed outside to round up the chickens for the night. She fancied a bit of fresh air and she also wanted to be alone for a while. Anyway, it would give her a chance to phone Ava.

'How are you bearing up?' Ava asked sympathetically, as soon as she heard Emily's voice.

Emily puffed out her cheeks. 'I don't know, to be honest. My head is all over the place.'

'I expect it is.' Ava's voice was loaded with sympathy. 'I can't believe Zelda has moved into Cole's house already.'

'*So soon!?*' Bloody hell, that was quick, Emily thought in disgust: she hadn't been gone a week!

'Apparently, Cole told Ben that Zelda hates the colour scheme in the living room, and Ben got the impression that she intends to scour the whole place. She's already started, Ben said.'

'I bet she has,' Emily replied grimly. 'I don't blame her though – if I'd stepped into another woman's shoes the way she had, I would want to get rid of anything that might remind me of how badly I'd behaved. And I'd want to obliterate any hint that the other woman had ever lived there, because neither would I want Cole to be reminded of her every time he drew the curtains or sat on the sofa.'

'He's an arse,' Ava said, and Emily wholeheartedly agreed.

It was only after she'd rung off, still seething that Cole was allowing Zelda to redecorate when he used to make a fuss if Emily had wanted to hang as much as a single picture on the wall, that she realised she hadn't told Ava that she would be staying in Glynafon for good.

CHAPTER 9

'Your mother is so good to me,' Bea said, taking the cake tin out of Emily's hands. 'She bakes me a cake every week, without fail. What have we got today, I wonder?'

Emily didn't have the foggiest. All she had been thinking, when her mum had asked her to drop something off to Bea after Sunday lunch, was that this was what her life was going to be for the foreseeable future – running errands for her mother.

But even as the thought entered her mind, Emily felt guilty. Of course she was more than happy to help out, it was just… she had envisioned a more exciting future, for herself, that's all. The fact that her life hadn't been terrifically exciting to date, was neither here nor there. It would have *become* exciting – or so she had thought, when she had been dreaming of white weddings and happily ever afters. It wasn't her fault that the dream had turned to ashes. She lay the blame for that firmly at Cole's door.

'Come in, have a cup of tea with me and keep an old woman company for a bit,' Bea urged, ushering Emily inside. 'And while I'm putting the kettle on, you can tell me why you've got a face like a slapped arse. Is it Mac's fault, because if it is, he'll feel the sharp end of my tongue.'

Emily gave a tiny smile as she thought of Macsen getting a stern telling-off from his gran.

'It's nothing to do with Mac,' she assured her, keen to make sure Bea didn't think her grandson was responsible for her woes.

Emily didn't know whether Bea was aware of Mac's reputation, but even if she was, Emily didn't want him to carry the blame for this. She was no jilted lover (actually she *was*, but it hadn't been Mac who had done the jilting), and neither had he given her the runaround, although, she acknowledged, he probably would have done if she'd given him the slightest encouragement.

'Good. What is it, then?'

'Nothing important, just a few things to sort out,' Emily said.

Those 'few things' were weighing heavily on her mind; she needed to resign from her job, and she should also let Frankie know that she wouldn't be viewing the house tomorrow. She had been so excited to see it, too…

She would do both of those things today, she vowed. Delaying handing in her resignation wasn't going to change anything, considering she hadn't come up with any other solution to her parent's problem.

'Is that ex of yours giving you gyp? Your mum told me what he did.'

'Not really.'

'Have you found yourself a place to live yet?' the old lady persisted.

Bea fixed her with a beady-eyed look, and Emily knew she wouldn't let the matter drop. Besides, she may as well tell Bea now, because when Emily informed her mum of the change of plan, her mum would tell Bea anyway. And telling her mum was another thing she would do as soon as she returned to the farm. Emily said, 'I'm staying here. I'm not going back to Worcester.'

Bea's eyebrows shot up. 'I didn't see that coming.'

Neither had Emily. Over these past seven days there had been several things that Emily hadn't seen coming. Bloody Cole! If he hadn't—

'Your face will stay like that,' Bea warned, and Emily realised she was scowling and hastily rearranged her features. 'And don't look so pleased about it,' Bea added sarcastically.

Emily had already blurted, 'I'm not!' before realising what she'd said.

Bea sighed. 'You'd better give me the full story. Sit down, have a slice of whatever is in this tin, and tell me all about it.'

Emily dutifully sat, wondering how much she should divulge. She didn't want to blab about her mum and dad's financial situation, but she desperately wanted to talk to someone, and she knew that whatever she told Bea would remain confidential: Bea wasn't a gossip. Lilian hadn't been either, and many a time Emily had shared her childhood worries with her godmother when she hadn't felt able to tell them to anyone else. It had usually been silly stuff that she had forgotten about shortly after, but which had seemed so important to her younger self at the time. Maybe this was the same? Perhaps in a few months, Emily would be wondering why she had set so much store in returning to Worcester.

Bea was gazing at her expectantly, so Emily began, and when she had finished explaining why she was staying in Glynafon, Bea patted her hand.

'You're a good girl and what you're doing is commendable, but I know your mum, and she would be upset to think that you are staying on the farm because you felt you had to, and not because you wanted to.'

Emily replied, 'Which is why I'm not going to let on that I know. If my staying here means they get to keep the farm, then that's what I'll do. I can't see any other way.' She gave a sad laugh. 'I've got some savings, but it's not enough to keep the wolf from the door for long. And I thought about selling the jewellery Lilian left me, but I'm not sure how much I'd get for it and I'd hate to be ripped off. Besides, it's got sentimental value, so I don't want to get rid of it if it isn't going to help matters.'

Bea squinted at her. 'I hope you got a decent price for that book.'

'What book?'

'The little one with the black cover. Lilian reckoned it was worth a pretty penny. A first edition, I think she said. It was in the box with the others.'

Emily was frowning. 'I can vaguely remember a small black book, but I can't remember the title. I'm sorry to say, I didn't look at them too closely.'

Lilian had once told Emily that she would leave her some jewellery and a box of books when she died, and Emily remembered her saying something like 'it's worth a pretty penny', but Emily hadn't paid too much attention. Back then, she hadn't ever imagined Lilian dying. Her godmother had been as much a part of the village as the pub, and her not being around had been unthinkable.

But Lilian *had* died, and she had left Emily all her jewellery and some books, just as she'd promised she would.

The jewellery had some value, Emily knew, especially the pretty Victorian brooch, but she didn't believe it to be worth a great deal – after all, not many people wore brooches these days. But as for the books... Emily had taken a cursory glance, noticed that they were all old, and had promptly put them out of her mind, and when she had moved in with Cole, the box had gone straight into the attic.

She had assumed the dusty old tomes must have been from Lilian's youth, and therefore had held some sentimental value for her godmother, which was why Emily hadn't disposed of them.

'It was thin, leather-bound...' Bea scrunched up her face. 'I can see it now... What was it called? Hang on, it'll come to me... its name sounded like Glynafon. Glenfarnon... Glenamon... *Glenarvon!* That's it. Phew! Don't you just hate it when something is on the tip of your tongue? Glenarvon,' she repeated triumphantly. 'Lilian said the story was rather gothic and melodramatic, I believe, and the title also reminded her of Glynafon.'

Emily raised her eyebrows.

Bea carried on, 'She bought it from a second-hand bookshop in Hay on Wye, years ago. She paid a good bit for it then, if I remember rightly. I told her she must have been off her rocker, but she never listened to me.'

'Who was it written by?' Emily asked. She was intrigued now, and wanted to know more.

'A woman called Lady Caroline Lamb, in around 1815 or 1816. I can't quite remember exactly. But I do recall Lilian saying that Lady Caroline had a very public affair with Lord Byron, the poet. It caused quite a scandal at the time. Anyway, after she wrote the book people said that Lord Glenarvon, who was the main character in the story, was based on Byron. Lilian did a bit of research and found out that the first edition caused such a furore, that Lady Caroline was forced to quickly bring out a toned-down second version. But – and here's the important thing – this particular book has been annotated by *Lord Byron* himself! Glenarvon wasn't released until a few weeks after Byron left England, but Lady Caroline must have sent him an early copy. When you look inside you will see for yourself what he thought of it. Put it this way, he wasn't complementary. It's his inscription and signature that makes this copy so valuable. And Lilian wanted *you* to have it.'

'How much…?' Emily coughed, her throat suddenly dry, and tried again. 'How much is it worth?'

The question earned her a sharp look. 'I hope you've still got it and not thrown it away. Or given it to a charity shop,' Bea tutted.

'I've still got it,' Emily rasped.

'Good. I suggest you get it valued, because if Lilian was right, it might be the answer to your mum and dad's problems.'

'How much do you think?' she asked again, and when Bea told her, Emily almost fainted from the shock.

***

How Emily managed to say goodbye to Bea and stagger out of the house, she'd never know. But once outside, she leant her backside against the low wall surrounding Bea's lovely front garden and took several deep gulping breaths.

'Are you OK?' Macsen asked, and she almost leapt out of her skin.

She had been so deep in thought (or was it shock?) that she hadn't heard his jeep pull up.

'You look like you've seen a ghost,' he added.

She stared at him wordlessly, and he stepped closer.

'Are you hurt?' he asked, then his gaze shot to the house behind her and he muttered, 'Oh, shit!' and Emily realised he had jumped to the wrong conclusion.

'Bea is fine,' she gasped. 'She's drinking tea and eating cake.'

Mac slapped a hand to his chest. 'You scared the crap out of me,' he said, relief spreading across his face before his expression quickly turned to one of concern again. 'If Gran is OK, why do you look like you've just had an almighty shock?'

'That's because I have,' she replied.

'Do I have to beat anyone up?' Mac looked so serious and determined that Emily smiled.

'Not today. I could have done with your services last Saturday though.'

'Was that the day you found out your boyfriend was doing the dirty with another woman?'

Emily straightened up. 'You have such a nice way with words. And he's not my boyfriend. Not any longer.'

'Glad to hear it. I don't go on dates with women who are already in relationships.'

'Glad to hear it,' she shot back at him.

His mouth twisted into a sardonic smile. 'So you *do* admit that Friday was a date!'

Emily rolled her eyes. 'I'm not talking to you anymore.'

'Not even to tell me what's bothering you? I'm pleased to see you've got a little more colour in your face. I was worried there, for a second.'

'I'm fine,' she began, then sucked in a deep breath as the astronomical amount of money that Bea had mentioned flashed into her head once more. If the book really was worth that much, her parents need never worry about money again.

Macsen was giving her that look, the one where he was wondering whether she was about to fall over. 'You're clearly *not* fine. How about I take you home?'

'No!' she cried, then toned it down. 'Not yet. I need to um… er…' She stared at him helplessly. Maybe she needed a sit down and a stiff drink. 'The pub,' she blurted.

'It's a bit early, isn't it? It's only five o'clock.'

'Not too early for me.'

Mac was scrutinising her intently. 'I don't think it's a good idea for you to drink on your own, so I suppose I'd better come with you.'

'What about Bea?' Emily's eyes shot to the living room window. A movement from within made her frown and Emily knew that Bea was watching this little exchange.

'I'll call in on Gran later,' Mac said, taking her elbow. 'Come on, let's get a glass of wine inside you and you can tell me all about it.'

'What if I don't want to?' she asked, brushing his hand off.

'You will.' He seemed very confident.

With a shake of her head, Emily followed him to the pub, but instead of going inside, he made for the garden. Glad to sit down because her knees were shaking, Emily sank onto a bench.

'Wine?' he asked.

'Brandy. A large one.'

'Is it that bad?' The concern was still there, and his voice was gentle.

'Yes. And no. It depends how you look at it.' She rested her elbows on the table and put her head in her hands.

'Don't go anywhere. I'll get us both a brandy.'

'Aren't you supposed to be driving me home?'

'I'll walk you home instead.'

Emily watched him saunter away, wondering how much she should tell him – *if* she told him anything at all. She knew Bea wouldn't betray a confidence, but would she have already mentioned the book to Mac? It wasn't any secret that Lilian had left the house to Mac and a few bits and pieces to Emily, but the question was, did Mac have any inkling of how much one of those items was worth? And if she didn't mention it now and he spoke to Bea later…?

He returned with a double brandy for her, and a single for him.

She took it eagerly and drank a large mouthful, then spent the next minute coughing as the liquid burned its way down her throat and set fire to her stomach.

'Better?' he asked, but she ignored the sarcasm.

'Do you remember that Lilian left me some jewellery and a box of books?' she began.

Puzzlement spread across his face. 'Yes?'

'Apparently one of the books is worth quite a bit.'

'I knew Aunt Lilian used to collect old books and she once told me that some of them were very collectable, but…' Mac trailed off and shrugged. He was silent for a while, then he said, 'They couldn't have been worth much.'

'Are you thinking that if they *had* been worth something, she would have sold them and spent the money on the house?'

'Exactly! It needed a complete overhaul,' he said. 'I've put a new kitchen and bathroom in, and it's had a new roof.'

'Maybe she liked it just the way it was,' Emily replied cautiously. But maybe Macsen had a point, and the little black book wasn't worth much at all.

'There is that,' he agreed. 'She never did like change. Gran reckons that was why she never married. Too set in her ways, Gran used to say. Apparently, she was like it when she was a girl. Anyway, why are we discussing old books, when we should be talking about the reason you are upset?'

'I'm not upset, as such. It's more a case of being in shock.'

'Why?' Mac persisted.

'I called in to see Bea earlier, and we got to talking about Lilian's books.' Emily took another substantial sip of brandy, but this time she was prepared for it and it slid down without any drama. 'She mentioned that one of them is a first edition – Glenarvon, written by Lady Caroline Lamb – and is worth a small fortune.'

'Wow! That's fantastic!' Then his face fell. 'Oh dear, don't tell me you've lost it, or got rid of it?'

'No, I know where it is, and it still belongs to me. Technically.'

He raised his eyebrows. 'Carry on…'

'It's in a box in my ex's attic.'

'And that's a problem because…? Can't you ask for it back?'

'Um, I could try, but I don't want to alert him. I'm sure he would give it to me if I asked, but he's moved his new girlfriend in and I've got it on good authority that she doesn't like me very much. She's already putting her own stamp on the place, and I've heard that she's getting rid of anything that might remind Cole of me. I wouldn't put it past her to throw it out if she knew it was mine.'

'She sounds a horrid piece of work.'

Emily sighed. 'She probably isn't. I expect she's insecure.'

'You're being far nicer than I would be, if I were in your shoes.'

'I did hate her, but now just I feel sorry for her. If Cole can do that to me, what's stopping him from doing it to her?'

'You've had a lucky escape,' Mac said.

'Yes, I have. If I never see that man again for as long as I live, I'll be happy. Which is why I'm going to Worcester tomorrow to get the book back.'

'And how do you propose to do that without seeing him?' Macsen was smiling indulgently at her.

Emily guessed he thought the double brandy had gone to her head. It hadn't. Before she knew about her parents' problems and the book, she had already decided to collect anything belonging to her and had worked out how she was going to go about it, so she saw no reason to change her plans.

It was a good thing she'd not yet handed in her notice, or informed Frankie that she wouldn't be able to make the house viewing. Because, if the book was worth as much as Bea thought, Emily could save the farm and return to the life she had made for herself in Worcester.

***

'Let me get this straight.' Mac was studying her, his expression bemused. He had just returned from the bar with another double brandy for her. She noticed he had yet to finish his first. 'You are planning to break into your ex's house and steal the book.'

Emily shook her head emphatically. 'I'm not going to break in: I've got a key. And how can you steal what already belongs to you?'

'OK, I'll give you that last one. But entering a house which you don't have permission to enter, is wrong. And you mightn't be 'breaking in', but you will probably be trespassing.'

'Only if I'm caught, and I don't plan to be.'

'What if he's got a day off, or comes home unexpectedly?'

'I'll ring the bell first to check he's not at home,' Emily said. She wasn't stupid. But she *was* desperate to get her hands on the book.

'You're determined to do this, aren't you?'

'Yep.'

'And I can't persuade you to ask him for it?'

'Nope.'

Mac took a deep breath and let it out slowly. 'Then I suppose I'll have to come with you.'

'Why?' Emily was puzzled.

'Someone needs to bail you out of gaol when you get caught.'

'I'm not going to get caught. And even if the worst happens and Cole does come home early, I'll just tell him that I'm picking up the rest of my things. What?' He was pulling a face, and she glared at him. 'It's the truth.'

'Fine. Have it your way, but I'm still coming with you.'

'I don't need moral support.'

'No, but you'll need a lookout guy.'

A giggle bubbled to the surface. 'A lookout guy? I'm fetching a few bits and bobs, not stealing the crown jewels.'

'Can I at least pretend that you're a spy and I'm your wingman? I always wondered what it would be like to work for MI6.'

'You're mad.'

'Probably.'

'Don't you have to work tomorrow?'

'I expect so.'

'So you can't come with me, can you?'

'I'll book a day off.'

'Isn't it a bit short notice?'

'Didn't you do the same thing last weekend?'

'That's different, I was in distress.'

'Are you still in distress?' His expression was kind, but Emily preferred his sassy look. She neither wanted, nor needed, his pity.

'No, I'm not.' It was true: she wasn't. But what did that make her? Fickle? Shallow? Just last week she had been convinced she was heartbroken, but to have recovered so quickly…

Admittedly, she was still devastated by what Cole had done, but dismay, disbelief, disgust, and incredulity that a man who had professed to love her could have treated her like that, took precedence over heartbreak.

So she guessed she couldn't have loved him as deeply as she'd thought. Had she loved him at all, or had she loved the idea of being in love more than the man himself?

And if she hadn't really been in love, would she be able to trust her own feelings and judgement the next time? If there *was* a next time, because the way she felt right now, she would be happy if she never had a romantic relationship ever again.

'Penny for them?' Mac said.

'I hate men.'

'Okaaay…'

'Not all of them, obviously, I love my dad. And you're all right, too.'

'Thanks, I think.'

'But most of them are arseholes.'

'You're probably right.'

'They want to have their cake and eat it.' She was getting into her stride now, righteous indignation flowing through her, warming her from the inside out. Or might that be the brandy? Her glass was empty, but she couldn't remember finishing it.

'Are you ready to go home now?' Mac asked.

'I haven't got a home.' There was a tiny puddle of dark liquid in the bottom of her glass and Emily tipped her head back and opened her mouth wide to let it trickle in. She brightened. 'I'm going to see a woman about a house tomorrow.'

'Is this before or after you've broken into your ex's place?'

Emily shot him an irritated glance. 'I told you – it's not breaking in if you've got a key.' She wrinkled her nose. 'After. I'm seeing the house at six. I hope she likes me.'

'She would be daft not to.' His tone was deadpan, and his expression gave nothing away.

'Do *you* like me?' she burst out. Then she flushed profusely. Oh, God, was she seriously asking Macsen that?

His lips twitched. 'Yes.' He got to his feet. 'I'll drive you back to the farm.'

'You can't, you've been drinking.'

'I think you'll find you drank mine.'

'I did?'

He nodded.

'Shit. I'm drunk, aren't I?'

'Not drunk as such. Tipsy, maybe.'

She groaned. 'I don't want a hangover.'

'Who does?' He took hold of her elbow and guided her out of the beer garden and onto the pavement.

As they began walking towards Mac's car, she said, 'I mean, I've got a long drive tomorrow.'

'What time do you want to set out?'

'Mid-afternoon would be the best time.'

'Isn't that a bit late? I've never been to Worcester, but even I know it's at least a three-hour drive from here.'

'Not *leaving* – getting there.' She rolled her eyes and tutted loudly. Macsen was supposed to be a bright guy. 'Six hours.'

'You've lost me.' He opened the car door for her, and she clambered into the passenger seat.

'It took me six hours to travel from Worcester to Glynafon last Sunday.' She stabbed at the clicky thing that the seatbelt went into and missed. When she missed again, Mac gently took the buckle out of her hand and clipped it in.

'I was perfectly capable of doing that myself,' she objected.

'You were,' he agreed, but she had a feeling he was humouring her.

The journey took all of five minutes, and soon Emily was unbuckling herself: an easier task than doing it up.

'I'll pick you up at nine, shall I?' he suggested, as she carefully got out of the car.

'No. *I'm* driving. My book, my ex, my problem.'

'Fine, you drive but I'm still coming with you.' He had got out, too.

Did he expect to kiss her?

The thought sent her tummy into a spin, and when he stopped in front of her, a rush of desire sizzled through her veins and settled south of her belly button.

The disappointment when he indicated she should walk to the house, was acute.

Dear God… she vowed not to drink so much again. At least, not in Mac's presence, because she hadn't forgotten the way she used to fantasise over him all those years ago. What was that thing called, where you did something automatically without thinking… muscle memory? Except hers was emotional memory. Echoes of teenage hormones, that's all this was. And too much brandy. A large glass of water, some precautionary painkillers and a doorstep sandwich to soak up any remaining alcohol in her stomach, and she would be as right as rain.

'I'll be here at nine on the dot,' he said, as she came to a halt on the step.

'You don't have to come with me. I'm a big girl.'

'I know you don't need my help, but indulge me. Please?'

'Why would you want to spend what could be over twelve hours stuck in a car with me?'

'Let's just say that I enjoy your company, Nuts.'

'Do you want to get into my knickers?'

Mac guffawed. 'That wasn't my aim, but if you're offering…?'

'Gah! You men are all the same. Can't keep it in your pants.' Emily turned away in disgust, but froze when he placed a hand on her arm.

His voice was soft as he said, 'I most definitely can keep it in my pants. I'm going with you as a friend, nothing more – although I'm not going to deny that I'm attracted to you. *Very* attracted.'

Emily gave him a sideways look, her heart bumping against her ribs. His eyes had darkened as his gaze snared hers, and his lips were curved into a sexy half-smile. The sight of them sent a jolt of unbridled lust right through her.

Drawing in a sharp breath, she let it out in a hiss. Him coming with her tomorrow was *so* not going to work. She was still far too attracted to him, and to learn that he felt the same way…

But she was off men for good (for a good while, she amended) and he had a reputation, so he was probably attracted to any woman under the age of forty.

Mac held up his hands. 'I'll back off, I promise. I know you're still hurting and I know you're only in Glynafon for a few more days. Just friends, OK?'

Emily hesitated: company on the trip would be nice. He could help keep her awake on the long drive back, for starters. He could also help keep her calm on the way there, because whenever she thought about unlocking Cole's front door, she broke out in hives. It would be hard stepping into the house she had happily lived in for the past year. And it would be even worse if Cole's new girlfriend had already moved all her stuff in.

Emily would never have believed she could be so easily replaced, and the way Cole had treated her had hit her confidence hard. Although... hearing Mac say that he found her attractive was a boost to her self-esteem. But then again, he probably used that line a lot. It had certainly made her sit up and take notice for a moment.

'Nine a.m. on the dot,' she agreed. 'But if you don't behave yourself, I'm leaving you at the side of the road and you can walk home. Agreed?'

'Agreed.' He strolled to his car, chuckling, but he just had to get in a parting shot and she heard him say, 'I'll wear my hiking boots just in case.'

Goddam it! He was ruddy insufferable.

CHAPTER 10

'What are you doing!' Emily exclaimed in exasperation, as Mac twisted the dial on the car's blower this way and that, and a blast of hot air hit her in the face.

'Trying to find the air-con.'

Emily snorted. 'It's that button, there.' She jerked her chin at the dashboard, and Mac found the one she was referring to. He pressed it and the passenger window glided down.

'That's not it, that's for the window— Oh.' The penny dropped. 'You don't have air-con, do you?'

'No. That's what windows are for,' she retorted. Hers was already half down, and a welcome breeze ruffled her hair.

The threatened heatwave had finally arrived, and half of the population of the UK must be on the move, if the traffic was any indication. The roads were ridiculously busy, and she dreaded to think what it would be like when schools broke up for the summer holidays in a week's time. Which was why Emily had decided to turn off the main arterial roads and use the ones less travelled. It was a more direct route but would normally be a slower one, because many of the roads were narrow and twisty. But with the number of vehicles on the main roads slowing traffic to a crawl in places, this route might prove quicker in the long run, and it would be better for her nerves if she didn't have to concentrate so hard.

Emily and Mac had set off early enough, so time shouldn't be an issue; as long as they arrived before Cole got home from work, that was all she cared about.

'You should have let me take the jeep,' Mac grumbled, as he fiddled with the radio again.

He wasn't proving to be the world's easiest passenger. In fact, he was downright annoying. He kept fidgeting and couldn't seem to sit still.

Emily gave him a sideways look and stifled a giggle. He'd had to fold his body into the seat, and he filled the inside of the car so thoroughly that whenever she changed gear, her hand brushed against his thigh, making one or the other of them apologise.

The first time it had happened, Emily had felt a sizzle of desire travel up her arm, flow through her chest and settle in her lower stomach. The feeling had yet to dissipate, and she was beginning to wish she'd let him drive after all. Being so close was affecting her concentration. Not only did she run the risk of touching him every time she reached for the gearstick, but his scent invaded her nostrils and made her head spin.

She risked another glance.

He was staring at the road ahead, a frown teasing his brow. 'Are you sure this is the right way? This road seems awfully narrow.'

They were trundling along a single-lane road which had been steadily climbing for the past ten minutes. To either side was rough moorland, dotted with clusters of trees. They appeared to be in the middle of nowhere, but she knew where she was going. More or less.

'I'm sure. This is the most direct route, and you've seen how bad the traffic is on the main roads.'

'We're going to end up in some farmer's backyard at this rate.'

'If all you're going to do is complain, I'll let you out now and you can walk back,' she threatened. She had checked out his footwear before he'd got in the car, noticed that he hadn't been wearing his hiking boots, and had felt a pang of disappointment. The thought of Mac not behaving himself had been quite appealing.

Too appealing…

'I'm *not* complaining,' he argued. 'I'm sure you know what you're doing.' However, the look on his face suggested that he was sure she *didn't*.

'I do,' she insisted. 'It took me six hours to get from Worcester to Glynafon last time, and I don't want a repeat performance, thank you. I don't think I could take another six hours stuck in this car.'

She was aware of the slow smile spreading across his lips. 'Is that because I'm so irresistible that I drive you crazy with lust and you're finding it difficult to keep your hands off me?'

'You're driving me crazy all right,' she shot back, as he fiddled with the radio yet again. The signal wasn't the best, and once more the noise coming out of it was mostly static.

Emily had to admit that there was a semblance of truth to his words. She was finding it awkward being in such close proximity, and she was so acutely aware of him that it made her whole body tingle.

Flippin' heck! She was behaving like a love-struck teenager. Anyone would think she was eighteen, not twenty-eight – although her eighteen-year-old self would have found this experience far more overwhelming. Past-Emily would probably have fainted with excitement. Present-day Emily, however, was merely irritated that he still had such an effect on her.

There was one good thing, though: Mac took her mind off what she was about to do, because whenever she thought of sneaking into Cole's house, her gut twisted into a knot of apprehension.

Emily proved her point when it came to the traffic and B-roads as the car joined the A49 near Craven Arms, and she was quick to gloat.

'Ta-da!' she cried triumphantly. 'See, I knew what I was doing.'

'I'm glad one of us does,' Mac grumbled.

She smiled smugly. 'We've made such good time. I think we can afford to stop off for a coffee. I don't know about you, but I could do with a break.'

'Coffee would be good. I'm looking forward to stretching my legs, too.' He shifted in his seat, but at least he didn't mention his bloody jeep again.

Emily kept her eyes peeled for somewhere suitable, and it wasn't long before she spotted it. Pulling into a layby, she brought the car to a halt beside a burger van.

'This will do,' she declared, cutting the engine. 'I hope they do hot dogs. What do you fancy?'

'You?'

Emily tossed her head. 'Good luck with hitching a lift.'

Mac gave her a cheeky grin. 'You can't blame a guy for trying.'

'I can. Behave.' She scanned the chalkboard on the outside of the van. 'Yippee! A hot dog for me, and a latte, please.'

Mac gave his order, and while they waited he gazed at his surroundings. 'How far is Worcester from here?'

'About fifty minutes.'

'We should be there by about two o'clock,' he said, and suddenly Emily felt nervous again.

She was really going to do this. It wasn't idle talk or wishful thinking. She was an hour away from sneaking into Cole's house; or coming face-to-face with him if he was at home. She knew which one she preferred, so after she'd finished her hot dog, she wiped her hands on a serviette and made a phone call.

'Ben? It's Emily. Can you speak?'

'Er, yeah. What's up, Em—'

'Shh! Don't say my name – I don't want Cole to know you're talking to me. Are you at work?'

'I'm always at bloody work.'

'Is *he* there?'

'Cole? Yeah, I—'

'Shh!!'

Ben lowered his voice until it was little more than a whisper and continued, 'I can see him. He's at his desk.'

'Is he planning on leaving the office, do you know?'

'Not that I'm aware of. Look, E— er, what's all this about? You're being very cloak and dagger. Does it matter if he knows you're on the phone?'

'Yes, it does,' she hissed, although she didn't know why she was whispering too. 'Has he said anything about leaving early? Or will it be the usual time?'

'The usual time, I think.'

She let out a sigh of relief. 'Thank God. I'm going round to his house in about an hour, to collect the rest of my things, and I didn't want to bump into him.'

'You're in Worcester?' Ben's voice rose and she shushed him again.

'Not yet, but I will be soon.'

'Are you staying? Ava didn't say anything.'

'That's because she doesn't know. Don't worry, I'm not about to descend on you. I'm going to grab my stuff, view a house I hope to rent a room in, then I'm going back to Wales straight after.'

'You're more than welcome to stay with us.'

'I know, and thank you. Tell Ava I said 'hi' and I'll phone her tomorrow for a catch-up. Before I go, would you do me a favour and give me a ring if Cole leaves the office?'

'I'll try, but I'm going into a meeting shortly, so I mightn't be able to.'

'That's OK. I won't depend on you to tip me off.'

'Take care, E… er…'

Emily chuckled. 'I will.' She ended the call to find Mac gazing at her. 'That was Ben, Ava's partner.'

'I guessed as much.'

'Cole is at work and Ben doesn't think he's got any plans to leave early.'

'That's good.'

'See, I told you I didn't need my hand held.'

'I never said you did. I'll still play lookout, though. I should have worn a disguise.'

Emily shot him a quizzical look. 'Why? No one knows who you are. *I'm* the one who should wear a disguise.'

'Stop spoiling my fun.'

'You call this *fun*?'

'Spending time with you *is* fun,' he countered. His expression was serious, but she felt fairly certain he was winding her up. Or coming on to her.

She narrowed her eyes, but let it go. She had more important things on her mind. Like praying that Cole hadn't thrown out her little black book.

***

It was strange to be driving up Rainbow Hill, over the bridge spanning the canal and under the railway. To Emily, it felt as though she had been away far longer than a week. For some silly reason, she almost expected the area to look different, but the road was exactly the same as the last time she had driven along it, as was the street where Cole lived.

And as she turned the corner, her eyes automatically coming to rest on his house, she felt very odd indeed. This used to be her home, the place where she had felt safe, loved, and secure.

Now though, it felt like a snake's lair, and Cole was the viper.

She pulled into the pavement, a short distance down the street on the opposite side of the road. Coles's house was roughly in the middle of a terraced row, and she gave an involuntary shudder when she saw it.

Mac noticed. 'Would it be easier if I went in instead? You can tell me where to look and I'll fetch it.'

That was very nice of him, but this was something she had to do herself. 'Thanks, I appreciate the offer. But I want to get a few other things as well, and it'll be easier and quicker if I do it myself.'

'OK, but be careful. No setting off any alarms.'

'Cole doesn't have one.' She sniggered nervously. 'Although he might get one when he discovers all the soft furnishings are missing. They *are* mine,' she added hurriedly, in case Mac thought she was stealing them.

'I didn't doubt that for a second. Go do what you have to do, and if you need me, just shout. I'll be right here, watching your back.'

Despite her protestations that she would be fine on her own, Emily was grateful Mac was here. 'If you see a man driving a pale blue BMW with the numberplate beginning CO13, phone me,' she said.

'You can count on it,' Mac replied, and she could tell from his expression that he was sincere. She knew he wouldn't be sitting there playing on his phone. She knew he would be keeping watch, as promised.

Not that he would be able to prevent Cole from entering his own house, but any advance warning would be better than none. It would give her time to steel herself – and shove the book into the waistband of her jeans, just in case her ex decided to play dirty. She didn't care if he seized the box and refused to allow her to leave with it, as long as she had the little black one.

'Be careful,' Mac repeated as she got out of the car after checking the street.

'I will. You make it sound like I'm about to do something dangerous.'

She walked towards the house, trying to act as though she didn't have a care in the world and that it was completely natural for her to be there. Which, in the eyes of her neighbours, it probably was. She doubted if any of them had the slightest inkling she no longer lived there, except for Mr Dodds opposite. He was always up for a bit of gossip and liked to spend most of the day peering through his net curtains. Emily always made a point of stopping to speak to him because she suspected he was lonely.

From the outside Cole's house looked exactly as she remembered. Same blinds, same trophy on the living room windowsill. He had won it playing football when he was seventeen, and it had pride of place.

As she sauntered past the bay window, she kept her head to the front, but her eyes swivelled right as she desperately tried to see inside.

It was no good – she couldn't tell whether he was there or not. She just had to hope that her ex hadn't managed to sneak out of work since she'd spoken to Ben: however, with his car not being here, she was as certain as she could be that the house was empty. Praying there would be no answer, she rang the bell, hearing the chime deep inside. Thank God it wasn't one of those camera doorbells, she thought, then her breath caught in her throat as she checked to make sure he hadn't changed it.

He hadn't. It was the same bell.

She had another panicky moment as she worried that he might have changed the locks. If the shoe had been on the other foot, she would have got a locksmith out faster than a greased pig, as Lilian used to say.

But he hadn't. Her key slid easily into the lock, and the mechanism clicked as it opened.

With another furtive glance up and down the street to make sure no one was watching, she caught Mac's eye. He nodded once.

Then she went in.

And came to an abrupt halt.

What the…?

The walls in the hall sported a swathe of arcs painted on them in a variety of colours. Some were bright (too bright) and others were almost the same bland beige shade but with a small variation in tint. On each arc, written in pencil, was what Emily assumed to be the name of the colour and the make of paint.

She leant forward to peer at two identical ones. Mushroom Meadow said the one, and the other sported the words Stone Éclair. They were both horrid, beigy, nothing shades, and she was tempted to find a pencil and write exactly that but thought better of it.

Eyes wide, she wandered into the living room and gasped.

All the furniture was piled into the centre of the room, and there wasn't a single cushion or ornament in sight. The lava lamp had gone, and so had the rug. There weren't any pictures on the walls, either. Apart from the furniture, all that remained were the curtains and that damned trophy.

The kitchen appeared to be stripped bare, too. Gone were the colourful fridge magnets, and there was no sign of the rail of snazzy utensils that had hung from the ceiling. Even the hooks had been removed.

Filled with dismay, Emily opened the cupboard where her pink mixing bowl had once lived and came nose-to-nose with a high-tech food processor.

Don't tell me Zelda can cook, Emily thought savagely. Or was the machine just for show?

Anger building, she checked the rest of the cupboards, but the bowl was nowhere to be seen. Apart from a few things, most of the items behind the cream-coloured cabinet doors were unfamiliar.

Dear God, that woman hadn't wasted any time, had she? Emily's side of the bed was barely cold!

Thinking about the bedroom had her scuttling upstairs to check out the damage, and she stopped dead when she saw a four-poster monstrosity in place of the one that she used to share with Cole. Emily wondered if it was new, or whether Zelda had brought it with her from whichever rock she had crawled out from under. Not only that, but there was further evidence of the woman's influence everywhere Emily looked, from the framed photos of Cole and Zelda together (there was one of the pair of them in the snow – so when the hell had that been taken?!), to the impressive array of lotions and potions on the dressing table.

Emily stepped forward to have a closer look.

Good grief – the woman had more moisturisers, cleansers and toners than a decent-sized branch of Boots.

The more Emily saw, the more incensed she became, and her previous thawing towards Zelda suffered such a severe cold snap that it was equivalent to a mini Ice Age. Zelda had certainly made herself at home.

And Cole hadn't hung about, either. No sooner had the door shut behind Emily on her way out, than he had moved this other woman in.

When Emily had fled back to Glynafon, tears streaming down her face, she'd held the vain hope that Cole might try to fight for her. She should have guessed he wouldn't, but she couldn't help being affronted that he hadn't even bothered. It wasn't as though she had been difficult to track down – he had probably guessed that she had gone to Ava's, but Emily knew that he hadn't sought her out there. So the only other place she could be was Glynafon, and he hadn't contacted her there, either. Which made her believe that he must have been glad to see the back of her.

Resisting the urge to take some scissors to the contents of Cole's wardrobe, she checked out Zelda's side of the built-in cupboards instead, and wasn't surprised to see it rammed full.

Emily had just reached out a hand to take a closer look at a sparkly blue dress, when her phone rang.

'Argh!' she screamed, her feet leaving the floor as she almost leapt out of her skin.

Oh, shit, she thought, when she saw Mac's name on the screen. With her heart in her mouth, she scrambled to answer it.

'How long have I got?' she demanded.

'Pardon?'

'Twenty seconds? Ten? Oh, buggeration.' She took the stairs two at a time, stumbling down the last one and nearly headbutting the wall when she reached the bottom.

'Buggeration?' Mac sounded amused.

How dare he think this was funny! 'I'm coming out. Start the car – we might have to get away fast.'

'Do you want any help bringing stuff out? I can load the car while you—'

'*Is Cole here?!*' she screeched.

'What? Has Ben phoned?'

Emily sagged against the door. 'No, I thought that was why you were calling. Cole's not outside, is he?'

'No.'

'Can you please not ring me again unless he is? I almost broke my neck coming down the stairs.'

'Sorry. Do you need any help?' Mac repeated.

'No. All my stuff has gone.'

She heard his sharp intake of breath, then he said, 'The box of books, too?'

'I don't know. I haven't been up the attic yet.'

'Don't you think you should?' She heard the recrimination in his voice.

'I was just about to do that when you phoned,' she lied. Then she ended the call, annoyed that he was right: she should have gone up the attic first, and not wasted her time on the rest of the house. If the book was worth as much as her godmother had suspected, Emily could buy a load of new cushions and as many lava lamps as she wanted.

With renewed purpose, she headed back up the stairs.

The hatch to the attic was in the spare bedroom, and Emily only took a cursory glance at the room as she pressed the leaver which would open the hatch and release the ladder.

Wincing at the noise it made as it slid down, Emily waited impatiently for it to extend fully then climbed up, switching the light on as she reached the top.

A blast of heat hit her, and she gazed around. It was stifling up here, and already she could feel the sweat beading on her forehead and gathering in the small of her back.

From what she could tell, the loft hadn't yet been touched by Zelda, and it looked much the same as when she'd put the Christmas tree and decorations back, which was the last time she had ventured into it.

Now, where was that box?

She could have sworn it was in the far corner, so she gingerly made her way across, stepping warily on the boards. Although she knew they wouldn't collapse under her weight, she couldn't shake off her distrust. There was something about attics that she didn't like...

Was that the box?

Squinting, she moved closer, and realised with relief that it was indeed her box of books. Thankful that it was still there and apparently untouched, she opened it and examined the contents.

At first she couldn't see the one she wanted and her heart plummeted as she frantically hunted through them, then... *there it was.* Hidden between a brown book with gold lettering and a tome with a faded red binding, sat a slim, black, leather-bound book.

Reverentially, she lifted it out and gazed at it.

The front of it was blank, no title, nothing. Just embossed leather which had a raised design in the middle and around the edges. It was the same on the back. However, the spine had the word Glenarvon in tiny letters written on it, and when she opened it up, the front plate had the title, the author, the publisher's name and date... and some faded handwriting, complete with ink blots. And a name. *Byron.*

Emily drew in a shaky breath, her heart thumping. It was here, it was really here. To think that this thin little book could be worth so much. Goodness!

Gently she closed it and held it to her chest, as she struggled to compose herself, then when she felt ready, she carefully put it back.

Picking the box up, she made her cautious way back to the hatch, and had just put the box down so she could edge herself onto the ladder, when her phone rang again.

It was Mac, probably wondering if she needed help bringing the box out. How big did he think it was?

Or he could be calling her because Cole had just pulled up outside…

'Mac?'

'Get out, get out!' he hissed. 'A woman has just pulled up outside Cole's house. Didn't you say he'd moved his new girlfriend in? I'm sure it's her – she's faffing around with something on the back seat, but she keeps glancing at the house.'

Effing hell, it must be Zelda! Emily had been so focused on Cole, that she had forgotten about Zelda.

Emily groaned. 'Shit!'

'Hurry, she's heading for the front door.'

'I'm still in the sodding attic.'

'Can you hide?'

'I'll have to – she's coming in!' Emily heard the sound of a key in the lock and her blood froze.

She was about to get caught!

CHAPTER 11

There was no time to pull the ladder up, even if that were possible. All Emily could do was switch the light off, turn her phone on silent, and hope Zelda didn't realise anyone was up here. With any luck, the woman might think Cole had been in the attic and had forgotten to close it, or maybe Zelda would assume that the lever was kaput and the ladder had come down of its own accord.

Emily prayed that Zelda had only popped in for a couple of minutes and would leave again soon.

She held her breath as the front door banged shut and strained to hear as Zelda walked along the hall, following her footsteps as the woman's heels clip-clopped from the tiles and onto the wooden floorboards of the living room.

Breathing out slowly, Emily felt a flutter of relief that Zelda hadn't immediately ventured upstairs, but she knew it was only a matter of time.

What if she was home for good and didn't go out again? Even if Zelda didn't realise that someone was hiding in the attic and she closed the hatch, Emily would be stuck here until tomorrow.

The thought of being discovered and the police being called made her feel sick. She wished she had simply asked Cole for the books. She wished it had been *him* who had arrived early and not Zelda: Emily might have stood a chance of talking her way out of this ridiculous situation if it was Cole who found her. She had a feeling Zelda would want to throw the book at her.

Oh… *the book*! How the hell would she smuggle it out of the house if she was being dragged away in handcuffs? She had seen enough TV to know that all her personal possessions would be confiscated at the station. She might never see the book again, especially if she was accused of stealing it.

She had no choice. She would have to make a run for it.

Shit! Emily froze as she heard a familiar sound. It was the creak of the third stair from the bottom. *Zelda was coming upstairs.*

Oh, God, she thought, panic filling her. *I'm done for.*

A loud bang made her jump, and she stifled a squeal. It was swiftly followed by another, then another. It sounded as though someone was hammering a large saucepan with a rolling pin. The noise was coming from outside, from the rear of the house Emily guessed, and it was one hell of a din.

Where was Zelda? The noise was obliterating any sound from inside the house, and Emily was desperate to know where the woman was.

Plucking up her courage, she risked a peep through the open hatch.

She couldn't see Zelda herself, but she could see the woman's shadow on the wall of the stairs, and Emily realised she was about halfway up. Zelda wasn't moving though, and Emily crossed her fingers that she was wondering what that awful racket was and would be sufficiently curious to go and investigate.

When Zelda's shadow slowly retreated, Emily almost cried with relief, but her relief quickly turned to worry again when her phone vibrated with an incoming call and she saw it was Mac.

Keeping her voice low, Emily pressed the phone to her ear and whispered 'Hello?' then she snatched it away as her head was filled with a terrible cacophony.

The banging was now coming at her from two directions, from outside and from her phone. It was almost as though Mac was smack bang in the middle of whatever was making the—

Mac! He was creating a diversion to give her time to get out.

Emily had no idea what he was doing but she was bloody glad he was doing it.

And just before she hung up, she heard him yell, 'She's outside, in the garden! *Run!*'

So that was what she did.

Scuttling down the top few rungs of the ladder, she hoisted the box onto her shoulder whilst trying to hang onto the rail with the other hand, got a more secure grip on the box as she hit the ground.

Charging out of the bedroom, she hurtled along the landing and threw herself at the stairs, skidding down them, wildly off balance and clinging onto the box for dear life.

But as she dashed towards the door the noise stopped.

Keeping her fingers crossed that it would take Zelda a couple of seconds to come back inside, Emily grasped the door handle, yanked it open and darted into the street,

Running as fast as she could, she pelted full tilt down the pavement, towards her car. Catching sight of Mr Dodds's confused expression, she gave him a wild grin, and was vaguely aware of his baffled wave, then he was behind her. Other neighbours had also come out to see what all the ruckus was about, but she ignored them, too intent on reaching the car.

Emily took valuable seconds to ease the box onto the backseat, before sliding behind the steering wheel. Shoving the key into the ignition, she took her phone out, dialled Mac's number and jammed her mobile to her ear as she started the engine.

Mac answered on the first ring.

'I'm out!' she yelled. 'Meet you at the end of the street.'

'Roger that,' she heard Mac shout as she tossed the phone onto the back seat.

Bloody hell! He thinks he's a goddam special agent, she thought, laughing hysterically as she pulled away from the kerb far faster than was wise.

Unfortunately, she hadn't specified which end she meant... Because when she got to the end of the street, Mac was nowhere to be seen.

Frantically, Emily scanned left and right wondering where the hell he could possibly be, then movement in her rearview mirror caught her attention.

There he was, at the other end of the street, standing in the middle of the road, waving his arms.

Letting out a little cry of frustration, Emily threw the car into reverse and hurtled back up the road, the engine screaming in protest as she floored the accelerator.

Mac tore down the middle of the road, and they met almost back where they'd started.

Not waiting for Emily to bring the car to a complete standstill, Mac yanked the door open and dived into the passenger seat.

'Drive! Drive! Drive!' he shouted, and Emily was more than happy to oblige.

Only when they were on the main road again did she slow down. And only then did she realise that Macsen was laughing like a loon. He was doubled over, his arms around his middle and his shoulders shaking, and when he looked up, he wore a huge grin and tears were streaming down his face.

It took him a couple of seconds to calm down enough to catch his breath, and when he did, he said, 'That's the most fun I've had in ages. Did she see you?'

'She didn't – thanks to you. What was that awful noise?'

He snorted with laughter. 'A plank of wood against one of those metal bins people use to burn their garden waste in. I was hoping she would come out to see what all the fuss was about before she clapped eyes on you. I thought that if I could keep her occupied long enough to let you escape....'

'You did! You were marvellous.' Emily grinned.

Mac grinned back. 'You ought to have seen her face when she saw me in the garden. I thought she was going to lynch me! Thank goodness one of the neighbours is a keen gardener.' He dissolved into hysterics once more.

It was infectious, and soon Emily was laughing almost as hard as he, and had to pull into a carpark because tears were streaming down her face.

'I thought I was going to be stuck in that attic for hours. Or arrested,' she spluttered.

'It was a wonder someone didn't call the police on *me*,' Mac chortled. 'The only way I could get into the garden was by climbing over the fence. I must have looked like an utterly inept cat-burglar. I didn't have a clue what I was going to do – knock on the back door and ask if she wanted her windows cleaned, perhaps. But then I saw this metal bin thing in next door's garden.'

'It did the trick,' she said, giving him a grateful smile as she dabbed at her damp cheeks.

'Aren't you glad I insisted on coming along?'

'Absolutely!' And with that she leant across and threw her arms around him. 'I don't know what I would have done without you,' she cried, her voice muffled because her face was buried in his neck.

He tensed, then she felt his arms go around her and she relaxed into him, suddenly feeling incredibly shaky and more than a little overwhelmed.

As though he sensed how she was feeling, he held her close, one hand stroking her hair as he murmured, 'It's OK,' over and over.

Drawing strength from him, she finally gathered herself enough to pull away. But as she settled back in her own seat, she caught his eye, and her breath hitched in her throat. For a second he looked as though he wanted to devour her, but the expression was quickly replaced by concern.

'Are you all right?' he asked.

She nodded. 'I'm fine. Honestly. It's the adrenaline.'

'What you need is a nice cup of tea.'

'You sound like Lilian. She always thought a cup of tea could cure anything.'

A smile hovered around his lips, and Emily's gaze dropped to his mouth. He had a nice mouth, a kissable mouth, and she wondered what his lips would feel like.

Realising what she was doing, she dragged her eyes away.

'It won't hurt, and it might help,' he said, and it took her a beat or two to refocus on the conversation.

'Er, yeah, OK. Good idea. It's too early to see the house, so we may as well take a stroll into the city centre – it's not far, only over the road – and I'll treat you to a cuppa.'

He stared at her, and she thought he was going to say something, but she must have been mistaken or he had changed his mind, because all he did was give a curt nod and get out of the car.

Had she said something to upset him, she wondered, as he stalked off, and she was about to follow him, when she dithered over what she should do with the book. Should she leave it in the car or take it with her? Both had their risks…

She was still dithering when he came back into view, wielding a ticket.

'I assumed we'd leave the car here,' he said, handing her the ticket to display on the dashboard. His voice was normal, as was his demeanour, so she must have imagined it, which was quite likely considering her emotions were all over the place. A near miss, such as the one she'd just had, could do that to a person.

'I'm not cut out to be a spy,' she announced, as she locked the car, having placed the box in the boot out of sight.

'Neither am I,' Mac admitted. 'When I saw Zelda go inside with you still in there, I…' He trailed off.

Emily searched his face for a hint of what he might have been going to say, but his expression didn't give anything away and neither did he meet her gaze. He was staring into the distance, and a tiny muscle in his jaw twitched.

Was he annoyed with her for putting him in that position, she wondered, as they left the carpark and crossed the road. All the drama could have been avoided if she'd only waited for Cole to come home from work.

She didn't blame Mac if he was. In hindsight, she had been incredibly stupid. She was lucky to have got away with it.

On second thoughts, luck hadn't had anything to do with it. It had all been down to Mac and his quick thinking.

'Your idea was brilliant,' she said. 'You're not just a pretty face, are you?'

'I've got brains as well as beauty,' he shot back, with a sardonic grin. 'I'm glad you think I'm 'pretty'.'

'OK, not pretty: handsome.'

He arched an eyebrow and warmth crept into Emily's cheeks.

'I mean, good looking,' she amended, realising she was making things worse when she saw him biting his lip. She assumed he was trying not to laugh as she dug a deeper hole of embarrassment for herself. 'I'll stop talking now,' she said.

'Please don't. It's entertaining.' His mouth was curving into that sexy half-smile of his, and she let out a snort of exasperation.

'I'm so glad I amuse you.' Her retort was sharper than she intended. 'Sorry, I'm still a little shaken up.'

'It's only to be expected. Shall we try here?'

'Here' was a pretty double-fronted café on New Street.

Emily didn't answer; she just darted inside, eager to sit down and collect her wayward emotions. Coffee would probably make her even more jittery, so she settled for a raspberry tea.

By the time she had drunk half of it, she was feeling more herself, and when Mac asked her what the book was like, she was more than happy to answer.

'It's about this big and this wide,' she said, indicating the size with her hands. 'I'll show it to you later. It doesn't have anything on the cover, only the spine, but it's got a lovely front page.' She glanced around the café to make sure no one was taking any notice and lowered her voice. 'Byron has written something inside. I couldn't quite make out what it was, but his signature is clear enough.' She sat back and hugged herself, as the realisation that she had the means to put an end to her parents' financial problems sank in.

She had the tricky problem of selling it, but she was sure it would be fine. She would do her research and get a few valuations before she took the next step.

'Fancy another?' Mac asked, as she drained the cup.

'I'm good, thanks. Shall we take a stroll? It's lovely down by the river, and if we've got time we can have a wander around the shops.'

Mac pulled a face.

Emily hazarded a guess. 'Shopping not your thing?'

'Not so much. I'll happily look around the cathedral, though, if it's open to the public.'

Surprised, Emily said that it was. She knew Macsen was the outdoorsy type – he'd told her as much – but she wouldn't have put him down as a culture buff. She was happy to go along with his idea though: she rather liked the cathedral. It was humbling to think that it had been built hundreds of years before she was born and would probably still be standing hundreds of years after she was gone.

As she and Mac entered the impressive monument, she had a sudden image of her own children, grandchildren and great-grandchildren walking where she was walking, seeing what she was seeing, and it made her feel rather tearful, because before that could happen she first had to find a guy to have those imaginary children with.

Now that Cole was out of the picture, her plans to marry and have kids had well and truly flown out of the window.

But then she glanced over at Mac...

He was standing in front of the magnificent west-facing stained-glass window. His head was tilted back as he studied it, and shafts of multi-coloured light speared the air around him. One of them was illuminating his face.

Unbidden, a thought popped into her head – what would *their* children look like...?

Oh, no you don't, she told herself. She wasn't going to go there. Not now, not ever. He might be gorgeous to look at, and she might be extremely attracted to him, and – even more worrying – he seemed to have been genuinely concerned about her today, but that didn't mean she was going to have any kind of romantic relationship with the man.

Her heart had only just narrowly escaped being broken, so there was no way she was going to risk it being smashed to smithereens – because she had a feeling that was precisely what would happen if she allowed him to get anywhere near it.

CHAPTER 12

'I'll meet Frankie, take a look at the house, then how about we have dinner before we head home?' Emily suggested, as she drove the short distance to the house she hoped to be living in. It was in an area of the city not far from the cathedral or the river, and she was pleased to see that the road the house was on sloped gently down towards an expanse of playing fields. The street itself consisted of terraced houses, similar to the one Cole lived in, but that's where she hoped the similarity ended.

'Good, I'm starving,' Mac announced. He turned his attention to the house, as they pulled up outside. 'It looks nice.'

'It does,' Emily agreed, beaming.

She cut the engine and got out, surprised when Mac got out too. 'You don't have to come in with me,' she said.

'I want to. I'd like to see where you're going to be living.'

'*If* Frankie likes me,' Emily reminded him. 'This isn't a given.'

'I'm sure she'll love you. But if, for any reason, the two of you don't hit it off, what will you do?'

'Look for somewhere else.'

'You wouldn't consider staying in Glynafon?'

There was a tone to his voice that made her hesitate just as she was about to ring the bell, and she shot him a sharp look. 'No, I don't think so. I never wanted to be a farmer.'

'You don't have to be. There are other jobs out there, you know.'

'My life is here. There isn't anything for me in Glynafon,' she stated, but once again she doubted her own words.

'You'd better ring the bell before the neighbours think we're casing the joint,' Mac pointed out, his expression inscrutable.

'Right.' Putting on her best smile, Emily pressed the button, then waited. She felt nervous, knowing that she was about to be evaluated, and she hoped she wouldn't be found wanting in any way.

The door opened, Emily's smile grew wider… then faded.

In front of her stood a bloke. He was around forty years old, had alarmingly white teeth gleaming out of an overly-tanned face, receding hair, and was wearing a white vest top and faded jeans. To top it all off, Emily could see wiry black hairs poking over the neckline of his top, like fat spider legs.

'You must be Emily,' he said, wiping his right hand on the backside of his jeans and holding it out to her.

'That's me.' She took it and gave it a shake, but the brief contact she had hoped it would be, became rather more extended as he held onto her hand for longer than was necessary.

When he finally released her, after scanning her from top to toe and all parts in between, Emily resisted the urge to wipe her palm on her own jeans.

'And you are…?' the man asked Mac.

'Mac, a friend of Emily's.'

'Right. You do know this room is for one person only?'

Emily noticed that he didn't offer to shake Mac's hand.

'I do know, and I'm not looking to move in,' Mac replied in an even tone, but Emily noticed his jaw clench.

'Good.' The chap rubbed his hands together. 'In that case, you'd better come in.' He stepped to the side to let Emily pass, but he didn't step far enough, so she was forced to squeeze past him, shrinking away as she did so.

As soon as she was inside, the bloke followed, leaving Mac to bring up the rear and close the door behind them.

'Um… I thought I was meeting Frankie,' Emily said, walking into the sitting room. 'Is she here?'

As she glanced around, her heart sank. The room bore only a fleeting resemblance to the one in the photo. The décor was the same, but where the photo showed a clean, tidy room that was tastefully furnished and sported nice touches such as throws, cushions and candles, this room looked as though a wild party had been held in it the night before and no one had got around to cleaning it. There were dirty plates on the floor, on the sofa and the side table, as well as several glasses, some half full. And squashed beer cans were everywhere. There wasn't a throw or a cushion in sight either, and the curtains were half-closed, casting the room into gloom.

Faintly, Emily thought that maybe the gloom was a good thing – she suspected the place might look even worse in a better light.

'Sorry about the mess. I haven't had a chance to clean up yet,' the bloke said.

'Frankie?' she reminded him, ignoring Mac who was loudly clearing his throat behind her. She had an awful feeling she knew where this was going.

'*I'm* Frankie,' the man announced, confirming her fears. 'The name's Frank, but my friends call me Frankie. And if I let you move in, we'll be good friends, won't we, so you can call me Frankie.'

Mac let out a strangled noise, which turned into a stifled yelp when Emily stamped on his foot.

Mac might have come to her rescue once today, but she could deal with this herself.

'Me and the missus have split up, so I need someone to help with the bills,' Frank was saying, oblivious to Emily's dismay or Mac's simmering anger. How Frank failed to notice the tension coming off Mac in testosterone waves, Emily didn't know.

Frank carried on, 'And if you could help a bit around the house, I'd be very grateful.'

'*Oh?*' Emily was starting to simmer. To think she had pinned all her hopes on a dive like this.

'Yeah, like if you are doing a load of washing, maybe you could shove some of my clothes in with yours? And I'm hopeless at ironing.' He gave her what he must have believed to be a winning smile.

Emily winced. No wonder his wife had left him. He was obnoxious.

She gazed around the room again, and her expression must have given away how she felt, because he added, 'As I said, you'll have to excuse the mess. I had some of the lads around on the weekend. The missus never liked the lads coming around, but now she's gone it's party time! And to show I'm a fair man, I don't mind if you have a few friends around, either.'

His eyes tracked up and down her body again, resting briefly on her chest, before moving up to her face. Dear God, the letch was licking his lips!

She heard Mac utter a growl, and this time she elbowed him in the stomach. He let out a grunt.

Frank was still oblivious. 'I suppose you want to see your room? We'll have to share the bathroom. Sorry.'

He didn't sound sorry in the slightest; he sounded positively delighted, and the thought of him creeping across the landing in the hope that she had forgotten to lock the bathroom door, was the last straw.

'No thanks, *Frank*—' she emphasised his name '—I've seen enough.' She drew in a steadying breath, willing herself not to lose the plot.

But before she could say anything further, he leapt in with, 'Great! When can you move in?'

'How about never?' she hissed, through gritted teeth. 'I wouldn't move in here if *you* paid *me*. This place is a tip.'

'It won't take you long to clean it up – you would soon have it ship shape.'

'*Me?*' Emily spluttered. 'You want *me* to clean up *your* mess. Over my dead body!'

'OK, perhaps we can come to some arrangement?'

'No, no arrangement. I'm going now. Come on, Mac.'

Mac seemed to have grown a couple of inches and was glowering at Frank. His hands were clenched into fists by his side and Emily prayed he wasn't thinking about punching the guy. If there was any punching to be done, she would be the one to do it. She shoved Mac in the chest and when he failed to move, she shoved him again.

'Out,' she commanded.

After a final glower, Mac looked at her and nodded. She pushed him ahead of her, not trusting that he wouldn't take a swipe at Frank if the odious man uttered another word.

Frank scuttled after them, too close to Emily for comfort, but she ignored him and hurried outside.

Taking a deep breath of clean air, she let it out in a sigh of relief.

But Frank, the idiot, couldn't resist one last comment. 'Don't be hasty. Think about it, eh? But don't take too long because a place like this will be sure to be snapped up pronto.'

Emily stepped between a furious Mac and an oblivious Frank, as Mac snarled, 'The only thing that's going to be snapped around here, is your scrawny neck.'

'Get in,' Emily commanded. 'He's not worth it.'

'You can say that again,' Mac spat. 'No wonder his wife left him. The obnoxious creep.'

She quickly hustled him into the car and hurried around to the driver's side before he decided to leap back out and go all macho on her. She appreciated the sentiment and thought it was lovely that he was looking out for her, but she could do without any more drama today. She had already come far too close to having the police called on her, and the last thing she wanted was for Mac to be arrested for assault.

'I wouldn't actually have wrung his neck,' Mac said as the car pulled away from the kerb. His eyes glittered dangerously and he continued to radiate anger, but some of the tension had left his face and he had relaxed into the seat.

'I did get a bit worried there for a minute,' she admitted. 'I thought you were going to deck him.'

'I was tempted. I don't agree with violence and it never solves anything, but for that man to suggest... Actually, I'm not entirely sure what he was suggesting, but it sounded sleazy. If he had so much as laid a finger on you—'

'He didn't dare.' *Not with you there,* she thought. It might have been a different story if she had gone to view the house on her own, and a shudder went through her. This was the second time today she had been grateful for Mac's presence.

Suddenly she giggled. 'I can't believe he expected me to do his washing and ironing. His poor wife. And I pity anyone else who goes to view his house. I bet he only picks women. *Frankie* indeed! I was imagining some trendy professional woman: instead I got a nasty, creepy guy.'

'I bet you're now doubly glad you brought me.' Mac's smile was once again smug.

'I didn't need you to hold my hand. I was more than capable of dealing with him on my own.'

He barked out a laugh. 'I didn't doubt you were. At one point I thought you were going to knee him in the balls.'

'I would have if he had got any closer.' She blew out her cheeks. 'What a day.'

'It's been fun. Are things always as interesting around you?'

'You'll have to stick with me and find out,' she shot back.

His tone was oddly sombre, as he replied, 'I would, if you were staying in Glynafon.'

Her heart missed a beat. Did he mean what he said, or was he merely flirting? She didn't know him well enough to tell. *But you'd like to get to know him an awful lot better, wouldn't you?* a voice in her head said, and she silently told it to shut up. Getting to know him better wasn't an option.

'I'm starving,' she announced. 'I know a little pub a couple of miles out of the city centre. How about I treat you to dinner?'

'I thought you were all for going Dutch?'

'I am, but I owe you one.'

'You don't have to buy me dinner: I'll settle for a thank you.'

'Thank you,' she parroted back. 'But I'm still going to buy you dinner.' She jerked her head towards the rear of the car. 'After all, I think I can afford it.'

'In that case, I accept – on one condition. I buy dinner the next time.'

There wouldn't be a next time. In six days she would be heading back down this road and preparing to stay in Ava's house for the duration. Although it wasn't an ideal solution to her homeless situation, it was the best she could do and she hoped it wouldn't be for long.

Mac seemed to have an uncanny ability to read her mind. 'What will you do now that you won't be renting a room from Sleazy Guy?'

'Keep looking and move in with Ava and Ben for a while.'

He frowned. 'You do realise that when you sell the book, you'll be able to afford to buy somewhere? You might not have to stay with your friends for long.'

'Er... yeah. You're right.' He wasn't, but that was only because he didn't know the full picture and Emily had no intention of sharing it with him.

'Don't sound too enthusiastic,' he drawled. 'Although, I suppose you do have to get it valued first.'

'I've been thinking about that. I'm planning on taking it to a few different places to compare.'

'Have you thought about an auction house? They might be more impartial. I'm only saying that because you hear stories of people taking valuable items to jewellers or antique dealers, and they're offered a low amount because they want to scam you.'

'It is a risk,' she admitted. 'I wonder if I could get it valued by the *Antiques Roadshow* experts?'

'That's an idea! Let me see...' Macsen's thumbs flew over his phone screen. 'Here we go... Oh, no, sorry. You need a ticket, and the application date is long gone. Apparently, you can't just turn up on the day.'

'Bummer.' She indicated to turn left and drove into a small carpark next to a quaint little pub. 'I'll look online tomorrow, but I would like to get it valued as soon as possible.' She got out. 'You haven't seen it yet, have you? Do you want to take a look?'

'Yes, please. It would be nice to see what I risked life and limb for.'

'Ha, ha.' She opened the boot and eased the cardboard flaps aside. Carefully lifting out the slim volume, she passed it to him.

Mac took it with the respect it deserved and turned it over in his hands. 'It's smaller than I thought, and quite ordinary and nondescript.'

'I know. But look inside.'

Slowly Mac opened the cover. 'That's more like it,' he said, reading the print, then brought it closer to read the inscription. 'You can see the name Byron easily enough, but the rest of it is a bit of a scrawl. Either the man was in a hurry, or he was as mad as hell.'

'I think it was the latter.'

Emily watched him place the book back in the box. After locking the car, she double-checked to make sure, then they made their way inside.

'I'm so hungry,' she moaned. 'I'm having a starter, a main course *and* a dessert.'

'Go for it. I think I'll join you. Have you been here before?'

'Once or twice. The food is good and it's not too far from where I used to live.'

'You used to come here with Cole?'

'Why do you want to know? Are you jealous?'

'Yes, if you must know.'

'Ha, ha, very funny.'

'I'm not joking.'

Emily was fairly sure he was, but before she could reply a member of staff claimed her attention, and she said, 'A table for two, please?'

'Certainly, if you'd like to follow me.'

Emily poked her tongue out at Mac and fell into line behind the waitress as she showed them to a table before handing them a menu.

'Can I get you any drinks?' the woman asked.

'Lemonade, for me,' Emily said.

'Make that two, please.' Mac smiled up at the waitress, and Emily watched as she simpered at him.

Bloody hell, he really was a player, she thought. A second ago he had been pretending to be jealous that she had frequented this place with Cole, and now here he was, flirting with the staff. No wonder Lucy and Jo had warned her about him. She would do well to remember that, and not allow his charm and good looks to get under her skin.

However, she was forced to acknowledge that his presence had been invaluable today, so she hid her irritation behind the menu.

With drinks and orders sorted, Emily returned to the subject of how to get the book valued. It seemed the safest topic of conversation, and the one least likely to set him off in flirting mode.

'*Antiques Roadshow* would have been perfect. What about *Flog It!?*' she wondered.

'The last series was filmed several years ago. The ones they're showing on TV now are all re-runs.'

'You watch *Flog It!?*'

'Gran does, therefore I get to watch snippets of it. There's another programme that's been doing the rounds. It's called *Heirlooms*. They do a similar sort of thing, where people take their antiques along to be valued. If they like the valuation, *Heirlooms* sells the items on the person's behalf at that fixed price. But the catch is that the valuation might be lower than it would fetch at auction (or it might be higher, in which case the owner is quids in) and the items are only on sale for twenty-four hours.'

'That's not very long.'

'It's all about the drama, dahling,' he drawled.

'I'm not sure I like that. What if you don't think the valuation is high enough? Are you obliged to go through with selling it?'

'Not at all, you get to take your item back home with you.'

'Hmm.' Emily took a gulp of her lemonade, as Mac played with his phone again.

She slumped back, suddenly exhausted. The day certainly had been a busy and emotional one, not to mention all the travelling. She would be lucky to keep her eyes open on the way back. Thankfully it would still be light for a couple more hours yet, which might keep her alert, but when it began to grow dark she might have to ask Mac to prod her every few minutes.

Mac let out a low whistle. 'Well, well, well,' he said. 'Guess where *Heirlooms* will be filming on Friday.'

'I haven't got the foggiest.' And neither did she care. She had about as much chance of getting tickets for that, as she'd had for *Antiques Roadshow*.

Mac beamed. 'Powys Castle.'

'So?'

'You can take the book there.'

'Tickets?' she reminded him.

'Don't need any. People can just turn up.'

'Sounds like a free-for-all to me,' Emily grumbled.

'Do you have any better ideas?'

'Go to a proper auction house.'

'Will it do any harm to try *Heirlooms* first? At least then you might have more of an idea of its worth.'

'I don't know… What if I'm turned away, or they don't have anyone specialising in antique books?'

'Of course they will.'

Emily wasn't convinced, but what did she have to lose? And it was a step in the right direction. 'Powys Castle, you say?'

He nodded, his eyes alight with eagerness.

'This Friday?' She had to double-check because if it was next Friday she would be at work.

'Yep, gates open at nine a.m., but I'd bet my right arm you'll need to get there much earlier if you want to be anywhere near the front of the queue.'

'How early?'

'Middle of the night early?'

Emily sighed. If that's what it takes, she thought. 'I suppose I could give it a go.'

'Want some company?'

'Don't you have a job to go to?'

'Yes, but I don't work nine-to-five. And I've got some holidays to take.'

'Why would you want to waste a day's holiday on something like *Heirlooms*?'

'It might be fun.'

'It might not. It'll probably be lots of standing around, for nothing.'

'I've never been to anything like that before, and neither have I been to Powys Castle. An episode of *Antiques Roadshow* was filmed there a few years back.'

'You watch *Antiques Roadshow* as well as reruns of *Flog it!*?'

'Guilty as charged.'

'I wouldn't go telling people that. It'll ruin your reputation.'

Mac laughed. 'What reputation?'

Emily gave him a knowing look, but didn't reply.

'Well? Can I come with you or not? I'll bring a picnic.' He waggled his eyebrows. 'There'll be pork pies and sausage rolls, and maybe even a cheese triangle.'

'Who can resist a cheese triangle?'

'I knew I could tempt you.' His mouth curved into a slow smile, and suddenly her heart was racing as she imagined that same mouth claiming hers.

Yes, she thought unsteadily, he certainly could tempt her – but it wasn't food she was referring to.

CHAPTER 13

Emily was sitting bolt upright in the driver's seat and peering intently through the windscreen. Although the car's headlights were on full beam, they barely pierced the darkness. She was having difficulty seeing more than a few metres ahead, and she cursed her silliness in insisting that they return to Glynafon on the same B roads that they'd travelled on earlier today. Actually, it was *yesterday*, because midnight had already come and gone. And right now she wasn't entirely certain these *were* the same roads. Emily had a sneaking suspicion she was lost; a little piece of news that she would have to share with Mac before they became even loster (she'd just made that up – lost, loster, lostest...?)

And now she was procrastinating like a good 'un, attempting to delay the inevitable by playing silly word games in her head.

'Er, Mac?'

'Yeah?' Mac hadn't said a word for the past hour, and at one point she'd thought he was asleep because he had been so still and silent. But when she'd risked a glance at him, she had realised that he was keeping quiet to allow her to concentrate.

'I... er... think we might be lost.' There, she'd admitted it.

'Ah.'

'Don't just say 'ah'. Use the map thingy on your phone,' Emily urged.

Mac sighed and got his phone out.

'Well? Where are we?' she demanded. The road was narrow, with overgrown verges on either side and was barely wide enough for a single vehicle. The most recent indication of civilisation had been a sign for a farm and some lights in the distance, but that had been about ten minutes and several kilometres ago. And with its potholed, rutted surface and the grass growing along the middle of it, Emily feared that this road was swiftly becoming a dirt track.

'Are we on the right road?' she asked.

'Not exactly. I think we need to find somewhere to turn around and go back the way we came.'

'Damn it!' Emily blew out her cheeks. 'How far out of our way are we?'

'Quite a bit. We'll have to backtrack to hit the B4396.'

'What are we on now?'

'It's not called anything.'

'Great.'

'Do you want me to drive for a bit? You must be exhausted.'

She *was* tired. Her eyes felt gritty, and her neck and shoulders ached from the tension of driving on unfamiliar roads in the dark. She could also do with a drink. Thankfully, after they'd left the pub, Mac had suggested stocking up on a couple of bottles of water when they'd stopped for fuel, so at least she wasn't going to die of dehydration.

The track widened into a passing place, although she didn't think there was enough room to execute a three-point turn, but she pulled into it anyway, deciding to take Mac up on his offer.

Emily cut the engine but left the headlights on, as she clambered stiffly out of the car.

The abrupt silence was unnerving. Although she was used to very little noise on the farm, this lack of sound was almost complete. Apart from the tick-tick-tick of the engine as it cooled, the night was as silent as the grave.

Despite not feeling the slightest bit cold, Emily shivered.

Mac had unfurled himself from the passenger seat and was rolling his shoulders. She watched him tilt his head from side to side, then he bent forward to touch his toes.

'I think your car must be used by M16 as a form of torture,' he grumbled.

'What is it with you and spy stuff?'

Mac lowered his voice. 'Bond, Mac Bond, at your service.'

'Stop arsing about and get in the car. At this rate it'll be light before we get home. It's all right for you, you can bugger off to bed, but I've promised to help Dad with the shearing.'

Mac stretched again, wincing as his knees popped, making Emily jump.

'Good grief,' she muttered. She stomped around to the passenger side, took a long glug of water, then buckled herself in.

Mac struggled to get into the driver's seat, as he had to readjust its position first. Even then, his knees were almost touching the steering wheel.

'Should have brought the jeep,' he grumbled under his breath.

'Shut up and drive.'

'Yes, ma'am.'

He turned the key in the ignition.

Nothing happened.

He tried again

The engine uttered a wheezing cough, and for a second Emily hoped it would catch.

It didn't.

Mac tried a third time, but the engine remained stubbornly unresponsive. Then the headlights dimmed and faded, before going out completely.

Darkness reigned.

'Wonderful. Just wonderful,' Emily snapped, slapping her palm on the dash.

'It's okay, just phone the AA or the RAC, or whoever you're with.'

Emily closed her eyes and let her head drop back. Buggeration, as Lilian used to say.

When she failed to answer, Mac sighed. 'You don't have any vehicle recovery, do you?'

'No.' God what a mess. How were they going to get out of this? Wait for a passing farmer with a tractor to take pity on them?

She opened her eyes and sat forward, scanning the darkness. 'This is how it starts,' she said ominously.

'How what starts?'

'Horror films. You break down in the middle of nowhere in the middle of the night, then you see a light in the distance.'

'What light? I can't see a light.'

'Not yet, you can't,' she replied ominously. Any second now a figure would appear at the window, offering to help...

Mac's face was abruptly illuminated by his phone's screen. 'I have roadside assistance,' he said, 'but mine is on the vehicle, not the person, so that's no good to us. We'll just have to see if we can find a local recovery service and get them to take us to the nearest garage.'

'That's going to cost a fortune,' Emily wailed. Not only that, but they would also be stuck in wherever-it-was until the car was fixed – which could take hours. Days, even.

'Do you have a better solution?' Mac asked.

'No...?'

'Okay, then. Beggars can't be choosers. Unless...' He tapped the phone '...you want to give your dad a ring? It'll take him a couple of hours to get here, but I'm sure that old Disco of his can tow us back.'

That was debatable. The Land Rover Discovery, or 'Disco' as the vehicles were commonly referred to by Land Rover owners, was ancient. She wasn't sure whether it would make it this far, let alone drive all the way back whilst towing her car.

'I don't think that's going to be an option,' she said. The last thing she wanted was for her dad to drive all this way and have the Disco break down too. He relied on that old thing to do the donkeywork around the farm, and she was acutely aware that her parents would struggle to find the funds to get it repaired, let alone replace it.

'In that case, I'd better start phoning around,' Mac said.

'Will anyone come out at this time of night?'

'Maybe.' He didn't sound too sure.

As he began scrolling, Emily tried to peer at the screen.

Realising she was crowding him, she sat back and stared out of the window, and although it was too dark to see anything her senses were on high alert for the slightest movement. Yep, this was definitely the classic start to a horror movie.

He dialled a number and Emily crossed her fingers.

It went to answerphone.

He tried another.

It rang and rang, but no one picked up.

Two further attempts were equally disappointing.

Mac sighed and shook his head. 'I should have thought of this sooner.'

'What?' she asked, wondering whether she wanted to hear the answer.

He said, 'I'm going to call Gran. Not now, obviously because it's the middle of the night. I'll wait until six o'clock – she's usually awake by then. She's an early riser, like me.'

'Phone Bea? How will that help?'

'I'm going to ask her to jump in the jeep and come rescue us.'

'Jump in the jeep,' Emily repeated flatly.

'Okay, not *jump*, as such. But she's perfectly capable of driving it, and it's perfectly capable of towing your car. I'll drive the jeep back, and you can steer your car.'

Emily blinked. Bea, rescue them…? Emily wasn't sure whether it was the most ridiculous thing she'd ever heard, or the most brilliant. She knew Bea could drive – she had a little silver hatchback – but Mac's jeep was a formidable beast for an elderly lady to handle.

Mac mistook her silence for trepidation. 'If you're not confident being behind the wheel of a car that's being towed, I'll ask Bea. She's done it before, when she got stuck in Crampton Lane when we had that awful rain last year.'

Emily was dumbstruck. Mac's idea was a perfectly sensible solution.

But there were two – no, three – things that irritated her about it. The first was the implication that a woman in her eighties was prepared to do what Emily mightn't be, and that was to sit behind the wheel of a car whilst it was being towed. Although (and she would never admit this to Mac) she was rather nervous. What if the jeep had to stop quickly and she didn't brake in time and went into the back of it, or she oversteered whilst going round a corner, straight into oncoming traffic?

The second thing that irritated her was the unspoken I-told-you-so that was coming off Mac in waves. She was immensely cross that if she had listened to him and they had driven to Worcester in the jeep, this wouldn't have happened.

And the third thing was that with the best will in the world and a hurricane-force tailwind, Bea wouldn't arrive until at least eight-thirty in the morning. Which meant that Emily and Mac would have to spend the night in the car.

Mac didn't say anything further, but she sensed he was waiting for a reply.

'What if Bea has got plans?' she asked.

'If she has, we'll phone for a tow truck. We won't be any worse off timewise, because I highly doubt one would come out in the middle of the night, even if we could get hold of someone – which we can't.'

He was right. They had nothing to lose. 'OK, let's ask Bea,' she decided. 'And if she's otherwise engaged, we'll just have to go down the tow-truck route.'

'It looks like we're here for the night, then,' Mac said cheerily. He didn't appear to be the least bit bothered.

'Yeah.' Emily was most definitely bothered. Spending a night in the car wasn't her idea of a good time, no matter who she would be spending it with.

'Bagsy the passenger seat!' Mac cried.

She shrugged, even though he probably couldn't see her. It was only fair, she thought, considering she was smaller than him.

So with the sleeping arrangements sorted, and both of them in their respective seats, Emily settled down to try to get some rest. Tilting the seat until it was back as far as it would go, she scooted down and stretched out her legs. This is doable, she thought, trying to convince herself that she was comfortable, when she quite clearly wasn't.

Neither was Macsen. Every few seconds he shifted in his seat, and every time he did so, Emily let out an irritated breath. At this rate, neither of them were going to get a wink of sleep.

Not that she felt much like sleeping: she was too worried about what might be out there in the darkness, for one thing. For another, she was too aware of the man beside her, and her growing feelings towards him.

After what was probably only ten minutes, but which felt like a couple of hours, Mac sat up. 'This isn't working,' he announced.

'No sh—' Emily began but stopped herself. No part of this situation was Mac's fault. This was solely down to her. So, ashamed of herself for her attitude, she was about to offer to clamber into the tiny backseat to give him more room, when he opened the car door and got out.

'Where are you going?' she cried. He wouldn't leave her here on her own, would he? She knew she was being arsey, but… Anyway, where would he go?

'I'm going to sleep outside.'

'You can't! It's…' She trailed off, her objections fading. Actually it *was* a good idea. Macsen Rogers seemed to be full of them.

Yes, it was dark outside, and yes it was the middle of the night and they were in the middle of nowhere, but it was incredibly mild, the heat of the day still lingering. And it was far more comfortable sitting on the grass than it had been in the car, Emily discovered when she got out to join him.

'I can't believe how dark it is,' she whispered. 'I mean, it's hardly the Blackpool illuminations where we live, but it's never as dark as this.' There wasn't a light to be seen, although a glow on the horizon indicated the possibility of civilisation in one of the distant valleys.

From Glynafon Farm, the lights of the village were usually visible, except when the mist was down, and there was also the caravan park near the headland, plus a scattering of isolated houses and other farms. Here there was nothing, apart from the swathe of stars overhead.

She had felt uneasy in the car, wondering what might be out there in the darkness, but now that she was outside all she felt was awe. The stars were bright, the sky a clear inky black, and the grass was soft and springy. She wouldn't be able to sleep, but star gazing was a pretty good way to spend the time. Anyway, it wouldn't be dark for long: in about three hours the sun would start to rise and they would be able to see where they were.

Emily sank back into the grass and put her hands behind her head. Mac lay down beside her, and she was acutely aware of how close he was. They weren't exactly touching, but a slight shift in her position would bring her into contact with him.

Under any other circumstance, this would be romantic.

Actually, it *was* romantic: breaking down in the middle of nowhere and having to spend the night under the stars with a seriously good-looking man could be a scene from a romantic movie. This could be where the guy kisses the girl for the first time, or where he admits that he's loved her from the moment they met.

That was a quick about-change, she thought wryly: horror to dreamy in the space of a few minutes.

'I'm sorry,' she said. 'We should have taken your jeep.'

'I'm not.' Mac turned to face her, propping himself up on one elbow.

Uh-oh, here it comes… He's going to take advantage of the situation and try to come on to me, she thought.

'I've had a great time,' he said. 'I haven't had this much fun in ages.'

'So you keep saying. You must live a boring life if you call this fun.'

'I do,' he insisted. 'Work and the occasional visit to the pub doesn't make for an exciting life.'

'That's not what I've heard.'

'What have you heard?' He sounded amused, and she wished it wasn't so dark. She would have liked to see his expression. All she could make out was the pale oval of his face, and the glitter of his eyes.

Emily turned over, so she was lying on her side and facing him. Her head was resting on her outstretched arm, and grass stems tickled her face. Should she be honest with him? Would his feelings be hurt, or would he revel in having a reputation as a player?

'You've got a reputation as a bit of a dude,' she said.

'A *dude*?'

'Yeah, you know… play the field, a heartbreaker, a ladies' man…'

His guffaw of laughter took her by surprise. '*A ladies' man*? That sounds like something Gran would say. Ladies' man indeed! That's so last century.'

'What would *you* call it?'

'It depends on what you mean. Are you telling me that you think I sleep around?'

'Do you?'

He snorted. 'No. Do *you*?'

Emily was taken aback. 'I've just come out of a long-term relationship, so no.'

'So have I.'

'You *have*? When?'

'About six months ago.'

'Do I know her? Does she live in Glynafon?'

'Unlikely, and no. She's from Broughton-in-Furness, and we met at work.'

'What happened, if you don't mind me asking?'

Mac took a while to answer and when he did, he sounded sad.

'We wanted different things out of life.' He sighed softly. 'I wanted to get married and have kids. Verity didn't want any of that. I just wished she'd told me before I…' He sighed again. 'Let's just say I felt fragile for a while.'

Emily was surprised, and was also regretful that she had told him about his reputation. He was clearly still hurting. 'I'm sorry. It's not easy being dumped, is it?'

'I was the one who did the dumping. There didn't seem any point in carrying on with the relationship after that.'

She suspected that his decision to move back to Glynafon might have been driven by splitting up with his girlfriend, and she wondered how, in such a short amount of time, he had earned himself a reputation for being a love-em-and-leave-em sort of guy.

'How do you feel now?' she asked. 'Still fragile?'

'Not as much. It gets easier, especially when there is some emotional distance and you realise it would never have worked. I'm a bit further along that particular road than you.'

'Oh, I don't know...' Emily said. 'I was incredibly upset when I saw Cole slobbering all over that woman, but after a few days I realised I was more angry than heartbroken. I think I was more in love with the idea of being in love, than I was actually *in* love. If that makes sense.'

'If anyone else had said that I would be scratching my head and wondering what they were on about.'

'But not me?' She rolled onto her back once more. The stars appeared to be even brighter, and she stared up at them, mesmerised.

'No, Nuts, not you. You always were weird.'

'Thanks!' she huffed.

'It's a complement. I like weird.'

'Doesn't that make you just as weird?'

'Probably.'

Emily was silent for a moment, then she said. 'I reckon I had a narrow escape. Zelda is welcome to him.'

Mac sniggered. 'She was seriously pissed off when she saw me in her garden.'

'I bet she was. Thanks, again.'

'You're welcome.'

'I'll buy you dinner when we get back to Glynafon.'

'You've already bought me dinner, but how about we grab some breakfast on the way? I expect we'll both be in desperate need of coffee by then.'

'Ooh, yes! You're full of good ideas.'

He didn't answer straight away and when he did, he said, 'Not always.' He dipped his head towards hers, blocking the stars. 'I don't think *this* is the best idea I ever had.'

Then he kissed her.

She gasped, the unexpectedness of it catching her off guard, and he immediately began to draw away, but she grasped the back of his head, pulling him down to her.

He hesitated, then his mouth was on hers again, teasing her lips apart with his tongue. Emily tangled her fingers in his hair, a shiver of delight surging through her as he deepened the kiss.

Her eyes were closed, and she was being swept away by the desire cascading through her, when he stopped abruptly.

Tension snapped in the air as he drew back with a muttered, 'Sorry. That should never have happened.' He was breathing hard, and his voice was hoarse.

Emily nearly groaned aloud with frustration, desire sweeping through her. Her own breathing was ragged and her pulse pounded in her ears.

Don't stop, she wanted to say, but she had no intention of begging. And he was right, it shouldn't have. There was no future in this, even if she did fancy him rotten. She would be returning to Worcester in less than a week, and he was still smarting from a failed relationship. She supposed she should be smarting from one of those too, but all she felt was annoyed that she had wasted so much time on a man who hadn't loved her at all.

But, considering she hadn't loved him as much as she had believed, maybe she and Cole had had a lucky escape from each other. The only difference between them was that she would have ended their relationship before beginning another with someone else.

Emily lay there stiffly, not knowing what to say.

Mac was sitting with his knees up to his chest and his arms wrapped around them. His posture indicated that he wanted to be left alone.

So that was what Emily did. She closed her eyes and tried to ignore the tingle of her lips, the thudding of her heart, and told herself that she hadn't enjoyed kissing him and that her girly crush was definitely *not* going to turn into anything deeper.

***

'Wake up, sleepy head.' The voice was male and gentle, and rather sexy. It didn't belong to Cole. And neither did the arm that was firmly wrapped around her, or the chest that her head was lying on.

'Mac!' Emily's eyes shot open as she remembered where she was and who she was with.

'That's me.'

She pushed her hair out of her eyes and sat up. Mac was gazing at her, a hint of humour in his eyes and a smile playing about his mouth.

The same mouth that had kissed her so passionately in the middle of the night…

It wasn't night now, though. The sun had risen, and she covered her embarrassment by checking out their surroundings.

Moorland, mountains and stands of trees dominated the scene. The track disappeared into the distance in both directions, but aside from some sheep in a field below and a wind turbine on a far hill whose slowly turning blades looked like an alien machine, there was no sign of human habitation.

She really had got them well and truly lost, hadn't she!

'What's the time?' she asked.

'Time I phoned Bea.' He took his phone out of his pocket and stood up, brushing bits of grass off his jeans and T-shirt.

Emily watched him take a few steps along the track, envying his composure, and was annoyed that he looked much the same as he always did, whereas Emily's emotions were all over the place, and her hair was an utter mess to boot.

How had she fallen asleep? The last thing she remembered was peeping at Mac through lowered lashes, as he sat there, staring moodily into the darkness.

To wake cuddled up next to him had been unexpected. So had the kiss.

But even more unexpected had been his revelation about his previous relationship. The powerful attraction she felt for him aside, it had been that, more than anything, that had led to her kissing him back.

It had been silly, on both their parts, but she put it down to the stressful events of the day and the rather romantic setting of the night. They had both been tired and somewhat emotional, that was all.

He turned towards her, the phone pressed against his ear and gave her a thumbs up.

Bea was coming to get them.

That was a relief. Only a couple more hours of just the two of them, then his grandmother would be here.

And Emily was certain that with some good food inside her and a decent night's sleep, she would be able to forget all about that kiss.

She would have to, because no matter how enjoyable it had been or how much she had wanted him to kiss her again, she wasn't prepared to put her heart on the line for a brief fling.

CHAPTER 14

What with all the excitement of seeing Mac's jeep trundling up the track, Bea looking tiny behind the wheel, followed by the fun and games of getting it into position and attaching the tow rope to Emily's car, and not to mention driving further into the wilderness until they found a suitable place to turn around (Emily was desperately trying to erase the memory of that from her mind), then a long, slow drive home – with a stop off for breakfast – Emily had forgotten to show Bea the book that had caused all the trouble in the first place.

As soon as the car had been dropped off at Potters garage, all she had wanted to do was go home, have a shower and fall into bed for a couple of hours.

Mac had driven her back to the farm, Bea happily ensconced in the passenger seat, and Emily had waved him off with relief.

What an ordeal!

Carrying the box of books, Emily let herself into the house, to be met with her mother's cross expression.

'Fancy dragging poor Beatrice all that way. You should have called your father. He would have fetched you and you wouldn't have had to wait until this morning, either.'

'He's got enough to do, without rescuing me and my car. Besides, he probably wouldn't have found us in the dark. Mac's jeep has got satnav. How is the shearing going?'

'Slowly, and stop trying to change the subject. Was Mac part of the reason you were happy to be stranded all night?'

'No, he wasn't,' Emily retorted, ignoring the blush stealing into her face.

'Hmm. What have you got there?'

'The books Lilian left me.'

'Can I give you a hand to unpack the car?'

Emily had told her parents that she wanted to retrieve a few items from Cole's house but hadn't gone into details. There would be time enough to tell them about the book once she'd got it valued and knew how much she could realistically expect to get for it. She had also told them she was going to look at a house, with a view to renting a room there.

'I don't have anything to unpack,' she said, injecting disappointment into her tone. 'I reckon Cole's new girlfriend threw everything out.'

'They weren't hers to throw. You should invoice Cole for them, or demand he replaces them like for like. Are you hungry?'

'No, thanks. We stopped off on the way for a cooked breakfast.'

'How was the house you went to look at?'

'Um, it wasn't the best, so I'll have to keep on looking.' She thought about Mac's comment that she might be able to afford to buy somewhere of her own, and she knew she would have a fight on her hands when she came to sell the book. Her parents would be very reluctant to take the money: persuading them was going to be difficult, but she would cross that bridge when she came to it. 'Right, I'd better get changed. There's a sheep with my name on it.'

She was dog-tired and in desperate need of a shower and a nap, but she had promised to help her dad with the shearing, so that's what she was going to do. She had already lost half a day, she couldn't afford to lose the rest of it.

***

Several hours later, Emily's back was in bits, her legs felt as weak as a kitten's and blisters were beginning to form on her hands from gripping the clippers. She was dirty, sweaty, knackered and she stank of sheep.

But after a long-overdue shower she felt considerably better, so when she received an invitation to pop along to Lucy's house for a barbeque, it was gratefully received. Charcoaled food and an ice-cold beer would go down a treat, and would be her just reward for working so hard today.

First though, she wanted to have a quick chat with Ava to tell her about yesterday, so while she was getting ready she gave her friend a call.

'You're not going to believe what happened,' Emily began.

She heard Ava laugh 'I think I can! Cole is furious. A neighbour told him he'd seen you racing down the street, then driving off like an idiot.'

Oh dear, sorry Mr Dodds, she thought.

'He told Ben to tell you that he's had the locks changed,' Ava added.

'As if I want to go back to that house: Ben was right, Zelda has practically gutted the place already. She's certainly making herself at home. Anyone would think the house belonged to her, not Cole. It really cheeses me off that he made such a fuss if I wanted to put up so much as a picture, yet he's letting her repaint the whole house.'

'Believe me, you're well out of it. Ben said she's a right witch: she's got Cole totally under the thumb, but he doesn't realise it. He's madly in love at the moment, but just wait until he wants to go to the footie with the lads and she plays her face. He won't be so loved-up then. I reckon she'll keep him on a tight leash, because she doesn't want what happened to you, to happen to her. Hyenas don't change their spots.'

'Don't you mean leopards?'

'Nah, hyena suits him better, and they have spots too.'

'If you say so,' Emily chuckled.

'Anyway, why were you racing down the street and driving like an idiot? Ben said something about a *ruckus*?'

When Emily told her about the attic incident and what Mac had done to get her out of the sticky situation, Ava laughed so hard that Emily worried she was having an asthma attack.

'That's priceless,' she cried, braying like a loon.

'That's not all…' Emily went on to recount the horrid Frank story, which had her friend howling with laughter again, and Ava couldn't contain herself when Emily told her about getting lost and the car breaking down. The only bit she didn't share was the kissing-Mac part.

'You never had this much fun when you were with Cole,' Ava chortled. 'See, you're much better off without him. You get to have adventures.'

'I'm not sure it could be described as fun,' Emily replied. Mac had said the same, though, so maybe she was looking at things from the wrong perspective.

Fun wasn't how she would describe that kiss, either. Unsettling would be a better description, although romantic also came to mind. And afterwards, awkward would be the word of choice.

'This Mac you keep mentioning. What's he like?'

'He's OK.'

'Just OK?

'He's not bad looking, I suppose, but he's just a friend. Someone I used to know from school. He's Lilian's nephew.' Emily had told Ava all about Lilian. What she had failed to tell her was that she'd once had a crush on her godmother's nephew. And neither was she going to tell her now. The least said about it, the better.

'You should have called in on the way back. I would have liked to have met him,' Ava said.

'As I told Ben, it was only a flying visit. I just wanted to pick up some stuff I'd left in the attic and anything else I'd bought for the house.'

'Send me some photos of him, then.'

'Why?'

'Because he sounds nice.'

'He is nice.'

'Ah-hah! You *do* like him.'

'You don't give up, do you?'

'Nope. You can do so much better than Cole.'

'Mac might be better, but he lives in Glynafon and I live in Worcester.' *And I could get seriously hurt if Lucy is telling the truth,* she thought.

'So? That shouldn't stop you from having a bit of fuuun.' Ava drew out the word.

'Behave yourself. Gotta run. I'll speak to you later in the week.'

'OK, but don't forget those photos,' was Ava's parting shot.

Telling her mother that she was popping to Lucy's for a while and not to wait up, Emily wrapped the precious book carefully in a sheet of bubble wrap, then placed it in her bag and set off towards the village. She would pop in to see Bea on the way, and show her the book.

It was another lovely evening, and Emily enjoyed the twenty-minute stroll across the fields and down the lanes to Bea's house. The route took her past Mac's place, but his jeep wasn't there, and she wondered where he could be, before recognising that it was none of her business and telling herself that she didn't want to see him anyway. She had seen more than enough of him over the past thirty-six hours or so, and she would be seeing him again on Friday when they went to Powys Castle to get the book valued.

Her tummy grew a handful of butterflies at the thought of spending another day with him, and it turned over again, but this time with disappointment, when she rounded the corner into Bea's lane and saw that Mac's jeep wasn't there either.

Telling herself to get a grip, she knocked on the door, going inside when she heard Bea yell, 'Come in!'

She found the old lady in the kitchen with her head under the sink.

'Pass me that doo-dah, will you?' Bea said.

'This?' Emily picked up the spanner sitting on the worktop near the sink.

'Ta, love.' Bea held out her hand for it.

'What are you doing?'

'Tightening up the stopcock.'

'Riiight.' Emily puffed out her cheeks and nodded sagely. What else would a woman in her eighties be doing on a Tuesday evening? 'Can't Mac do that for you?'

'Why? I'm perfectly capable of doing it myself.' Bea let out a grunt. 'There. All done.' She eased her head out and sat creakily back on her haunches.

'Do you need a hand getting up?'

'No, I don't. If you insist on doing something, put the kettle on.'

Emily didn't wait to be told twice. She was coming to realise that Bea was a force to be reckoned with.

As soon as they had a cup of tea in front of them, Emily brought out the book.

'Ah, yes…' Bea took it and turned it over in her hands, examining it. 'Who'd have thought such a plain little thing could be worth anything?'

'Do you know what Lilian paid for it?'

'Not exactly, although I did tell her it was too much for a tatty old book. But she wanted it, so she bought it.' Bea looked inside, her gaze lingering on the front page. When she glanced up at Emily, she had a tear in her eye. 'Some days it's hard to believe she's gone,' she said. 'And other days it feels as though she's been gone forever.'

'I know.' Emily blinked back a tear of her own.

'She loved you just as much as if she had been your grandmother.' Bea sipped her tea, looking wistful. 'Did you know that her greatest wish was that you and Mac got together?'

Emily drew in a sharp breath. 'No! She never said.'

'She was so disappointed when you stayed in Worcester and Mac buggered off to the Lake District.

She never liked that Verity. Mind you, she never liked your Cole, neither. She used to say he had shifty eyes.'

'She only met him the once.'

'Once was enough for her.'

'Wow. She should have said.'

'Would you have taken any notice if she had?'

Emily pulled a face. 'I doubt it.'

'People have to find these things out for themselves. Which was why I told her to leave well alone when it came to you and Mac. If you were meant to get together, you would.'

Emily held back a snort, thinking that Bea needed to take her own advice, remembering how she had railroaded her and Mac into going for a meal together at the Smuggler's Rest. Thinking about him brought a whoosh of colour to her cheeks, and she winced, knowing Bea would notice. There were no flies on her.

Bea gave Emily a sly look. 'I hope my grandson didn't behave himself last night,' she said.

Emily blinked several times. 'Sorry, I thought you said *didn't* behave himself.'

'That's right. That's what I said.'

To Emily's consternation, her blush deepened until she thought that her whole face must be on fire.

Bea grinned wickedly. 'Our Mac always liked you. He used to talk about you all the time when you were teenagers. That's probably where Lilian got the notion that you two would be perfect together.'

'Stop it, Bea. You can't matchmake me and Mac. I'm leaving at the end of the week, remember?'

'More's the pity. Are you sure you don't want to stay? I bet your mum would love to have you on the farm. Your dad, too,'

'Stop trying to guilt trip me. I don't want to take over the farm. It's too much like hard work. I've been shearing ever since you and Mac dropped me off this morning, and Dad reckons it'll be another two days before all the ewes are done. I'm knackered. I just want to fall into bed and sleep for a week, but Lucy has invited me to a barbeque, and you know what they say about all work and no play. I had to get away from the farm for an hour.'

'Is it only you and Graham doing the shearing?' Bea asked.

'Yes, Mum's back is playing up again.'

Bea grunted and said, 'I think you'd better get that book sold sharpish, my girl.'

And Emily wholeheartedly agreed with her. It wouldn't be sold in time for this year's shearing, but Emily sincerely hoped she would never have to do another.

***

Lucy handed Emily a paper plate. 'I got you a hot dog. I think my dad incinerated the burgers. The corn on the cob looks edible, though.'

Emily bit into the sausage. Thankfully, it was cooked all the way through and not too badly charred on the outside.

'You were saying?' Lucy prompted.

Emily had been telling the Worcester story, as she was beginning to think of it, for the fourth time that day. Bea had been the first recipient, and hopefully Lucy would be the last, although every time she told it, it became funnier. *I mean,* she thought, *you couldn't make this stuff up.*

Emily had been about to get to the part where she and Mac had broken down, when Lucy's dad had called Lucy over to the barbeque to collect some food for the two of them.

Jim was a lovely chap, and Lucy worshipped him. He lived on the other side of the village, so he and Lucy saw a lot of each other. Emily often wondered how Jim would cope if Lucy became serious about a fella, but she hoped he would accept him.

Lately, Emily wished her own dad hadn't been so accepting of Cole: not that it would have made any difference. Emily wouldn't have heard a bad word said about him. Now, though, she was more than happy to say several bad words of her own.

'Where was I,' she mused, licking the grease from her fingers. 'Oh, yes, we were on this mountain – not a high one, it was more like moorland – and it was pitch black, the road had turned into a narrow track and the car broke down.'

'Oh, no! How did you manage to get home?' Lucy took a bite of her own hotdog, and tomato sauce oozed out of it. Titch, her dad's ponderous Basset hound, licked up the resulting splodge.

'I'll come to that in a minute. What I wanted your opinion on – and promise me this won't go any further – is something that happened with Mac.'

Lucy's eyes were wider than the paper plate she was holding, and she paused mid-chew. 'I promise,' she mumbled, holding out her pinkie finger.

Emily curled her own finger around it to seal the promise and took a steadying breath. Even thinking about Mac's lips on hers made her feel dizzy. 'Mac kissed me,' she announced.

Hastily Lucy swallowed her mouthful. '*He didn't?!* I hope you slapped his face! Fancy taking advantage of you like that.'

Emily's heart sank. That wasn't the reaction she had been hoping for.

Lucy totally misinterpreted her expression. 'What a bastard!'

'Lucy, stop! It wasn't like that.' Emily lowered her voice. 'I *enjoyed* it.'

'You *did*? Then what happened?'

'He apologised and said it never should have happened. He seemed to really regret it, but I've just come from Bea's house and she said Mac has always liked me and when we were younger he couldn't stop talking about me. So why is he regretting kissing me now?'

'Are *you* regretting it?'

'I didn't at the time, but I did after he pushed me away.'

'I told you he had a reputation,' Lucy said. 'I'm just surprised he didn't try to take it further.'

'I don't think he's as bad as people make out,' Emily replied. She wondered whether she should tell her friend that Mac was still smarting from breaking up with his girlfriend, but she decided it wasn't her place to say anything.

'Because he stopped before he ravished you?' Lucy arched a sarcastic brow.

'Maybe,' Emily muttered.

'You fancy him, don't you?'

'What's not to fancy?' she countered lightly, not wanting to admit how much the kiss had affected her. She had gone from being quite attracted to him, to having all those old emotions resurfacing. If she wasn't careful she could seriously fall for him. But could *he* fall for *her*?

She had gone from believing him to be heartless and uncaring, and only out for a good time and what he could get, to realising that he might still be heartsore and hurting, and that he mightn't be as bad as Lucy had led her to believe.

Emily gave herself a mental shake. Why was she thinking like this? She would be better off concentrating on what she needed to do to keep her parents' farm afloat and get her own life back on track. There was absolutely no point in revisiting her past, because there was absolutely no future in it.

CHAPTER 15

Emily brushed a stray strand of hair off her sweaty brow and straightened up to ease the kinks out of her back. Bending over to shave a sheep which weighed nearly as much as she did, whilst trying to keep it from struggling, was no mean feat. As a workout, it was a damn good one, and she knew that by the end of the day she would be in an even worse state than she had been yesterday.

She had lingered at the barbeque for another hour or so yesterday evening, but tiredness had eventually overtaken her and she had staggered home, barely able to put one foot in front of the other. Maybe going out last night hadn't been such a good idea after all? She would have been better off having a seriously early night – like retiring to bed straight after dinner – and catching up on the sleep she had missed.

She had already been hard at it since the crack of dawn today and was on her last legs, and it was only just gone lunchtime. The thought of doing this until supper, and then again tomorrow (because they had only sheared half the flock so far) made her want to cry. How her dad kept going was a mystery.

As she took a swig of too-warm water, she gave him a quick look.

He had an ewe on its back wedged between his legs, and the clippers flew over its exposed belly, swiftly separating the heavy fleece from the animal's soft pink skin underneath. The sheep had a long-suffering expression on its face: her dad had a determined one on his.

With a sigh, Emily went to the holding pen to select another ewe.

When she opened the gate, the animals milled together, trying their utmost to get away from her, but she grabbed the nearest with expert ease (she had been helping with the shearing since she was old enough to wield a sweeping brush) and hauled it over to her workstation.

Upending it with the minimum of fuss so the animal was sitting on its bottom and wedging it securely between her knees with its chin under her armpit, Emily began to remove its thick woolly coat, starting at the chest and working her way down its belly and the inside of its back legs. Ideally, she would aim to remove the fleece in one piece, but right now she didn't care how it came off, just as long as it did. It wasn't worth anything anyway. Years ago, the farm would have got a decent price for its wool, but now they had to practically pay someone to take it away.

She turned the animal on its side and clipped its left flank, then turned it again to expose its back, working her way around to the right side until most of its fleece came away. Finally, she tidied up the bits she'd missed, such as the tail and around the face, and she was done.

As soon as she released it, the ewe scrambled to her feet and bounded off to join those of her flock who had already been shorn.

Emily watched it go, wondering if it felt relieved to be rid of its heavy coat, or whether it felt naked and exposed. Whatever it felt, it must surely be cooler.

The heatwave was into its third day, and the shed was stifling. The air was ripe with the smell of the animals and the aroma of lanolin from the wool itself. Oh, well, she thought as she bent to roll the fleece and tie it up, at least her hands would be wonderfully soft, even if it did take a week to wash the stink of sheep off her skin.

A movement at the far end of the shed caught her eye and she saw her mum approaching. She was carrying a tray, and Emily let out a sigh of relief. She didn't feel the least bit hungry despite the intense physical activity, but she could murder a cold drink.

Smiling, she took a quick selfie and pinged it off to Ava, with the caption, ***Getting down and dirty in wild Wales. Envy me much?!*** She received a reply immediately – a row of crying laughing emojis.

She put her phone away and saw her mum set the tray down on a bale of straw. Emily hurried over to it: homemade lemonade – bliss.

'Look who I found,' Dina sing-songed, and Emily, who had just picked up the jug of iced lemonade and was about to pour it into a glass, looked up and nearly dropped the jug – Mac was standing behind her mother.

He was gazing at Emily, but his expression was unreadable.

Emily wished she didn't look as dirty, hot and bothered as she felt. She wished she had taken the time to brush her hair this morning before scooping it up into a dishevelled bun. She wished she had put a slick of mascara on her lashes, because without it Cole used to say she looked tired. But more than anything, she wished she didn't stink of sheep.

Mac nodded to her dad.

Her dad nodded back.

But all three of them stared open-mouthed at Mac when he picked up Emily's discarded clippers and checked the blade. And they continued to stare as he sauntered over to the holding pen, opened it, caught a sheep, and wrestled it to the shearing area.

'What's he doing?' Dina hissed in Emily's ear as he upended the animal onto its bottom and began clipping it.

Emily found her voice. 'He's shearing a sheep.'

Why would he be shearing a sheep? Was it a dare? A bet? Was he bored? Did he secretly want to be a barber, and this was the next best thing?

Mac glanced across at her dad.

Her dad inclined his head, then fetched a sheep of his own.

'Well, I never,' Dina said. 'Has he come to help?'

'He must have.' Emily's reply was disbelieving.

'That's nice of him.' She nudged Emily with her elbow. 'He must really like you.'

Emily doubted that. She knew he must like her to have gone with her to Worcester, and to go with her to Powys Castle. But she didn't think he liked her in the way her mum was suggesting. Bea must have sent him. Bea could be a determined lady when she wanted to be, and Emily suspected that Mac hadn't been able to say no to her. That was the most logical explanation, because she honestly didn't think any man would go to such lengths to get into her knickers.

'I didn't realise he knew how to shear sheep,' Emily said, ignoring her mother's comment.

'Neither did I, but I'm not surprised. Lilian once told me that he would turn his hand to anything for a bit of spending money when he was younger. I knew he used to help out on Winett's farm in the summer holidays when he was a teenager, so he probably learnt how to shear there.'

Emily drank the lemonade, grateful for the coolness of the liquid as it slipped down her throat.

Another elbow in the side. 'You're wanted,' her mum said.

Mac had almost finished with his sheep. He had kicked the discarded fleece to one side and was checking the ewe over for any bits he might have missed.

Emily hurried forward, removed the wool so she could deal with it in a minute, and went into the holding pen to bring out another sheep.

Mac took it from her with a wry quirk of his lips, but he didn't say a word. Instead he got on with the job of clipping it, whilst she rolled and tied the fleece before throwing it into a large metal bin with the rest of them.

Swiftly she grabbed a broom and swept up any remaining scraggly bits of wool, then she repeated the whole performance for her dad.

No sooner had she dealt with that, she was back to Mac, and before she knew it, she was part of a shearing production line, with the two men doing the backbreaking shearing and Emily doing the only marginally less back-breaking job of sorting out the fleeces and catching the sheep.

Finally, and sooner than Emily could have hoped, they were down to the last few animals for today. Never had Emily been so happy to see an empty pen. The shorn sheep and their well-grown lambs were milling about in the paddock, eager to get back to their field, and as soon as the last ewe had been clipped Emily whistled to the two farm dogs.

Eager to do some work, they headed straight for the paddock, and the second Emily opened the gate they herded the excitable sheep up the lane, chivvying at their heels.

The noise was deafening, but Emily was glad to escape the hot, stuffy shed, and the hot, sweaty man inside it.

And she didn't mean hot in the sense of being too warm — although Mac undoubtedly must be. His T-shirt was damp and clung to him, outlining the muscles in his chest and back, and she'd had to work hard at not watching him working hard.

It had been a sight to behold, and if she hadn't already been hot and sweaty herself, he would have

225

heated her from the inside out. Heck, she'd almost been on fire watching him bend and stretch, dip and turn. He had made shearing a sheep look easy – not as easy as her dad made it look, but he'd had far more experience. Her father's shorn animals were neater too, but Mac's were perfectly acceptable, and they looked better than hers had done.

Emily had to admit that the three of them had made a good team, and she was immensely grateful for Bea sending Mac to the farm. They had made great inroads into the shearing and although they had the sheep in the top field still to do, the prospect was no longer as daunting. She felt guilty though, because Mac had a full-time job of his own, and she hoped he wouldn't get into trouble for bunking off.

Emily lingered in the field for a while longer than was necessary, the sheep now happily grazing, looking fresh and clean without their tatty woolly coats. She knew she should get back to thank Mac for his hard work, but she was reluctant to see him. It wasn't because she looked a fright (how annoying that he looked good covered in sweat, dirt and bits of straw, whereas she looked like she had been dragged through a hedge backwards, forwards and sideways). She was reluctant because every time she saw him, her attraction to him grew exponentially.

When she had bumped into him in the Smuggler's Rest last week, she had felt a fizz of remembered teenage excitement. By the time he had kissed her, she had been doing more than fizzing. She had been lusting. And today, she was falling for him. His kindness touched her heart: a heart that had had enough upset lately and didn't need any more. A heart that had emerged from her relationship with Cole surprisingly unscathed, and which she wanted to keep that way. Because, as far as she was concerned, Mac was most definitely heartbreak material.

As she neared the house, she scanned the yard. His jeep wasn't there, and the relief she felt was mixed equally with disappointment because Mac had left without saying goodbye.

Emily could hear her mum in the kitchen, and the aroma of frying onions was in the air. Hopefully dinner wouldn't be long, but first she needed a shower.

She darted up the stairs and into her bedroom, casting off her stinking clothes before leaping into the shower. The first blast of lukewarm water on her superheated skin was bliss, and she turned her face into the stream, letting it flow over her. The water in the bottom of the shower tray quickly turned black, and she waited for it to run clear before she lathered herself with soap and washed her hair.

Feeling clean at last, she wrapped her body in a towel, wound another around her head, then stepped out of the bathroom.

And ran full tilt into Mac.

'Eek!' she squealed, gripping the front of the towel and hoping he hadn't caught a glimpse of anything he shouldn't. 'Get out!'

What was he doing upstairs, almost in her bedroom? She should feel safe here, yet this man had appeared on the landing and was grinning wickedly.

'The towel suits you,' he drawled, and she would have slapped him if she hadn't been clasping the towel so bloody hard. She might have risked it anyway, if his gaze had dropped from her face, but his eyes were on hers and not on her barely concealed body.

'What do you want? You shouldn't be up here!' she shrieked, desperate to make a dash for her bedroom, but he was in the way.

'Your mum sent me. She wants your dirty clothes because she's going to put a wash on.'

Emily shook her head in disbelief. *Her mum had sent him?* Couldn't she have waited *five* minutes? Emily would have brought her clothes down with her if she'd have known that her mother was desperate to wash them. She could have asked, not sent Mac upstairs to fetch them. What the hell was her mum playing at?

'You can tell my mother that if she's so keen to put a load on, she can come get them herself. Now go away. I want to get dressed.'

Mac chuckled, but he backed away towards the top of the stairs. 'I quite like you as you are.'

'Get lost.'

Another chuckle. 'I'm going.'

'Home, I hope,' Emily shot back.

'Not for a while – your mum has invited me to dinner.'

What? Dinner? That meant she would have to put up with him for at least another hour.

'Have you had a shower?' she demanded, suddenly aware that he looked far cleaner and smelt so much better than the last time she'd seen him.

'I thought it wise. I was rather grubby.'

'When? Where?'

'I popped home for one. Why the interest? Did you want to share it with me?' He was still grinning, and heat flared in the pit of her stomach at the thought.

The heat spread up her chest and neck, and into her face, until she was fairly certain she must look like a red traffic light.

'You wish,' she retorted, then she could have kicked herself when he said, 'Yeah, I do actually.'

Emily shot him a sour look, stalked into her bedroom and slammed the door so hard that the wall rattled.

She was going to have some stern words with her mother.

***

'Shouldn't you have been at work this afternoon?' Emily demanded, her eyes boring into Mac as he tucked into an enormous bowl of chilli.

'I did a couple of hours this morning.' He wiped his mouth with a napkin (Emily had raised her eyebrows when she saw them, because they were only ever brought out at Christmas). 'I've taken the rest of the week off,' he added.

'Doing something nice?' Dina asked.

'If Graham doesn't think I did too bad a job, I'd like to come back and give you a hand in the morning. With two of us shearing and Emily doing the catching and rolling, the rest of the sheep should be done in a couple of hours.'

'Oh, that's so kind of you,' Dina gushed. 'But we can't let you spend your day off working on our farm, can we Graham?'

'No, we can't. You've done more than enough today. You've been a great help, and we're very grateful.'

Mac glanced at Emily, then said to her dad, 'I'm not being kind – I've got a selfish reason for wanting to get the shearing done. I'd like to take Emily to the beach tomorrow afternoon.'

Emily almost choked. She chewed frantically, waving a hand in front of her face, before hastily swallowing what was in her mouth. 'I can go to the beach any time,' she said, sending him a furious look. 'It's on our doorstep,' she reminded him.

'Yes, but how often do you do anything other than stroll on it?'

She pressed her lips together, not wanting to admit he was right.

'We can paddleboard or windsurf, or just mess about in the water.'

Her mother beamed. 'Ooh, that would be nice. You'd enjoy that, wouldn't you, Emily? I don't want her to think that she had to work on the farm whenever she comes back home.' Dina leant forward. 'And after that awful Cole business... well, she deserves to enjoy herself. I was only saying to Graham that she should get out more. She doesn't want to be stuck here with a couple of old fogies. Before she knows it, she'll be back at work and wishing she wasn't.'

Emily raised her eyes to the ceiling. Her mum sounded as though she was trying to arrange a playdate for a five-year-old.

Mac smiled. 'She's doing something nice on Friday. Didn't she tell you?'

'No?' Dina turned to Emily. 'What are you doing?'

'Ow.' Mac reached underneath the table to rub his shin where she had kicked it.

Emily refused to meet his gaze. 'we're going to Powys Castle.'

Her mum said, 'It's lovely there. I haven't been in years. Are you going with Lucy?'

Through gritted teeth, Emily said, 'Mac.'

Dina's eyebrows shot up to her hairline. 'You're going with Mac?' She turned to look at him.

Mac was wearing a butter-wouldn't-melt expression. 'I thought it would be a nice day out.'

'I'm sure it will be. I hope you have a lovely time,' Dina replied.

Her mother sounded smug, and for the first time it occurred to Emily that Bea and her mother might be in cahoots.

'It's a business thing,' Emily interjected.

She didn't want her mum to get the wrong idea. It was bad enough Bea trying to set her and Mac up, without her mother joining in.

She did wonder whether her mum was hoping that if she and Mac were to hit it off, then maybe Emily would have a reason to stay in Glynafon, so maybe Dina had more selfish reasons to throw them together. After all, Emily had overheard her parents saying that there wasn't anything in Glynafon to keep her here, so perhaps her mum was trying to ensure there was?

CHAPTER 16

After another hectic morning in the shearing shed, followed by lunch eaten whilst sitting on straw bales surrounded by the satisfaction of a job well done, Emily jumped in the shower and Mac went home to get cleaned up.

She'd had a call from the garage to say that her car was fixed, so as soon as she was ready she walked into the village to collect it.

Having paid a small fortune (in her eyes – but it was in fact a fairly reasonable amount) to have the alternator replaced, Emily found a parking spot not far from the pub and wandered down to the beach.

Mac, dressed in shorts and a T-shirt and carrying a paddleboard under his arm and a rucksack slung over his shoulder, was sitting on a bench, waiting for her.

He gave her a slow smile as he watched her approach, and she was acutely conscious of his gaze on her as she walked towards him. It made her skin tingle and her heart thump.

Oh, that wasn't good. What was she *doing?* For a second it occurred to her to tell him that she had changed her mind and wouldn't go to the beach with him after all. He was a big boy, he could paddleboard on his own. He didn't need her to hold his hand. But the temptation to spend the afternoon with him proved too great, and as he was supposed to be accompanying her to Powys Castle tomorrow, she could hardly bugger off back to the farm without seeming churlish. She supposed she could always go on her own, but if she was honest, she could do with the company. He'd also booked the day off, so it would be downright rude of her to tell him she didn't want him to go with her.

Besides, she *did* want him there.

Oh dear, she was so confused. Her emotions were all over the place, which she shouldn't be surprised about considering the rollercoaster she had been on over these past couple of weeks. She had gone from being in love (or so she'd thought) and having a boyfriend, a home and a bright future – to not being in love, being boyfriendless, homeless, and totally uncertain about what that future might hold. Add to that, a resurgence of attraction for a man from her past, her discovery that the farm wasn't the rock she had always believed it to be, plus finding out that she was the owner of a valuable book… No wonder she didn't know whether she was coming or going.

'A penny for them?' Mac asked, and Emily gave herself a mental shake.

'Sorry, I was miles away. I've got a lot on my mind.'

'That's understandable. How about we try to forget our worries for a while, and enjoy ourselves this afternoon? I always find that a few hours on the beach helps ground me.'

Emily loved the beach, too. But lately whenever she had come back to Glynafon, she hadn't spent much time on it. The visits had been fleeting, as she was anxious to get back home to Cole, who had always been too busy to come with her. He'd only visited Glynafon once and he'd been like a fish out of water, clearly out of his comfort zone, not liking anything about the farm or the countryside surrounding it. The village had been too small with not enough to do, and the beach… let's just say, it wasn't The Bahamas.

Emily frowned. Sod him. What Cole thought or felt no longer concerned her. He was a total, utter waste of space, the polar opposite of the man who was currently gazing at her with concern in his eyes.

On impulse, she grabbed Mac's hand and tugged him towards the sand. 'You're right, let's just have fun.' she said, ignoring the bolt of desire that shot through her at the feel of his hand in hers, and telling herself that it was because she was unused to touching any man other than Cole.

But as soon as her feet sank into the warm golden granules, she used the excuse of needing to take off her sandals to let go of him.

'Got a towel?' he asked, as they headed for a spot further along the beach that had fewer holidaymakers.

Emily patted her large hessian tote bag. 'Two. I've also got suncream and a couple of bottles of water.'

'Snap!'

By unspoken mutual agreement, they found a spot they liked and plonked themselves down after spreading their towels out.

Emily's sunglasses were perched on her head, but the brightness of the day and the glittering sparkle of the sun on the water had her hurriedly reaching for them, and she put them on, hoping she looked sexy and enigmatic, rather than someone who was desperately trying not to squint.

Feeling self-conscious, she leant back on her elbows and gazed at the sea, wondering whether she should take her shorts and top off. She had a bikini on underneath, but she felt oddly shy about revealing her body.

Mac didn't. He was already stripping off.

Oh, my… Emily blushed and hurriedly looked away, but her gaze crept back, and she was thankful she was wearing her sunglasses so he couldn't see her ogling him.

His chest was sculpted with muscle, but it was subtle, not overdone, and had a smattering of dark hairs that trailed over his flat stomach and disappeared below the waistband of his shorts. He also had nice legs, long and slim but with defined muscles in his thighs, and she wondered how they would feel if she ran her fingers down them.

She'd like to run her fingers down his chest, too, and further south…

'Want to give it a go?' he asked, tapping the paddleboard.

Emily cleared her throat. 'Um… in a minute. You go ahead. I'll watch.' Cross with herself for having those kinds of thoughts about him, she bit her lip and tried to think about something else, like where she might be living in three months' time, for instance.

Mac didn't need telling twice. Picking up the board, he jogged to the water's edge. The tide was still in, so he didn't have far to go, and she had a perfect view.

And what a view it was! The sight of him wearing nothing but a pair of shorts was making her hot under the collar again,

Maybe she should have gone with him? The water might have cooled her off…

Emily sat up and reached for her phone. She took a few snaps of him, plus a selfie or two, which she sent to Ava along with a brief message that she was having fun on the beach with Mac.

Ava's reply came back immediately. ***What a hunk!***
I know!!!

I wouldn't say no…

I have to - for my own sanity

Aren't you just a teeny bit curious what he's like in bed? Lol

No!!

Bet you are. Do you think he'll be better than Cole?

Stop it. I'm not speaking to you anymore. Emily added several kissy emojis and tossed her phone into her bag.

Lying back on her towel, she propped herself up on her elbows once more, her eyes tracking Mac as he played in the waves. Hunk was a perfect description for him.

Water was cascading down his body as he rose from the waves and the words *Greek god* came to mind…

Ooh, this was such a bad idea… She should have known from being in the shearing shed with him for the past couple of days that he was going to look hot under his clothes. She should also have been prepared for him to take most of those clothes off when he was on the beach.

He strode through the shallows, the waves breaking over his legs, his board under one arm, and she recalled the Daniel Craig scene. Bond, Mac Bond…

Macsen would give Daniel Craig a run for his money, and she knew which guy she would prefer to look at, and it was the man currently strolling up the beach towards her.

Mac laid his board on the sand and ferreted around in his rucksack, bringing out two bottles of water. They were still cold, Emily noticed, as he handed one to her.

She unscrewed the cap and took a sip, her eyes on his throat as he swallowed.

He caught her looking at him and she bit her lip and dropped her gaze.

'It's lovely in there. Not too cold, but fresh. You should try it.' Mac sat down, his arm almost touching hers.

She could smell the sea on him, a tangy saltiness, and underneath was the scent of the man himself.

Turning away to stare at the headland, she watched the distant spray of white as the surf met the rocks. It looked wild out there, yet the water in the small bay was calm. A bit like her – she hoped she was projecting outward calm, even though on the inside she was a mess of mixed emotions and conflicting desires.

She was wildly attracted to Mac, yet she knew it was pointless starting anything that was going to fizzle out in a few days. But, boy, was she tempted. To add to her confliction, she liked him as a person, and despite the kiss and the mild flirting (she wasn't entirely convinced he was flirting – he might just be teasing her) he hadn't made another move on her. Did he look on her as merely a friend, someone he used to know back in the day, and was having fun hanging out with again? Their relationship appeared to have picked up where it left off, a decade ago, when they all used to hang out in a group together and life had seemed so much simpler.

Even though she had wanted desperately for him to ask her out, she had hidden her feelings well. As far as he knew, she had just been one of the gang: someone to make up the numbers in a game of rounders on the beach; someone to share a sneaky can of beer with when they had been too young to drink but used to do it anyway; someone to crib notes off when he'd missed school. He had treated her exactly the same as he had treated the rest of his friends, male and female. To coin one of Lilian's phrases, he hadn't pooped on his own doorstep. The girls he had dated had been outside of their friendship group, and usually outside of

Glynafon, and Emily had been jealous and envious of each and every one of them.

Then, one by one her friends had turned eighteen, and many of them had gone to university, and things had never been the same again. They had changed, had flown their nests, and although some of them had returned to Glynafon, like Jo and Lucy, Emily hadn't, and neither had Mac. Until recently.

And she still didn't know why he was spending so much time with her, unless he was trying to recreate some of his youth.

She could understand that. Adulting wasn't all it was cracked up to be, and sometimes she wished she hadn't bothered. She could have stayed on the farm and not gone to university, and her life would have trundled along much as it had always done – minus the inconvenience of having to go to school.

If she had stayed, would the farm have been in such financial straits?

Guilt ate away at her, but she tried not to let it gobble up too much. She had the means to put things right within her grasp, and tomorrow she would hopefully know just how much she'd be able to help her mum and dad. There might even be enough left over to rent a place of her own, without having to resort to sharing. Now, that would be bliss indeed.

'Are you OK?' Mac asked. 'You look as though you've got the weight of the world on your shoulders.'

'Just thinking about tomorrow,' she said. It wasn't a complete lie.

'Don't worry, we'll get there early. We will be one of the first in the queue.'

Bless him, he assumed she was worried about not getting in, so she let him continue to believe it.

She asked, 'What time should we leave? I've looked it up and it'll take about two and a half hours to get there.'

'The gates won't be open until nine, but as I said, I reckon people will start arriving well before then. My guess is that the carpark will be heaving by seven. We should aim to get there much earlier.'

'Leave in the middle of the night, you mean?'

'I fear so.'

Emily pulled a face. 'If that's what we've got to do, then so be it. You don't have to come with me,' she reiterated.

Mac fell silent and she turned to look at him. He was studying her sombrely.

She added, 'I mean, I'd like you to be there obviously, but it's your day off.'

'And I want to spend it with you, visiting Powys Castle. I thought we'd gone over this, but if you'd prefer to go on your own…'

'No, I want you to come. I just don't want you to regret it.'

'What is there to regret?' He reached across to tuck a strand of hair behind her ear. The breeze had picked up, and her ponytail was coming loose.

Her skin sparked at his touch, and she tried not to let her reaction show.

'It's just a day out with a… friend,' he continued.

She nodded slowly. Yes, that was exactly what it was. It was nice of him to clarify how he felt about it, considering she had been wondering.

Mac was staring intently into her eyes, and her heart stuttered, missing a beat. Then he seemed to collect himself and the lazy smile reappeared. He stood up.

'Come on, let's go for a dip. You look all hot and bothered.' He held out a hand.

She took it and let him haul her to her feet. Feeling incredibly self-conscious, she pulled her top over her head then shucked off her shorts. Risking a peep at him, she was glad to see that he wasn't taking the slightest notice of her. Contrarily, she also felt a little put out.

But after she had folded her clothes neatly and placed them in her bag, she became aware of his gaze on her body and her skin burned and tingled.

He looked away swiftly, but not before she'd caught the admiration in his eyes.

It made her feel emboldened, and she gave him a flirtatious look as she scampered towards the sea.

Laughing, she raced into the waves, the water splashing over her knees, and she gasped at the chill. 'It's freezing!' she cried, and he dived past her into an oncoming wave, to emerge on the other side of it as it broke over her thighs.

'Don't be a chicken, just get in,' he urged. 'It's lovely when you get used to it.'

Squealing, Emily threw herself forward, taking his advice. The water stole her breath, and she did a frantic doggy paddle in a circle to try to warm up.

'What are you doing?' he laughed.

'Trying to stay warm.'

'Are you doing a doggy paddle?'

'What if I am?' It was working, or she was getting used to it, because she didn't feel quite as cold, and within a few minutes she was diving into the waves and letting them carry her back to shore, before turning around, wading back out into deeper water and doing the whole thing all over again.

'This is fun!' She twisted onto her back, letting the water hold her up (with a little help from her hands scudding underneath her), and closed her eyes. If she didn't know any better, she could almost believe she was in the Med. The sun was gloriously warm and—

A wave washed over her face, making her splutter, and she spat out a mouthful of salty water. 'Bleh!'

Coughing, she righted herself and lowered her feet to the seabed, but she was further from the shore than she'd thought, and her head dipped under the water as her toes searched for the sandy bottom.

Surfacing, she paddled her arms frantically, trying to get her head clear before the next wave spilled over her, then suddenly she was being held in a firm grip.

Mac had hold of her. His feet were planted on the bottom so there was no danger of her pulling him under, but the water was deep enough for the waves to buffet him, and his body swayed to the rhythm of the outgoing tide as it pounded his shoulders. Relief filled her, as she wrapped her arms around his neck and her legs around his waist, and clung on with all her might.

'You're all right,' he told her. 'I've got you.' And he carried her further into shore, until the water was a chest height and she no longer felt they were in danger of being swept away.

With the threat alleviated, Emily was abruptly swept away by an altogether different tide, as a sea of emotion cascaded through her. Relief was paramount, but it was swiftly followed in quick succession by gratitude, embarrassment, then lust. Sheer unbridled lust.

Her arms were around his neck, but she was no longer clinging to him for dear life. They were curled around him, one hand on the back of his neck, the other resting lightly on his shoulder. Her legs had slithered south and were no longer holding him in a death grip around his waist, but were clasped around his hips. There were only two thin layers of material between her and Mac, and heat pooled deep within her, as she let out a slow languid sigh and buried her face in his neck.

He tensed, and she thought he was going to release her, but when he slid his hands down her back, gripped her thighs and settled her more firmly onto his hips, she understood what was causing his tension – he was as aroused as she – and she also realised he had no intention of letting go.

Unable to resist, Emily's lips teased the skin where his shoulder met his neck, and she nibbled her way along his collarbone until, with a deep groan that sent ripples through her, he said, 'I want to kiss you.'

His eyes were dark pools of hunger, and she could feel the desire thrumming through his body. She knew that if he could, he would take her there and then, and that she would let him.

Instead, she settled for the most passionate kiss she had ever experienced, and as she sank down into the depths of it, she feared that she had fallen for Mac all over again.

***

'We'd better go,' Mac said. 'I don't know about you, but I'm starving, and I'd like to get a couple of hours sleep before we hit the road.'

Emily sat up sleepily. The sun was still warm, but it was low in the sky and there were far fewer holidaymakers on the beach. She could quite happily stay here for the rest of the night, kissing and cuddling, but he was right. They did need to get a move on. And she was hungry too.

They had stayed in the sea until the chill of the water had cooled some of their ardour, and she had never been so thoroughly kissed in all her life. How she hadn't spontaneously combusted...

Careful to keep the heat levels down – after all, they were in public and there were families on the beach – Emily and Mac had contented themselves with the occasional relatively chaste kiss, and lots of snuggling and cuddling on their towels. She had particularly enjoyed half-sprawling across his chest and stroking the fine dark hairs growing there. For his part, Mac seemed perfectly happy to run his fingers up and down her spine until she'd begged him to stop.

It had been a delicious way to spend an afternoon. But the afternoon had now faded, and evening was creeping in. The sun would set in a couple of hours and the tide had gone way out.

'Do you want to have dinner before we head home?' he asked.

Emily was tempted, but she needed a shower. Her skin was sticky with sunscreen, and she could feel salt and sand in her hair. 'I'd like to, but I want a shower.'

'You could have one at mine.'

Her breath caught in her throat as she assumed he was offering more than a shower. Once more she was tempted, but self-preservation held her back. Her body was yelling at her to say yes, but her head was urging caution. And her poor heart had no idea what was going on. She needed time to think about what had happened this afternoon, and what, if anything, was going to be her next step.

She desperately wanted to make love with him, but the risk of losing her heart completely was too great. She was on the brink already...

'Better not,' she said, and the regret in her voice was very real.

'I understand.' He got to his feet and began packing his things away.

Emily watched him for a moment, hoping he would respect her decision, because if he decided to sulk, then he wasn't the man she hoped he was and it would confirm that she was right to turn him down. Despite having known him for most of her life, it was Mac the boy she knew; Mac the man was a relative stranger, and even if there had been any future for them, there was no way she would hop into bed with him so soon.

He didn't sulk. As soon as they began walking across the beach to the village, he took his hand in hers, his index finger stroking her knuckles. It was the gentlest of touches, but it had the desired effect of making her go weak at the knees.

'Behave yourself,' she giggled.

'Spoilsport.'

'I'll tell Lilian.'

'You wouldn't dare.'

Emily laughed. 'I would. A quick detour and I could be sitting by her headstone and telling her what a wicked man her nephew is.'

'I can be much more wicked than this.'

'I bet,' Emily retorted primly.

'Do you visit her grave often?'

'Not as often as I should. I miss her, you know.'

Mac said, 'So do I, but I can feel her in the house sometimes. It's as though she's watching over me.'

'Aw, that's so lovely.'

'Not if you can sense her displeasure because you couldn't be bothered to do last night's washing up,' he replied wryly.

'Are you glad you moved back to Glynafon?'

'Yes.' His reply was emphatic. 'I love it here. And if I hadn't, I wouldn't have met you.' He said it lightheartedly enough, but he sent her a sideways look that was loaded with more meaning than she could pick apart right now.

Her response was equally light. 'Can I let you into a little secret? We've already met. I've known you for years.'

'Not like this.'

He was right. Definitely not like this. What the hell were they doing? In three days, she would be out of his life, and she could kick herself for allowing things to get out of hand.

But the damage was done, and Mac knew the score as well as she. Assuming both of them looked on this as a kind of holiday fling, neither of them would be hurt.

They reached her car and she came to a halt, feeling shy and awkward. Should she kiss him goodbye? Were they a couple now, however briefly?

Mac solved her dilemma.

After she'd unlocked the car and tossed her bag into the back seat, he took her hands in his and turned her to face him.

'Nuts, I know you're leaving on Sunday so let's just take this one day at a time and enjoy it. No strings, no ties, no regrets.'

The intensity had returned to his face and his eyes were so deep she was scared she might fall into them and never find her way out. His mouth seemed to be saying that this – whatever it was they had – was just a bit of fun. Yet his eyes were telling a different story.

Suddenly it didn't matter, as his head dipped towards her, his mouth claiming her lips, and all she could think about was the way he made her feel—

'Ahem!' The cough was so close it startled her, and they leapt apart.

When Emily saw who it was, she said, 'God, Lucy, you didn't half give me a fright. I didn't see you there.'

'Evidently.' Lucy's eyes were flitting between Emily and Mac. Mac looked as uncomfortable as Emily felt. 'I'll, um, be off...' he muttered.

He was backing away, unable or unwilling to look at her. His gaze was downcast and there was a tightness around his mouth. Was he really so annoyed at being interrupted, she wondered. Maybe he had been hoping for a second go at trying to persuade her to go back to his place?

'OK, see you tomorrow,' she said, then, 'What time shall I pick you up?'

'Uh-uh, no way. Not after last time.' His eyes finally met hers, and she was relieved to see him back to his usual self. '*I'm* picking *you* up. We'll go in the jeep.'

'Mine's fixed,' she objected, patting the roof of her car.

'Have you joined the AA or the RAC yet?'

'No...'

'Case closed. I'll pick you up at two-thirty.' And with that he was gone, his long legs striding down the pavement.

Emily watched him walk away, conscious that Lucy was doing the same.

'Are you two an item?' Lucy asked. She was frowning.

'I'm not sure what we are, to be honest.'

'You seemed very... close.'

Emily shrugged: she couldn't deny it.

Lucy glanced in the direction Mac had taken. He was nowhere in sight, but her frown remained. She asked, 'Why bother if you're leaving on Sunday? Are you using him to get back at Cole? Or to get over him?'

'None of those things. I'm over Cole already. I was over him the second I saw him snogging another woman. It just took me a while to realise it.'

'A very short while,' Lucy snapped.

Emily blinked at her friend's obvious disapproval. 'What are you getting at?'

Lucy sighed. 'You might think you're over Cole, but you haven't given yourself enough time to grieve. You're vulnerable and Mac's taking advantage of that. Anyone can see he's using you. That's what he *does*.' Lucy put a hand on Emily's arm. 'I'm sure you know what you're doing, but be careful. You don't want to get hurt. Or catch anything.'

'I haven't slept with him, if that's what you're implying.'

'Not *yet*.'

'I'm grateful, that's all. He's been helping with the shearing.'

'I hope he's not expecting payment in kind,' Lucy snorted.

Emily was shocked that her friend could even think such a thing. 'Why are you being so horrid?'

'I'm not. I just don't want to see you get hurt.'

'I won't,' Emily replied firmly. 'I like Mac: he's fun to be with and as you said, he's a damn good kisser. But as you also pointed out, I'm leaving on Sunday, so there's no future in it.'

Lucy's expression softened. 'Just be careful, OK? You're in a fragile state.'

Trying to lighten the mood, Emily quipped, 'So you're not an advocate of the theory that the best way to get over one man is to get underneath another?'

'That's not even remotely funny.'

Emily puffed out her cheeks, wondering what had got into her friend to make her so grumpy. 'No, it isn't. And that's not what I'm doing. Rebound sex doesn't appeal.'

'Glad to hear it.' Lucy's eyes narrowed. 'Where are you going tomorrow?'

'Powys Castle.'

'Is it a date?'

'Not as such. More like business.'

'What business does Mac have in Powys Castle?'

'I'm not sure.' Emily hated lying, but until she'd had the book valued she didn't want to say a word to anyone. The only people who knew about it were Mac and Bea, and Mac wasn't aware of the full story, although maybe she *should* tell him – she trusted that it wouldn't go any further.

She would tell him after the valuation, she decided, and maybe he could help her find a way to sell it. It would also give her an excuse to return to Glynafon sooner than she otherwise might have done.

CHAPTER 17

Emily had to admit that Mac's jeep was far more comfortable than her little car, but there was no way she was going to tell him. It was so comfortable that she dozed for part of the journey, then woke feeling guilty that he had been driving while she had been snoozing.

They had left Glynafon in the dark, but it was light when she opened her eyes and sat up, although the sun hadn't fully risen yet. Hoping she hadn't been drooling or snoring, she ran her fingers through her hair and pulled the sun visor down to make sure her mascara wasn't all over her face.

'Hi, sleepy head.' Mac's voice was soft.

'Where are we?' she yawned.

'We've just driven through Welshpool, so about ten minutes away. As soon as we get there, we'll park and set up camp.'

'Pardon?'

Mac smiled, pleased with himself. 'I've brought a couple of folding chairs, two blankets in case it's chilly, and a picnic basket.'

'I'd love a coffee, but it's too early for sandwiches. Or cheese triangles,' she teased.

'I agree. That's why we've got scones with cream and jam, Danish pastries, bagels, fruit salad, egg muffins, yoghurt, and granola bars. I've also put in two flasks of coffee and some fresh orange juice.'

'No cheese triangles?' she pouted. 'You promised.'

'I did pack some actually, because I thought they'd be easy to spread on the bagels.'

'You've thought of everything,' she said, impressed.

'What can I say…? I like my food.'

'And here was I, thinking you had gone to all this trouble just for me.'

He indicated to turn right, and she noticed a sign for Powys Castle as they drove slowly up a narrowish road for a few minutes before, turning right again onto an even narrower one. A short while later they were pulling into a generous carpark.

To Emily's surprise, it was already about a third full, but she suspected some of the vehicles belonged to the film crew, as loads of metal boxes were being unloaded from a big lorry by a succession of people.

A man in a hi-viz jacket waved them to a stop. 'Are you here to have an item valued?'

Mac nodded. 'We are.'

'Here's a couple of tickets. You won't be allowed in without them. Those will give you access to the grounds and gardens, but not to the castle itself. If you want to have a look around while you're here, you'll have to purchase tickets from the office next to the main entrance. Once you're inside the grounds, someone will take a look at your item and advise you who the best person is to value it.'

'The gates open at nine?' Mac asked.

'Yes, but you'd better get in the queue long before then. People have already started.'

'That's our cue,' Mac joked, and Emily rolled her eyes.

'Don't make me regret bringing you,' she warned.

'I think you'll find that it was *me* who brought *you*,' he grinned.

'Only because you insisted.'

'Aren't you glad I did?'

She was actually. She never would have thought of bringing folding chairs or blankets, and her picnic would have consisted of a banana and a slice of cold toast.

Other people had the same idea she saw, as Mac unfolded the chairs and placed them side by side on the grass at the side of the road. There were probably about thirty or so people ahead of them, so not too many and Emily was quietly confident that she would be seen well before lunchtime. Maybe they could take a stroll around the castle afterwards? It would be nice to see inside.

The building was huge. Constructed out of red stone, it was perched on a hill and she wondered what the views were like from the top of the turrets. From where she and Mac were sitting, they could see little of the grounds and nothing of the activity inside, and she was eager to get her first glimpse of the various stands where the experts held court.

'I'm so excited!' she exclaimed as she settled into her chair.

Mac was ferreting about in the picnic basket, but he paused and glanced at her. 'Too excited for a scone?'

'Never! Gimmee!' She made a grabby motion with her hand.

'Patience, Nuts. I've got to get the plates out first.'

To Emily's surprise the picnic was in a proper wicker hamper, and when he opened the lid her eyes widened in delight because, attached to the underside and held in place with leather straps, were a selection of plates, cutlery, glasses and stainless steel mugs – as well as the food, some of which was in a small cool bag, whose material matched the fabric lining the inside of the hamper.

'Blimmin' heck, Mac, you've certainly pushed the boat out. I wouldn't have taken you for a hamper kind of guy.'

'I'm not. I'd normally shove everything in my rucksack, but I remembered seeing this in the attic and thought why not?'

Why not indeed! Emily felt rather posh as he unpacked everything, and when he handed her a loaded plate, she was aware of several pairs of envious eyes on them.

Around a mouthful of scone with cream and jam (jam first, obviously), she said, 'To think that Lilian probably used this.'

'I know. It's weird, isn't it? Although all her clothes and toiletries are gone, there's still so much in the cottage that is hers. I've kept most of the furniture, although I did send her sofa and those hideous armchairs to the charity shop.'

'Gosh, yes, I remember them. They were so uncomfortable.'

'I think sitting on the floor would have been preferable,' Mac agreed. 'But she liked them, so I didn't have the heart to tell her they made my back ache and my knees sore.' His mouth curved upwards, and he looked at Emily from underneath his lashes. 'I bought a new bed too. You're welcome to come bounce on it.'

'Mac, I—'

'Yeah, I know – you'll be going on Sunday.'

'It's not that I don't want to… you know… But it's just not wise.'

'You can say that again,' he muttered, and the mood was dampened for a while as they concentrated on their breakfast.

However, Mac soon perked up again, and to pass the time they played *I Spy* and when they had exhausted that, they played *Twenty Questions* until Emily ran out of steam.

By now the carpark was full and the queue stretched into the distance. She was mighty glad they had arrived early, even though she was tired.

'More coffee?' Mac offered and she readily agreed, hoping the caffeine would perk her up.

Every so often, she would pat her bag to make sure the book was still there, and whenever she did, her heart would leap.

It did more than leap when the gates finally opened and people started to trickle inside. Most of them were carrying bags or boxes but several had more substantial items, and Emily gazed at them with interest, especially an ornate harp that took three people to carry.

Mac hastily shoved everything back in the hamper and secured the lid, then hoisted a chair under each arm, and instructed Emily to drape the unneeded blankets over his shoulder before heading off to deposit them in the car.

She still couldn't get over how sweet he was, to think of her comfort whilst they queued. Although, a little voice in her head which sounded remarkably like Lucy, piped up that he had been thinking about his own comfort, too. It also pointed out that he had tried to persuade her into his bedroom again, and it wasn't to admire the duvet cover. That too, sounded like Lucy.

Emily understood that her friend was only looking out for her, but she wished Lucy would mind her own business. Emily didn't need reminding that this... whatever it was that was going on between her and Mac... was a non-starter.

She was nearly at the gates by the time Mac returned, and she beckoned him over with relief. 'I was worried that I'd have to go in without you,' she said, leaning into him.

'As if I would let that happen.' He slid an arm around her waist. 'I've got to come with you – I want to make sure Aunt Lilian didn't leave you more than she left me.'

'As if! Your cottage is worth a small fortune. Properties like yours are snapped up to be used as quaint holiday homes. I can't believe how expensive housing is in Glynafon. I couldn't afford to buy anything there.'

'You might, when you sell your book.'

Emily opened her mouth to tell him that the proceeds from the book were already earmarked, when he said, 'Our turn,' and fished their tickets out of his wallet as they were ushered forward.

Her excitement swelled and she could hardly contain herself as she was asked what the item was that she wanted valued.

'It's an old book,' she said, taking it out and showing it to the woman.

'You need stand number three. Remy Griswald is our book and document specialist today.' And she went on to explain what would happen if the producer decided they wanted to include her item and its subsequent valuation in the show.

Emily struggled to take it all in. She was far more interested in Remy Griswald's opinion on what it was worth, than her face being on TV. Although, if she did appear in the show and Cole got to hear about it, she would laugh her socks off. He would be well miffed if he realised that there had been a priceless book in his attic.

Emily joined the queue for Remy Griswald, Mac a solid and calming presence by her side as she fidgeted and fretted.

Eventually it was her turn, and she walked forward nervously, the unwrapped book in her hand. Remy Griswald was an older man, in his late fifties or early sixties, and was dressed somewhat bizarrely in orange trousers, a yellow shirt, and with a pink cravat around his neck. A porkpie hat topped off his ensemble.

'Hello, I'm Remy. Take a seat. What's your name?' He had a well-modulated, rather deep voice and spoke softly.

'Emily, and this is Mac.'

'Pleased to meet you.'

'Pleased to meet you too.' Emily said shyly. This was the closest she had ever been to a bona fide celebrity.

'What have we here?' he asked, taking the proffered book from her.

'I believe it's a first edition of Glenarvon by Lady Caroline Lamb. The unwatered down version.'

She watched him study the outside of it closely and held her breath.

'Ah, yes, so it is. Subsequent editions were published in three volumes, to maximise profits, I presume. This specimen is in quite good condition, and although it isn't particularly rare, it is rarer than the subsequent three-volume version. It's bound in treated calf hide and the colour is unusual. Calf is generally brown, but because of the despicable nature of the title character, the publishers may have thought it would have more gothic appeal if it had a black binding.'

He gently opened the cover and examined the title page, then he carefully looked at the rest of them.

'There's some foxing, which isn't unusual,' he said, looking up at her. 'Foxing refers to these brown blotches staining the paper. It's usually the result of impurities in the paper left behind during the paper-making process.'

'Does it affect the value?'

'It depends on the rarity of the volume and how extensive the foxing is. A very rare book, even with a significant amount of foxing, would not have its value impinged as greatly as a less rare book with less foxing.'

'I'm hoping this is one of the very rare ones,' Emily said. She was sitting on her hands to prevent herself from chewing her nails, but she freed them and twisted them in her lap instead. This was the moment of truth.

'Ah.' He frowned. 'Because of the handwritten inscription on the title page, I presume?'

She nodded, not trusting herself to speak.

Remy took out a loupe and inserted it into his right eye socket, then turned the book this way and that, holding it up to the light.

Slowly, he put it down on the table, removed the loupe and steepled his hands. 'I'm sorry to say that this inscription isn't original. This isn't written by Lord Byron's hand, although it is a fairly good facsimile. The signature might be old, but unfortunately it isn't old *enough*. I believe it has been added as much as a century later to increase the value of the book, and although I can't be one hundred percent certain, I suspect it was written by a fountain pen with a metal nib, and not a quill pen. Byron only used a quill pen and inkwell, I'm afraid.'

Emily was frozen. She couldn't believe what she was hearing, and she swallowed, her mouth suddenly dry with disappointment.

'I expect you would like to know its value?' Remy asked.

When she didn't say anything, Mac answered for her. 'Yes, please.'

'I would say, at auction, this would fetch somewhere in the region of fifteen hundred to two thousand pounds. Maybe more, if you have two buyers who are particularly keen. Thank you so much for bringing it in.'

Emily couldn't speak and neither could she move. Dimly she registered Mac thanking the valuer for his time, and she was aware of Mac retrieving the book and helping her to her feet, but the rest was a blur.

All she could think about was that her little black book wasn't nearly as valuable as she had prayed it would be.

Oh, God, what was she going to do?

CHAPTER 18

'I'm sorry. I know that wasn't the news you wanted to hear,' Mac was saying as he walked away, Emily tottering beside him on numb, wooden legs. Her mind was equally as numb and wooden.

'No, it isn't.'

'At least you're no worse off than you were before, so that's something.'

Oh, she was worse off all right. Very much worse off. 'I might have known it was too good to be true,' she said, bitterly.

She should never have pinned her hopes on a stupid little book. Good things didn't happen to people like her, and knowing her luck, she should have expected something like this. It just felt particularly cruel to have her dream of it being worth a fortune dangled in front of her nose, only to have it snatched away. She wished Bea hadn't mentioned it in the first place. To raise her hopes that she might have been able to solve the farm's financial crises, only for them to be dashed on the rocks, was something she could have done without this past week. She'd had enough to contend with, having found herself boyfriendless and homeless. Then there had been the drama of actually retrieving the damned thing. She didn't think she could take any more.

'Do you fancy looking around the castle, or have you had enough?' Mac asked, breaking into her morose and bitter thoughts.

'Do you mind if we go home?' She just wanted to curl up in a ball and wallow in her misery.

'Of course not. I must admit I'm rather tired myself, and you look shattered.'

Yeah, she was, and not just in the exhausted sense of the word. Her plan to inject a hefty dose of cash into the farm had been smashed to smithereens and lay in pieces at her feet.

The journey home took place in subdued silence for most of the way. Mac had attempted to make conversation but swiftly gave up when all he had received were monosyllabic replies.

Using the excuse that she was tired, Emily closed her eyes and pretended to sleep, but not before she sent an email to her employer. She may as well get it over with – there was no point in putting off handing in her resignation.

However, sleep was the furthest thing from her mind. Her brain was busy running through what her life was going to be like for the foreseeable future, and all she could see was sheep and mud, with the occasional drink in the Smuggler's Rest.

And Mac. She could see Mac. But would *he* want to carry on seeing *her*?

***

When Emily walked into the kitchen later that afternoon, her mother nearly dropped the basket of eggs she was holding. 'I didn't expect you back so soon,' Dina said. 'Did you have a nice time?'

'Yes, it was lovely.'

'Are you hungry? It's too early for tea, but I can rustle you something up.'

'No thanks; Mac brought a picnic.' She couldn't face food right now.

Her mother beamed. 'A picnic? How romantic. You're spending a lot of time with him.' She was pushing for details, but Emily didn't want to discuss it. She had other things on her mind.

'Mum, I've been thinking about what you said, and I don't want to go back to Worcester. I want to stay here, on the farm.'

Dina's eyes widened, then she pressed her lips together before asking, 'Is this anything to do with Mac?'

'No,' Emily replied honestly. It had nothing to do with Mac whatsoever.

Her mother took hold of her hand and sat her down at the kitchen table. 'I'm glad to hear it. I wouldn't want you to jump into anything – it's only been a couple of weeks since you and Cole split up. Are you sure this is what you want?'

'Spending time here, being with you guys and helping out on the farm, has made me realise that *this* is my home, not Worcester. This is where I belong.'

'But what about your job? Your friends?'

'I'll get a job in Glynafon or nearby, and I've got friends in the village. Not everyone has moved away; there's Lucy and Jo for starters.'

'You won't find it as easy as you think to get a job. You forget how rural we are.'

'Are you trying to put me off?' Emily was surprised, and more than a little hurt. She had expected her mum to be thrilled.

'Not at all. I just want you to make the right decision. We'd love to have you back, of course we would, but I want to make sure you are doing it for the right reasons, and it's not a knee-jerk reaction to what Cole did.'

'It's not,' Emily stated firmly. She was doing this for the very best of reasons. 'I've made up my mind. I want to stay in Glynafon for good. Anyway, I'll have to, because I've already handed in my notice. You're stuck with me, whether you like it or not.'

For the rest of the afternoon, Emily busied herself on the farm. She had plenty of chores to get on with, although doing physical things didn't necessarily occupy her mind, and her thoughts kept returning to what the expert at Powys Castle had said. Her disappointment was so acute that she wanted to burst into tears, but she managed to keep a lid on her emotions until after tea. She even managed to successfully pretend to be happy and upbeat, although maybe she had overdone it a tad, because her mum kept giving her odd looks.

Using the excuse that she may as well unpack everything now and find homes for all her stuff, she escaped to her room, hoping to catch Ava. But before she rang her friend, she checked her emails.

She hadn't expected to receive a reply from her employer just yet, and she fully assumed she would have to go back to Worcester to work her notice, despite asking if it was at all possible to forgo that.

But sitting in her inbox was a lovely email informing her they were sorry to lose her, but they fully understood that family came first (Emily had laid it on a bit thick) and wishing her all the best for the future. The email also said that, under the circumstances she didn't have to work her notice, and that if she needed a reference in the future, they would happily supply one.

This time she didn't hold back the tears. She let them fall, sobbing softly into her pillow until she was all cried out. It was the end of an era. She had cut her ties with the city and the life she had made for herself there, and she felt incredibly sad that it had come to this.

It took her a while to compose herself, but when she finally felt calm enough, she rang Ava.

'Where are you?' she asked when Ava answered. It sounded noisy.

'The Slug and Lettuce,' Ava shouted. 'Hang on.' More noises followed – voices, music, laughter – before abruptly diminishing. 'That's better. I've come outside. I couldn't hear myself think in there.'

'Have you got a few minutes to chat?' Emily asked.

'I have, but can't it wait until I see you on Sunday? We can have a proper catch-up then.'

'That's the problem. I won't be coming to Worcester on Sunday.'

'Oh, OK... What day will you be coming back?'

'I'm staying in Glynafon for good.'

'Pardon? I thought you said for good...'

'I did. I've found out that the farm is in trouble financially, and my parents need my help.'

'God, Em, that's a shock! How do you feel?'

'I'm not sure. I'm a bit numb, to be honest.'

'I'm not surprised. What will you do?'

'Get a job and do as much as I can around the farm, when I can. I've told them I'm staying, but they don't know that I know about the state of the finances.'

'How did you find out?' Ava asked.

'I overheard them talking. They were worried about paying for repairs on the tractor if Dad couldn't fix it himself, and Mum said if they had to get the garage to mend it, she'd not be able to pay the gas bill. And they had to let Ianto, their stockman, go because they couldn't afford to pay his wages, and now Dad is struggling to run the farm all by himself. Mum is doing as much as she can, but her back isn't the best.'

'That's a real bummer.'

'It certainly is.'

'I'm going to miss you, hun.'

'You can always come visit. Have a holiday on the farm,' Emily suggested.

'That's it! You can run a B and B, or rent out a field to campers.'

'There are already a couple of camping and caravan sites in the area, and loads of holiday cottages and guest houses, so I think the market is probably saturated. But keep the ideas coming – I'm open to any suggestions that could make the farm some money.'

'There is a silver lining to this,' Ava said.

Emily said, 'I know – the scenery is gorgeous, the village is idyllic, and I get to see my family all the time – although, I dare say Mum and I will butt heads more than once.'

'I didn't mean that. I meant *Mac*. If you're staying in Glynafon, there's nothing stopping you from seeing an awful lot more of him.'

Funnily enough, that very same thought had occurred to Emily…

***

The following day was another bright and sunny one. Although Emily was up early, it wasn't at ridiculous o'clock: thankfully their cows were beef animals and not dairy, so there was no herd to milk first thing in the morning.

She had slept for ten hours last night, the emotional events of the past week finally getting to her. But when she awoke this morning, she felt brighter and more positive than she had yesterday.

It might be Saturday, but it was just another day on the farm, and there were loads of jobs to be done. One of today's tasks was something she wasn't looking forward to in the slightest – muck spreading. It was an essential task, but a very smelly one. Her dad had managed to mend the tractor (for the time being) and he'd asked if she minded doing the lower field for him.

Emily had learnt to drive a tractor when she was a teen, and she knew how to operate most of the machinery that could be attached to it, so it was no hardship to sit in the cab and steer it up and down the field in orderly rows. The hardship came from the smell, and she wondered whether her dad was testing her commitment. He might even be trying to put her off, but, as she had told her mum, it was too late now. There was no going back. This was the start of a new phase in her life and it was up to her to make the most of it.

She was currently on the tractor, half of her attention on the field she was trundling up and down, the other half on the rear of the vehicle to make sure everything was operating correctly, when her phone buzzed with a message.

Deciding she needed a break anyway (she'd been at it for an hour), she came to a halt and stopped the machinery.

The silence was sheer bliss and she slumped back in the seat for a moment, relishing it, then she checked her phone.

The message was from Mac. ***Are you OK?***

I'm fine. I've got something to tell you. Can we meet later?

When and where?

Emily suggested they go for a walk, and they arranged to meet outside the pub and take it from there. She wanted to tell him face-to-face that she wasn't leaving, because his reaction would determine what she did next. After all, Glynafon was a small place and they would undoubtedly bump into each other on a regular basis. The last thing she wanted was for there to be any awkwardness or misunderstanding between them. If Mac had only viewed their little fling as a temporary thing, she didn't want him to feel obliged to carry on with it. She was conscious that Lucy still thought he was a bit free and easy when it came to relationships, and she didn't want to risk him riding roughshod over her heart.

That she was already half in love with him was a problem she would have to deal with, if push came to shove.

A few hours later, she set off into the village. She didn't bother taking the car: after all, she was now officially unemployed, so she had to start watching the pennies and had decided to only use her little car when it was absolutely necessary. The walk would do her good anyway.

Mac was already waiting for her. He had his hands in the pockets of his jeans and was gazing across the bay. The beach was busy, as was to be expected at this time of year, and there were people playing in the water, and further out several boats bobbed on the waves.

When he saw her, his face lit up, and Emily's heart melted at the sight of his wide sexy smile. He looked delighted to see her, and she hoped he would be just as delighted when he heard what she was about to tell him.

'Shall we walk along the coastal path?' she suggested.

Glynafon lay in a small valley with a little river running through it, hills rising above it on both sides and the views were spectacular from the clifftops.

He readily agreed and they made their way up a steep section of road, towards a gate. Beyond it was the coastal path, and as they began to walk along it, Emily turned to gaze back at the village and the sweeping expanse of beach below.

'I always forget how beautiful it is,' she said.

'It can be the same when you live here,' Mac pointed out. 'You forget to appreciate what's under your nose.'

'I don't want that to happen to me.' She carried on walking. There was a bench not too far away, and she made for that, sitting down on it and patting the seat next to her.

'It won't.' His reply was confident. 'Every time you come back, you'll appreciate it anew.'

'I'm not coming back,' she said, and a thrill went through her when she saw the sudden shock and dismay on his face. 'I'll clarify that – I'm not leaving.'

Mac was staring at her. 'Why not?'

Once again, she debated whether to share the farm's financial problems with him, but decided against it. Her parents wouldn't care for it to become common knowledge, and she wanted to ensure she wasn't just a number in his own little black book of bootie-call contacts and that their relationship would develop into something more than a fling, before she told him the real reason behind her decision.

'I belong here,' she said simply. 'The past two weeks have made me realise that this is my home.'

It wasn't a total lie. This *was* her home. She just hadn't expected to be living here permanently.

'I'm glad,' Mac said, simply.

He slung an arm around her and she relaxed into him, putting her head on his shoulder. Being with him felt so natural, so right.

'What about your job?' he asked after a few moments.

Her gaze rested on the village in the distance. 'I'll get another. In the meantime, there's always the farm.'

In fact, she should be updating her CV right now, rather than swanning around the coastal path with Mac.

'Is it a done deal?' he asked.

'I've handed in my notice.' She exhaled slowly. Although she knew she had done the right thing and that she hadn't had any choice, it had nevertheless been a difficult decision to make.

'I take it you've not got anything else lined up?'

'No, but something will turn up.'

'I admire your guts. I don't think I would be brave enough to jack in my job without having another one to go to.'

'Yeah, well, you know…' she hedged. 'Sometimes you've just got to follow your heart.'

His fingers had been idly stroking the top of her arm, but they stilled, and Emily sensed a sudden tension in him. 'Is that what you're doing? Following your heart?'

She lifted her head from his shoulder and gazed up at him. His eyes met hers, the expression in them serious and intense. Her tummy fluttered and her pulse drummed in her ears. It had only been a week since Bea had bullied them into going for a meal in the

Smuggler's Rest, yet it felt like a lifetime ago. So much had happened, and Mac had been at the heart of it.

Could she allow him access to the heart of *her*? He had always had a piece of it, but she had assumed it was an echo of the intense emotions of her youth, and nostalgia for a simpler time when she had been madly in love with her teenage crush, yet too scared and shy to do anything about it.

Was she too scared now?

'I'm sorry about the book,' Mac said, breaking into her thoughts. 'I know you were hoping it would be worth something.'

Emily made a face. Now would be the ideal time to mention why she had been so gutted, but she continued to hold her tongue. One day, she might share that with him...

'It doesn't matter,' she said, shrugging it off. 'I'm sorry I overreacted.'

'I didn't think you overreacted at all. I wish Gran hadn't got your hopes up, though. She should never have said anything.'

'And miss out on all the fun we had in Worcester?'

Mac chuckled. 'It was a laugh, wasn't it? I'll say that for you, Nuts... there's never a dull moment when you're around.'

'I don't think Lucy thinks so. She accused me of being sensible.'

Mac jerked, and Emily gave him a quizzical look. 'Bee,' he explained, flapping a hand near his face. 'Gone now. Lucy doesn't know what she's talking about.'

'That's what I thought – *she* was the sensible one, not me.'

'Do we have to talk about her? I would prefer to talk about us.'

Emily froze. 'Is there an *us*?'

'There could be, if that's what you want. Now that you're staying, there could definitely be an us.'

'As in, me and you dating?'

Mac smiled. 'That's exactly what I mean.'

'I would be your girlfriend?'

His smile faltered. 'Yeah… Look, sorry, I shouldn't have mentioned anything. It's only been a couple of weeks since you split up with your ex. It's just…' He drew in a deep breath and let it out in a rush, as he said, 'I've always had a thing for you, Nuts.'

Bea had told her as much, and her heart gave a little squeeze; maybe not going back to Worcester would have its upside. Hadn't she been kind of hoping for that, too?

'I had a thing for you, too,' she confessed.

'You did? Wow – I never guessed.'

'Me, neither.'

They beamed at each other. Emily suddenly felt like she was sixteen again, and the boy she had an enormous crush on had asked her to go out with him. Which, in effect, was exactly what had just happened....

'Bea will be pleased,' Emily said, with a giggle.

Mac replied dryly, 'I hope you aren't dating me, just to keep my grandmother sweet.'

'Not just her, my mum has also been trying to throw us together. Remember the incident on the landing when all I had on was a towel?'

Mac pretended to leer at her. 'How could I forget? You looked ever so cute with your wet hair and your pink cheeks.'

'Wait until I tell her about us – she already believes that you are the reason I'm not going back to Worcester.'

'Am I the reason?' His eyes were twinkling and there was a grin playing around his mouth.

'Er...' Shit! What should she say to that? Was he joking, or did he think he might actually be the reason?

'You don't have to answer that,' he laughed, letting her off the hook. Then his expression became serious. 'I'm very happy you're staying, Emily. Happier than you can imagine. I kept telling myself not to get too close, that you were still hurting, that you would be gone soon, but I couldn't help myself. I think I'm in love with you. I think I always have been.'

He was gazing deep into her eyes, and she saw the truth in them. This was no patter designed to lower her defences to get her to sleep with him: he meant what he was saying.

It made her heart sing.

Mac was *in love* with her.

And hearing him say that, Emily knew that she was in love with him, too. That she had never stopped loving him. That what she had believed to be a schoolgirl infatuation had been the real thing all along – but it had taken ten years and nearly three hundred kilometres to realise it.

CHAPTER 19

Bea was deadheading her roses when Emily unlatched the little wooden gate and strolled up the crazy-paved path. The garden was in full bloom, and perfume hung in the air. Emily breathed deeply, inhaling the scent of hundreds of flowers.

'You can't bottle that,' Bea said, straightening up. She had a wicker basket on her arm and was holding a wicked pair of secateurs.

Emily didn't think she had ever seen the old lady sitting still: she was always doing something, and Emily hoped she would be as healthy and lively when she got to Bea's age.

'Have you brought me a cake?' Bea asked, her eyes on the Tupperware box in Emily's hands.

'It's Sunday, so...' Emily held it up.

'No need to get sassy. I know what day it is. Here, you carry on deadheading and I'll make a pot of tea.

We'll drink it out here.' Bea handed her the secateurs and the basket, and swapped them for the plastic tub. 'Looks like carrot cake – my favourite!'

Bea gave her a one-armed hug, then went inside to make the tea, leaving Emily looking at the roses doubtfully. She had never been much of a gardener, and was scared of snipping off the wrong thing. After removing a couple of flowers that were past their best, her attention was grabbed by the sheer number of bees crawling over the petals. And as she looked closer, she could see the tiny pollen sacks on their legs. A fat bumblebee buzzed past her nose, and she reared back, marvelling at the size of it.

The garden was alive with butterflies, too. Loads of them – white ones, brown ones, blue ones… It was quite magical, and Emily imagined there might be bright red toadstools in the far corners and fairy doors hidden under the bushes.

'I love your garden,' Emily said, when Bea reappeared with a tray.

The old lady placed it carefully on the little wrought-iron patio table. 'So do I, especially at this time of year when it's a riot of colour. It's bloody hard work, though.'

'I could help, if you like. Just tell me what needs doing.'

Bea shot her a sharp look. 'You'll have more than enough to keep you busy at the farm.' She began to pour the tea into a pretty china cup, then stopped when she noticed a woman on the road outside. 'Clarice, you're looking better.'

Emily saw an elderly woman slowly walking along the pavement, coming into view behind a rather spectacular blue-flowered hydrangea.

She stopped and smiled at Bea. 'I'm feeling it,' she replied. 'Nearly back to my old self.' She squinted at Emily. 'Old age is no joke, not when you've got no family around you. Bea is lucky, she's got Macsen.'

Bea said, 'You remember Emily Oak? Dina and Graham's daughter, at Glynafon Farm?'

'I do.' Clarice was nodding. 'My, you've grown. I haven't seen you since you were a girl. You've turned into a proper little bobby-dazzler, haven't you!'

Emily blushed. She wasn't hideous in the looks department, but neither would she describe herself as a 'proper little bobby-dazzler'. Still, she'd take the complement!

Clarice shuffled along and was soon out of sight, hidden by a small lilac tree.

'That's another thing I love about my garden,' Bea said, returning to her tea-pouring duties. 'I get to see the world go by. If this was out the back, I wouldn't see anyone.'

Bea's cottage didn't have a rear garden: this was it, and although Emily loved it, she wasn't sure whether she would appreciate being on show, especially if she was guzzling her way through a bottle of wine on a Friday evening. People might get the wrong idea!

Bea passed her a cup and saucer, and Emily took a sip of the scalding liquid.

'Cake?' the old lady asked.

'Go on, then.' Lunch seemed a long time ago, and although she had stuffed her face with a substantial roast lamb dinner, all the outdoor work was making her perpetually hungry. A slice of cake wouldn't touch the sides!

Emily tucked in with enthusiasm, thinking that her mother's cooking was yet another reason why remaining in Glynafon wasn't such a bad thing. The reasons were adding up – Mac having been elevated to the top of the list.

Bea ate a mouthful, then said, 'Macsen told me that Lilian's book isn't worth as much as you hoped it was. He also said you were rather upset about it. I assume you haven't told him why?'

'I thought it best not to. I don't think Mum and Dad would like it if people knew the farm was in trouble.'

'Don't worry, your secret is safe with me. Do I take it that you won't be going back to Worcester after all?'

'How can I? They need me here.' Emily heaved a sigh. 'I just wish I could help them – even with me staying on at the farm I'm not sure it's enough to get them out of the financial mess they're in. If that flippin' book had been worth the thousands we thought it might be, it would have solved all their problems in one fell swoop.'

'And you wouldn't be here.'

'No...' Her heart clenched as she realised how close she had come to losing Mac. If she hadn't told him she was staying in Glynafon, he would never have told her that he was in love with her.

'How did Dina take the news? I don't suppose you told your parents the *real* reason you're not going back to Worcester either?'

'Hardly! Mum would be appalled if she thought I was staying here so they don't lose the farm. She thinks it's because of Mac. She's as bad as you when it comes to setting the two of us up. And all this gadding about with him, as Lilian would have said, has just added fuel to the fire.' She shovelled another forkful of cake into her mouth and briefly closed her eyes in bliss. 'Mmm, this is delish,' she mumbled.

She was about to tell Bea that although she had made the decision to stay based on the farm's finances, her grandson was an equal, if not more compelling reason to remain, when a volley of deep barks from the other side of the garden wall made talking impossible.

'Shush!' she heard someone say, and Lucy came into view.

Lucy glanced at Emily and Bea, pulled a face, then turned her attention to the dog.

'Titch! Be quiet!' Lucy looked up again as the barking resumed. 'I was just...er...taking him for a walk and...er, he saw a cat. He hates cats. Or rather, he likes cats, but only because he wants to chase them,' she stammered. Her face was pink and became even pinker when the dog began to bark again. 'Sorry,' she called, as she dragged the reluctant mutt away.

Emily caught a glimpse of the Basset hound as it slowly ambled after her, Lucy hauling on its lead as it stopped to sniff every section of the pavement.

'I often see Lucy taking Jim's dog for a walk,' Bea said. 'She's been doing it for a good few months. I must remember to ask her how her dad is, the next time I see her.'

'I saw him on Tuesday. He was manning the barbeque. He looked really well.'

'Ah, yes, Mac did say something about being invited to a barbeque at Lucy's house, but he didn't go because he was busy. Anyway, what were we talking about? Oh, yes, your mum and dad. How do they feel about having you home to stay?'

'They're delighted – I think. I keep catching them smiling at me and nodding their heads. It's quite unnerving, to be honest.'

'How do you feel?'

'I thought I'd be gutted, but I'm not. The only thing I'm not too happy about is the actual farming itself.'

Bea pursed her lips. 'You need to tell your parents that. They might think you've changed your mind and that you *do* want to run the farm after all.'

'But if I do that, they'll wonder what's really keeping me here.'

'From what you've told me, I think your mum can guess. Mac was beaming like a Cheshire cat yesterday.'

Emily blushed again, but she couldn't prevent a grin from spreading across her face.

Bea studied her. 'Do you know...' she began, thoughtfully. 'I've got a feeling that even if that book had been worth a fair bit, you wouldn't have left.'

'Maybe not,' Emily agreed. 'But at least I could have given them the money and be done with it. They would have been able to give Ianto his job back. As it stands now, I'll have to help them out for the foreseeable future. If I don't, they'll be forced to sell. Without my help they can't afford to keep it going.

'Maybe they don't want to,' Bea said slowly. 'Maybe they're sticking at it because it's all they know. As you've pointed out, your dad is at the age where most people are looking forward to retiring.'

'But he loves it, they both do,' Emily objected.

'Then you're going to have to figure out another way to keep the farm going if you don't want to be shearing sheep for the rest of your life. What's your degree in?'

'Business.'

'So, Emily Oak, go put your business head on.'

***

There were still a few people she had yet to share her news with – which was why Emily was currently standing at the bar in the Smuggler's Rest and getting a round of drinks in.

As she waited to be served, she pondered that a mere twelve days ago she had been in this exact same spot when she had set eyes on Mac for the first time in years. To Emily, that moment seemed to have been the starting point for the events which led to her being here this evening. Logically, she knew it wasn't, but when had she ever been logical?

She certainly didn't feel logical right now! What she felt was both excited and apprehensive at what the future might hold, and she tingled with the certainty that Macsen would be in it.

They had agreed to slow things down a little for the time being, because so far this new relationship of theirs could best be described as a whirlwind romance, therefore they hadn't made any definite plans for when they would see each other next. He had messaged her today though, and had promised to give her a call when she got back from the pub.

Emily paid for the drinks and with a strong sense of déjà vu, she spanned her hands around the three glasses and made her way to the table where Jo and Lucy were waiting.

'I can't believe you dragged me out on another school night,' Jo pretended to grumble. She had a twinkle in her eye that belied her moaning, and she made grabby hands, eager for her drink. 'I can't stay out long, though,' she warned. 'Nat has got work tomorrow, so I can't expect him to look after Oliver while I'm out partying.' She took a huge gulp of her vodka and smacked her lips.

'A quick drink in the pub is hardly partying,' Emily laughed.

'Anyway, I thought you would have left by now,' Jo said. 'Weren't you supposed to be going back today?'

'I was,' Emily replied slowly, 'but things have changed.'

'What things?' Jo was staring at her over the rim of her glass. Lucy hadn't touched hers yet.

'I'm not going back to Worcester,' she announced.

Jo said, 'What? Like, never?'

'No, I'm staying in Glynafon for good.'

'Bloody hell, Em, I never thought you would come back here to live. What brought that on?'

'Oh, I don't know… I fancied a change.'

'Is that so?' Lucy asked. She finally picked up her wine and sipped at it.

'Being in Glynafon these past two weeks has made me realise how much I miss it.'

'Have you got another job?' Jo asked.

'Not yet, but I updated my CV last night, and this evening I'll start looking to see what's about.'

'Not a lot,' Lucy said shortly. 'You would have been better off going back to Worcester.'

Emily frowned. Lucy seemed rather peevish and Emily wondered what was wrong.

'What sort of work are you looking for?' Jo asked, claiming her attention.

'Anything, I'm not fussy.'

'It could take a while,' Lucy warned.

'I know, but at least I've got the farm to keep me occupied until something comes up.'

'Are you going to be living there?' Jo asked.

'That's the plan. In fact, I want to pick your brains about it.'

'Not got any,' Jo shot back. 'I haven't been able to think straight since I got pregnant, and once I gave birth to Oliver it's been even worse.'

'I'll give it a go anyway,' Emily chuckled. 'Hit me with any and all ideas you might have: I know Mum and Dad love their sheep and cows, but frankly, I'd be happy if I never saw one again. And they're getting on a bit – my parents, not the livestock – so I thought I'd see if I could come up with a couple of things that would keep the farm ticking along but with less work.'

'Glamping?' Jo suggested immediately. 'Llama walks?'

'God, no! Not more sodding animals to look after.' Emily shuddered. Ava had already suggested glamping, but llama walks was a new one.

Lucy said, 'I'm surprised you considered moving back in with your parents if you hate farming so much.'

Emily blinked. 'I don't hate it exactly…'

'You could have fooled me.'

Picking up her drink, Emily paused, wondering how she should respond. Maybe she had overdone it with the negatives, bearing in mind she was supposed to be staying in Glynafon because she had missed it.

'It's not so bad,' she amended. 'I'm just a bit grouchy because I've spent the best part of three days this week shearing. I'd forgotten how hard it is.'

'On the bright side, it'll keep you in shape,' Jo said, grabbing a handful of her post-pregnancy tummy and squidging it. 'Got any left to shear?'

'No, thank goodness, all done. I was so sick of the sight of wool by the end of it, that I seriously considered throwing my knitting needles in the bin.'

'What are you working on at the moment?' Jo asked. Out of her and Lucy, she seemed to be doing all the talking. Lucy was unusually quiet. 'You used to make some fab jumpers, and that shawl you knitted when Oliver was born is gorgeous. I wish I could knit.'

'You can,' Emily insisted. 'I've offered to teach you.'

'Haven't got the patience, or the time,' Jo replied. 'Plus, I'd probably get bored if it took longer than an hour or two to make.'

Emily said, 'I've got a couple of things on the go, because I get bored sometimes, too, and I switch from knitting to felting, depending on my mood.' Thankfully, she had loads of scraps of wool for her felting projects, because wool wasn't cheap, and with her not working at present, she could hardly justify spending money on non-essentials. It was ironic that the farm had nearly one hundred fleeces to dispose of, yet—

Emily gasped. She'd just had the most brilliant idea!

CHAPTER 20

It felt strange not to be going to work, Emily mused, as she donned a pair of distinctly unattractive overalls. Today was her first proper day of her new life and overalls were going to feature rather heavily in it.

Before Friday and Powys Castle, she had been psyching herself up for her return to work, but now she had been forced into a completely different mindset.

Vowing to make the best of things, she entered the kitchen with a cheery smile and grabbed a mug. She would feel better after coffee and breakfast.

'Did you find anything?' her mum asked.

Emily had spent far too long scouring the internet for jobs last night after she'd arrived home from the pub, considering she had to get up early this morning.

'Yes and no,' she replied cryptically. She had looked at several job sites to see if there was anything she could apply for, and there had been one or two. So she had sent her CV in for one, and downloaded an application form for another (she would fill it in later tonight), but she had spent the remainder of the time doing research for the idea she'd had yesterday.

'What would you like for breakfast?' her mum asked. 'Scrambled egg, toast, cereal?'

'Just toast, please – but let me make it. I don't expect you to wait on me.'

'It's no bother. I'm putting some in for your dad, so adding two extra slices to the toaster isn't any hardship. What have you got planned for today, Graham?'

'We're going to worm the lambs and run them through the footbath,' he said, with a nod in Emily's direction.

Ooh, goody, she thought, *yet more messing about with the sheep*. She knew that both worming them and bathing their feet was essential, but neither activity was particularly pleasant – although they were rather more preferable to shearing.

He turned back to Dina. 'Can you arrange for the fleeces to be collected? I doubt we'll get much for them though – with the price of wool these days, I reckon we'll have to pay to have the damned things taken away before long.'

'Um, Mum… can you hold fire on that for a couple of days?'

'I can, but why would I want to do that?'

'I've got an idea – more than one – but before I say anything further, I want to know if they are feasible.'

Her mum and dad shared a look. Her dad shrugged.

Dina said, 'I don't have to do it today. But they need to be gone sooner rather than later. I don't want them hanging around.'

'But they're OK where they are for the time being, aren't they?' Emily asked. They were in big metal containers in the barn, and she didn't think they were in the way at all.

'For the time being,' her mum agreed. 'Now, I don't want you working on the farm all day – not when you could be spending the time looking for a new job.'

'It's OK, Mum, I can do both. I applied for one last night.' Mindful of what Bea had advised, Emily added, 'I don't want Dad to get too used to me doing all the grunt work, otherwise he might get the wrong idea and think I like it.'

'I won't,' her dad said. 'You've made it perfectly clear that farming isn't for you, but whilst you've got the time, I appreciate your help all the same.'

Emily thought she detected a note of resignation in his voice, and she felt bad. But although she was prepared to help as much as she could, her ultimate goal was to find some way to make the farm more profitable without her help being needed.

She knew it was only a stop-gap, because at some point in the future the farm would have to be sold when it finally became too much for her dad – even if he was able to employ a stockman or two. But – and this was the driving force behind everything she was doing – they would be able to sell it when *they* wanted, when the time was right for *them*; and not have the sale thrust upon them by their worsening finances.

She just had to keep things going until she figured something out...

***

Emily's heart was thumping with excitement as she trotted down the lane. She was heading to Macsen's house, and the takeaway he had promised her.

After putting in a full day's work on the farm, she was starving. However, her excitement stemmed from seeing Mac again, and not from the thought of tucking into a large bowl of noodles.

She passed Bea's house, but didn't call in, and when she spotted Lucy and Titch coming towards her, all she did was shout a quick hello and hurry on past. And the reason for her haste was because she strongly suspected (*hoped*) that she would spend the night, despite their agreement to take it slow.

On Saturday, he had told her he was in love with her. If he hadn't confessed to that, she might be a tad more cautious. But, darn it, she couldn't wait to kiss him senseless, tear his clothes off, and drag him upstairs to bed.

She hoped he felt the same way, because if he didn't and he tried to get her to take it easy, she just might explode.

'I haven't ordered any food yet,' Mac said, when he opened the door and saw her standing on the step. 'I wasn't sure what you wanted, so I thought I'd wait for you to arrive and we could decide together.'

Emily put a hand on his chest and pushed. Mac took a step back, then another as she propelled him backwards into the hallway and kicked the door shut.

'I know what I want.' Her voice was husky.

'You do? Good? I'm easy so—'

'Shh. Kiss me.'

Mac was laughing. 'OK, but should we order first, because it'll take at least half an hour to arrive?'

'No, we shouldn't.' She tilted her chin, her lips parting, and dropped her bag to the floor. Her hands went to the buttons on her floaty summer blouse, and she undid the first one.

Mac's eyes shot to the sliver of lacy bra peeking out from underneath the thin fabric.

He watched her undo a second button and drew in a deep breath, letting it out in a slow sigh. His gaze crept to her face and the desire she saw in his eyes made her melt. Liquid heat sizzled through her veins and her heartbeat ratcheted up a gear.

'Kiss me,' she repeated, and he didn't need telling again.

With a groan, he swept her into his arms as she moulded herself to him, his lips hot and hard as his mouth came down on hers. His hands roamed up and down her back, coming to rest on her waist, as he lifted her up and her legs clamped around him.

'I think we've been here before,' he said throatily.

'Not quite – this time there's nothing to stop us.'

And nothing did…

***

'Gosh, I'm stuffed.' Emily was glad she wasn't wearing the cut-off jeans she had arrived in, because she didn't think she would have been able to do them up. Instead, she was wearing a pair of Mac's pyjama bottoms and one of his old T-shirts. At some point, before she had got naked, she'd lost a button off her blouse and it needed to be sewn back on before she could wear it again.

Mac said, 'Me, too. The takeaway had arrived a half hour ago, and more than three hours since Emily had knocked on his door. The intervening time had been spent working up quite an appetite.

'Can you stay for a bit longer, or are you going to rush off now that you've had your wicked way with me and I've fed you?' Mac was teasing, but she sensed a seriousness beneath it.

'Do you want me to go? Be honest with me...' she warned. 'If you want me to leave, just say.' Her heart was in her mouth as she uttered the words.

'No! That's the last thing I want. Stay the night... please?'

Her relief was profound. 'If you insist,' she replied, primly.

'I do. And I want to carry you off to bed again, but I'm scared I might burst. I've eaten far too much.'

'We can always cuddle on the sofa and chat for a bit,' she suggested. She got to her feet with a groan and staggered over to it. 'I'll help you clean up in a minute.'

'No need, I've got it covered.' He piled the empty cartons into the bag the food had arrived in, and collected up the plates and cutlery, taking them into the kitchen. He returned with two glasses of sparkling water and sat down next to her. 'I thought you might be thirsty.'

'Thanks, I am.' She took one of them gratefully, and gulped half of it down.

'How are you feeling?' he asked.

'Pretty darned good.' She smirked at him.

'I meant about not being in Worcester. I've been thinking about you all day.'

'I'm fine,' she said. 'Better now that I've seen you. Oh, and I've had an idea.' She scooted around to face him. 'Wool. We've got loads of it at the farm, and I've been thinking about what we can do with it.'

'What do you normally do?'

'We sell it for pennies, but some farmers compost it or burn it. No one wants it, see? People don't buy as many wool carpets these days, and when it comes to clothes they prefer man-made fabrics. There's just not the call for wool that there once was.'

'What's your idea?'

'I've got a couple. But first, do you remember that Lilian used to spin her own yarn?'

'Now that you mention it, I do. It used to fascinate me when I was little. Gosh, I'd forgotten all about that.'

Emily's face fell. 'Bugger. I was hoping you might still have her old spinning wheel.'

A grin spread across his face. 'I don't have it, but *Bea* does. It's in her attic. I saw it at Christmas when I was getting the tree down. The daft old thing was going to climb the ladder herself. I keep telling her that she's going to do herself a mischief one of these days.'

'Do you think she would let me have it?'

'I don't see why not. Ask her tomorrow. I take it you're thinking about spinning your own wool, but then what are you going to do with it?'

'Sell it, of course. I'm also planning on dyeing it myself using plant and not chemical fabric dye. And if that fails, I'll make those wool logs you were on about! There are hundreds of things you can do with wool — that's only the tip of the iceberg.'

'You're really excited about this, aren't you?'

'I'm more excited about this than I've been about anything else in my entire life. Except for when I won the egg and spoon race in year three.' She wrinkled her nose. 'And *you.*'

'I was hoping you'd say that — although I'm not sure I want to be compared to an egg and spoon race, especially since I remember them not being real eggs.'

Emily studied his face. It was glowing with the memory of their seven-year-old selves, and her heart melted. They had come such a long way since then. She never would have thought that she and Mac would end up together, that he had felt the same way about her, and neither of them had realised.

Right now, she wanted to show him exactly how she felt...

'Are you ready for dessert yet?' she asked, glancing at him coyly from underneath her lashes.

He drew in a slow breath, his gaze boring into her. 'I believe I might be.'

And with that, he took her hand and led her upstairs...

CHAPTER 21

The shrill trilling noise was piercing and Emily woke with a start.

'Whassit?' she mumbled, opening her eyes to see Mac's hand reaching out to pat the bedside cabinet.

Feeling for his phone, he found it, blinked several times, then squinted at the screen.

Holding it to his ear, he croaked 'Gran?' then cleared his throat. 'What's up? It's early.'

How early, Emily wondered, rubbing her eyes. It was light outside, so she guessed it must be later than five a.m.

Mac abruptly sat up. 'You're not making sense. Gran, what's happened?' He turned stricken eyes to Emily. His summer tan had paled and she knew something awful must have happened. 'Don't try to move. Have you called for an ambulance?'

Oh, God... Emily's heart was in her mouth.

Mac flung the sheet back and leapt out of bed. 'I'm on my way. Give me five minutes.' He dropped his phone on the bed and grabbed the clothes he had abandoned on the floor last night.

'What's happened?' Emily swung her feet to the floor, scanning the carpet for her own discarded clothing.

'Gran's had a fall.'

'Can I do anything? Ring for an ambulance?'

'She's done it, I think. She wasn't making a great deal of sense.' He zipped up his jeans. 'On second thoughts, I'd better ring anyway.'

'Finish getting dressed, I'll do it.'

Whilst Mac searched for his keys and wallet, Emily dialled 999. 'They're on their way,' she said, after a brief conversation.

Hastily, she scrambled into her cut-offs, yanking the T-shirt she had borrowed last night over her head, and pounded down the stairs after him. As she reached the bottom step, she heard a siren in the distance.

'That was quick,' he said, and his already pale face grew even paler. 'They must think it's serious. Oh God.' He dashed into the kitchen. 'Where the hell did I put my keys?'

Emily spied them on top of the microwave. She snatched them up and handed them to him. 'Here you go. Don't panic, they said they received a call over an hour ago,' she told him.

Mac darted past her and into the hall. 'And Gran left it until *now* to phone me? That woman will be the death of me,' he growled. When he realised what he'd said, he flinched.

Flinging open the front door, he took off at a run, Emily sprinting after him. The siren grew louder, a rising, swooping call that made her stomach constrict and her blood turn to ice.

As she ran through the village, she was dimly aware that it must be later than she'd originally thought. The corner shop was already open, and two or three cars passed them with people on their way to work. She also noticed a few faces peering through their windows, and on rounding the corner onto the road where Bea lived, she saw one or two people emerge from their houses.

Sirens weren't common in Glynafon...

Bea's house was a five-minute walk from Mac's. They did it in just over two.

The ambulance was sitting outside, and one of the paramedics was pounding on Bea's door, the other peering through the living room window, her hands cupped around the glass to see inside.

'I've got a key,' Mac called, as he dashed towards the door. Unlocking it, he stood to the side to let them in, saying, 'I think she's in the bathroom.'

Emily hung back, reluctant to go inside in case she got in the way. Biting her lip, she waited on the path and strained to listen. She could hear voices, but not what they were saying.

'What's going on? Is Bea all right?' Lucy's voice called from behind, and Emily turned to see her friend standing on the other side of the gate. 'I was just on my way to work and I saw the ambulance.'

'Bea's had a fall,' Emily said, glancing over her shoulder at the house. Mac and the paramedics were still upstairs.

'I hope she's OK.'

'Me, too.'

'How did it happen?'

'I don't know. Mac got a call from her about ten minutes ago.'

Lucy frowned. 'You must have flown down the hill to get here so fast.' She glanced up and down the road, as though looking for Emily's car.

'I was already in the village,' Emily admitted. She thought about telling her friend about her and Mac, but now wasn't the time or the place. However, Emily didn't need to explain – for Lucy, the penny had dropped.

'You spent the night with *Mac*?' She sounded as though she couldn't quite believe it.

But then, Lucy had warned her about him, so maybe she was surprised that Emily hadn't heeded her advice. When she got the chance, Emily would tell Lucy that she was wrong about him.

'Uh, yes, I did.'

'I see.' Lucy's lips thinned. 'I'll leave you to it. Make sure to tell Mac I was asking after him, and I hope Bea is OK.'

So did Emily.

She turned her attention back to the house and continued her vigil.

Eventually, after what seemed like hours, Bea was brought out on a stretcher. With an oxygen mask on her face and connected to tubes and monitors, she looked weak and frail. Her eyes were closed, and she had blood on her forehead.

Mac followed slowly, his expression despairing.

'They think it's a heart attack,' he said, 'They're not sure whether she fell and banged her head first and then suffered a heart attack, or whether she had the heart attack, then fell. They think she might have a concussion, too.' He swallowed hard. 'At least she had the wherewithal to phone for an ambulance. I dread to think what would have happened if she'd knocked herself out. She might have...'. He swallowed again, fighting back tears.

Emily longed to wrap her arms around him, to comfort him, but she didn't know whether he'd welcome it, so she settled for stroking his arm.

'I usually call in before work,' he said, 'but I wasn't planning to this morning.'

Emily guessed why, and she also guessed he was being eaten up by the guilt of what might have been. 'You weren't to know.'

He said, 'I'm going to fetch my car and follow the ambulance.'

The paramedics finished loading Bea into it, the driver started the engine, and the ambulance pulled away, blue lights flashing. Mac set off up the road in the opposite direction, at a quick jog.

'Do you want me to come with you?' Emily called after him.

He didn't hear her, and within seconds he had rounded the corner and was out of sight, leaving Emily alone and feeling helpless.

The only thing she could do now was go home, wait for news, and pray that his grandmother would pull through.

***

'Thank God! I've been so worried!' Emily was clutching her mobile to her ear with one hand and trying to bolt a gate with the other. The mechanism was stiff, and she gave up for the moment, leaning against it to keep it from swinging open. The cows on the other side glared at her balefully.

'You and me both,' Mac said. He had phoned her to confirm that Bea had indeed suffered a heart attack but was now sitting up in bed. 'They operated a couple of hours ago,' he was saying. 'She's had a stent put in.'

'How about the injury to her head?'

'Superficial. She's not got a concussion, thankfully, because I don't think they would have been able to go ahead with the procedure if that had been the case, even though it's done under local anaesthetic.'

'How is she in herself?' Emily asked. She had been on tenterhooks all day, waiting for news. Several times she had reached for her phone, but hadn't called, knowing that Mac would ring her when there was something to report. She had kept telling herself that no news was good news, and trying not to cry.

He said, 'Hang on, I'm just getting in my car.' There was the sound of a car door shutting and the engine starting. 'She's putting on a brave face, but as you can imagine, she's shocked and scared. It has knocked her for six. I've been in contact with Mum and Dad, and they're on their way back, but it's going to take them two days to get here.'

'Is there anything I can do?' Emily asked. She hated feeling so helpless.

'Actually, there is. Do you think you can meet me at Bea's house? I want to pick up some things for her, because they're keeping her in for a few days. She'll need a nightie, and a toothbrush, and...' He ground to a halt, and Emily sensed he was overwhelmed by it all.

'Of course I can.'

'Thank you!' He sounded relieved. 'I didn't fancy rooting through her undies drawer.'

Emily was more than happy to help, and she guessed she might have a better idea of what the old lady might want. Mac was perfectly capable of packing some nightclothes and toiletries for Bea, but would he think to pack her comb, or the moisturiser she liked to put on her hands? And he was right – he wouldn't find it easy picking out knickers and a bra for his grandmother, or a suitable outfit for her journey home when they discharged her.

Emily was already waiting outside Bea's house when he pulled up in his jeep, and as soon as he got out, he enveloped her in a hug, burying his face in her neck.

'You don't know how much I need this,' he said, his voice muffled.

Emily held him tighter, breathing in his gorgeous scent and relishing the feel of his arms around her. Was it only this morning she had woken next to him, after having enjoyed the most wonderful night of her life. She hadn't had time to process it yet, too concerned about Bea, but now that the old lady was out of the woods, Emily felt able to think about what impact last night would have on their relationship – a damned good one, she decided. It would cement their commitment to each other, and not only that, it had been *fun*.

Feeling slightly hot under the collar at the memory, she thought it best not to dwell on that right now and she pulled away. 'Will you be at the hospital long?'

'No, visiting hours will be over by the time I get there. I'll drop the bag off and come straight home.'

'Shall I cook something for when you get back? I bet you haven't eaten all day.' Emily hadn't had much of an appetite either, but at least she'd had the opportunity to eat if she'd wanted. She guessed Mac wouldn't have moved from Bea's side or left the relatives' room if that was where he had been stationed.

He kissed her on the nose. 'That would be lovely. I'll message you when I'm leaving.'

'Tell you what, if you drop me at your house on the way to the hospital, I can start cooking now so it'll be ready for when you get back.'

'Good idea, if you're sure you don't mind.'

Emily arched an eyebrow. 'Stop being silly – of course I don't mind. Even if I wasn't your girlfriend, I would still want to take care of you.'

'You're so sweet.'

The complement made her blush. 'Let's get on,' she told him. The sooner we're done, the sooner you'll be back and I can get some food into you.'

Mac led the way into Bea's bedroom, looking around awkwardly, as though he didn't know where to start.

'You go find a bag or a small case, and while you're doing that I'll pop everything I think she might need on the bed,' Emily suggested.

He seemed to be relieved to have the responsibility taken off his shoulders. 'I think there's an overnight bag in the spare room,' he said, and went to retrieve it, leaving Emily to decide what to put in it.

She started with a couple of nighties, which she found in a drawer, and added the dressing gown which was draped over an ottoman at the foot of the bed. Then she gathered up a pair of slippers, some underwear, a skirt and a lightweight top. She was in the middle of choosing some shoes, when she heard a knock on the door.

'I'll get it,' Mac said, dropping a small suitcase on the bed. 'It's probably one of the neighbours wanting to know how she is.'

It wasn't.

Emily recognised Lucy's voice, as her friend said, 'I saw your car outside. How is your gran?'

'Better now, hopefully.' Mac's answer was gruff, and Emily guessed he was keen to get a bag packed and return to the hospital.

'What was it? I heard she might have had a heart attack.'

'She did. She's had a stent put in. Look, Lucy, I—'

Lucy cut him off. 'The poor thing. I hope she's better soon. If there's anything I can do, *anything at all*, just ask.'

That was nice of her, Emily thought.

'Thanks. I can manage.'

'I'm here for you Macsen, you know that, don't you? If you need a shoulder to cry on, I'm your girl. I'll *always* be your girl.'

Emily stiffened and stopped what she was doing. What an odd thing to say.

Curious, wondering what Lucy meant, Emily crept to the top of the stairs. She didn't know why she didn't make her presence known to Lucy, but a sixth sense told her to keep quiet.

Mac said, 'Lucy, not that again. I've told you, I'm not interested.'

Lucy's tone was sharp, 'You were *very* interested not so long ago, if I remember rightly.'

'That was wrong of me and I'm sorry. I was hurting and—' Mac had lowered his voice.

'You *used* me.'

'I didn't,' he protested. 'I genuinely care about you, Lucy, but it should never have happened.'

Emily gasped and her mouth dropped open. What was he *saying*? *What* should never have happened? Had Mac and Lucy kissed? Had they *slept* together? Had they been in a relationship?

The questions whirled around her head, making her dizzy. She put a steadying hand on the newel post, and quietly descended one step, then another.

Lucy spat, 'Why are you pushing me away? It's because of *her*, isn't it? Ha! Please don't kid yourself that she cares about you, because she doesn't, not one little bit.'

'That's where you're wrong – she does.' Mac sounded certain, as he should be. Emily more than cared about Mac, she *loved* him.

'Bullshit! You're *rebound* sex, that's all. Just like I was to you; a bit of nookie to help you get over being dumped. It serves you right to have a taste of your own medicine. I hope you don't think she's staying in Glynafon because of *you*. Emily is here because she doesn't have any *choice*, not now that the book she was counting on to get the farm out of a hole is worthless.' Lucy's laugh was devoid of humour. 'The only reason she's not in Worcester right now, is because her parents will lose the farm if she leaves.'

Emily heard Mac's sharp inhalation.

Abruptly, he glanced over his shoulder, his eyes widening when he saw Emily standing halfway down the stairs. His expression was as full of disbelief, shock and hurt as was Emily's own. *Mac and Lucy had slept together!* Why hadn't he told her? Why hadn't *Lucy*?

Emily stared back at him, shaking her head. This was not happening. She was not going to be the other woman, especially not when it was one of her best friends. When had their relationship ended? Before or *after* Mac had kissed her?

Slowly, she descended the remaining steps, her legs shaking. Lucy had been right all along. She had tried to warn her, but Emily had refused to listen. She had fallen for his story about having his heart broken – how could she have been so stupid?

She reached the bottom step, knowing that the pain would hit her soon, but right now all she felt was numb. How could he do this? He had *made love* to her, goddamit. But worse than that, he had led her to believe he had fallen for her, just to get her into bed. And to her shame, it had worked. Guessing he must have done the same to Lucy, her chin wobbled and she felt the acrid sting of tears.

Willing herself not to cry, she glared at him.

To her surprise, he didn't attempt to explain what he had done, or excuse it. Instead, the initial shock and disbelief she had seen on his face when he'd noticed her on the stairs, had changed to anger.

His eyes hardened, his jaw tensed, and he shook his head. 'Unbelievable,' he muttered.

Was that all he had to say for himself? She wasn't expecting him to apologise, but she expected him to say something more than 'unbelievable'.

Her heart breaking, tears threatening to spill over, Emily marched to the door, hardly registering the rather smug look on Lucy's face as Mac shrank to the side to let her pass.

A sob caught in her throat at his obvious reluctance to even touch her, now that she had discovered what he was really like and, biting it back, she stormed past both of them.

It wasn't until she was halfway home that she remembered something Lucy said… 'I'll always be your girl'… and she understood that just like her, Lucy was also in love with Mac.

'Damn him!' she yelled, scattering a flock of alarmed sheep as she stomped across a field. 'Damn him to hell.' Then she staggered to a halt and with tears pouring down her face, she sank to the ground and buried her face in her hands.

In the space of two weeks, she had lost not one, but *two* boyfriends, her house, her job and probably one of her oldest friends, and if that wasn't enough, her parents were in danger of losing the farm...

What more was there left to lose?

CHAPTER 22

Emily checked her phone for the umpteenth time: still nothing from Mac. Whilst she was furious at him for leading her on, a part of her (the heartbroken part) was desperate to hear from him. Thankfully her pride and sheer stubbornness wouldn't allow her to contact him first.

Anyway, what was there to say: thanks for not telling me you've been shagging one of my best friends? Thanks for breaking my heart, the way you have broken Lucy's? Because there was no doubt in Emily's mind that Lucy was in love with him.

Just as Emily herself was.

In a fit of temper, she threw her phone across the barn. Luckily for her it landed on a pile of loose straw and bounced gently.

This was all Cole's fault. If he hadn't done the dirty on her, she wouldn't be in this position. At this time on a Wednesday afternoon, she should be looking forward to leaving the office and debating whether she needed to pop into the supermarket on the way home. She wouldn't be up to her elbows in mud (yes, it had rained – torrential downpours falling from black, lowering clouds, the weather perfectly reflecting her mood) and sobbing in the barn where no one could hear her.

How had things fallen apart so quickly? On Monday she had been so utterly, blissfully happy.

Two days later, she was utterly, desperately miserable.

Emily recognised she was being unfair blaming everything on Cole. Allowing herself to fall in love with Mac had been down to her, and had nothing to do with Cole, even if Lucy accused her of having rebound sex with Mac.

She hadn't. She'd had first-love-never-got-over-him sex, and it had been glorious.

It had taken coming back to Glynafon to realise that she had never lost her teenage feelings for Mac. They had been lurking in the depths of her heart, waiting for their chance to emerge and show her what true love was really like – because what she felt for Mac was ten times what she had felt for Cole. A *hundred* times, even.

Maybe Cole had sensed something, which might explain why he hadn't been able to fully commit to her

– because *she* hadn't been able to fully commit to *him*, even if she hadn't been aware of it at the time.

It was sobering to think that if she and Cole hadn't split up, she probably wouldn't have met Mac again and she certainly wouldn't have rediscovered her feelings for him. She would have spent the rest of her life not knowing love could be like this.

Right now, Emily wished that was precisely what *had* happened, because whoever said it was better to have loved and lost than never to have loved at all, was an absolute arsehole and didn't know what they were talking about. And whoever said that the first cut was the deepest, got it spot on. Mac had stabbed her in the heart as surely as though he had plunged a knife into her chest. And twisted it, for good measure.

Poor Lucy… poor her.

They had both been played by the same man, had both been taken in by him, and now they were both paying the price in heartache and lost friendship.

Emily wished Lucy had just told her straight that she was in love with Mac, because if she had, Emily wouldn't have gone near him if she'd known how her friend felt. Maybe, in time, Lucy would forgive her.

'Here you are!' Dina exclaimed. 'I've been looking all over for you. Have you heard how Bea is? When are they discharging her?'

'I don't know.' Emily retrieved her phone and as she bent down she surreptitiously wiped her eyes. She pretended to look at it, as an excuse not to look at her mother.

'When are John and Ivy back? Would Mac like to pop in for tea this evening? I bet he's not eating properly.'

Emily remembered the meal she had offered to cook for him yesterday and wondered whether he had bothered to eat anything at all.

'Stop it with the questions, Mum,' she snapped, and immediately felt contrite for taking out her angst on her mother. 'Sorry.'

'Emily, what's wrong? Is it Bea? I know it was a shock, but she's already on the mend. So what is it?'

'Nothing.'

'Stop that at once, Emily Lilian Oak. I can tell when you're lying. You can't fool me, I'm your mother.'

'Yeah, right.' Emily huffed out a humorous laugh. Her mother definitely *couldn't* tell when she was lying, otherwise she would have realised there was more to Emily's story than her saying she wanted to stay in Glynafon because she had realised her home was here, not Worcester. She hadn't been telling an untruth, but neither had she told them the whole story.

'What's that supposed to mean?' her mother demanded.

'Nothing.' Emily knew she was being sullen, but she couldn't deal with this right now.

'Are you regretting packing your job in?' Dina persisted. 'Is that it? Look, I know you don't like working on the farm, but it's not going to be for long. You'll soon find another job: give it time, it's not been a week yet.'

'Mum, you guys can't manage this place on your own, so I'll have to help out even when I do find a job.'

'Good gracious, don't be silly! We don't expect you to do a full day's work *and* do chores around the farm.'

'You used to make me do chores when I was in school.'

'It was character-forming. Anyway, that was different. I didn't want you growing up thinking that everything would be done for you. But you're a grown woman now, you can make your own decisions. Besides…' Dina sat on the nearest bale. 'There's something you need to know – your dad and I are selling the farm.'

Emily froze. *'What?'*

'Wonderful, isn't it? I knew you'd be pleased. No more wrangling sheep or herding cows. No more working seven days a week without a break. No more mud!' Dina had a blissful look on her face as she uttered the last word. 'I *hate* mud.'

'You're selling the farm.' Emily was stunned.

'Yes, we heard yesterday that someone had put in an offer, which we've accepted, but with all the worry about Bea, we didn't get around to telling you.'

'But… but…'

'I know it's a shock, but you've got to admit it's for the best. Your dad and I are getting on and, frankly, I don't want to be working this hard when we're in our seventies and eighties. I know farming is a way of life and we will miss it, but life is for living, and that's what we intend to do.' She paused, lost in her own world as her expression became dreamy. 'When John and Ivy bought that motor home of theirs, it got me and your dad thinking. There are so many places we want to see, so many things we want to do, but we couldn't do any of them because we are tied to the farm. The solution was to sell it. We've got a decent price for it, too. We're going to buy a nice bungalow in the village. Don't worry, it's got three bedrooms, so you won't be homeless. It's even got a couple of nice-sized outbuildings, which you could convert into a house of your own if you wanted, further down the line. And there'll be plenty left for us to do what we've always wanted to do – go travelling.'

'Are you going to buy a motor home?' Emily's voice was flat.

'Good God, no! We've no intention of roughing it. We've had years and years of that! It'll be four- and five-star hotels for us. I don't want to have to lift a finger: I don't want to do so much as boil an egg. It's going to be luxury all the way from now on. Venice, Rome, the Amalfi coast – and that's just for starters.'

'You've sold the farm,' she repeated, then she began to laugh, tears streaming down her face as she doubled over, hysteria rippling through her. Emily had turned her whole life upside down for *nothing*.

***

'I wish you had told us about the book,' her dad said, a short time later after Dina had called him in from the field to take a look at their daughter, who appeared to be having a breakdown.

Emily had been alternatively laughing and sobbing for a good ten minutes, seriously alarming her mother.

The three of them were now sitting around the kitchen table, mugs of tea in their hands and the remains of a plate of Welsh cakes between them. Emily had managed to force one of the sweet treats down her throat, just to ease her mum's worry, but all it had done was made her feel even more nauseous.

'So do I,' Emily replied, with feeling. If she had told them as soon as she'd found out about it, and if she had shared with them her plan to plough the proceeds of the sale back into the farm, then all of the subsequent hoo-ha could have been avoided. And by hoo-ha, she meant the car crash of handing in her notice, sleeping with Mac and having her heart torn to shreds. She would have returned to Worcester and would have put her feelings for Mac to the back of her mind and never allowed them to see the light of day again.

'At least it's not totally worthless,' her mum soothed. 'And it's not as though we need the money.' She smiled at Graham. 'Not now.'

'And you won't be homeless,' her dad pointed out. 'You can live in the bungalow for as long as you like. In fact, we'll be away so often that you'll have the place to yourself for most of the time.'

Great, Emily thought – along with everything else, she would now also be lonely.

'Or I might just go back to Worcester,' she said. 'I should easily be able to find a job. But can I stay here until I do? I don't want to impose on Ava and Ben for longer than I have to.'

Dina reached across the table and squeezed her hand. 'I'm sorry, my lovely. Between us we've made a right hash of your life, haven't we? Although… I did think you and Mac might have something going on. How will he feel about you moving back to Worcester?'

Emily pressed her lips together before answering. 'He won't give two hoots. It will probably make his life easier.' She took a deep breath; she might as well tell them, because they would find out eventually. Glynafon was a small place…

'I thought we did have a connection,' she began, 'but it turns out he doesn't feel the same way.'

'I don't believe it! Bea said—' Dina stopped abruptly, spots of colour appearing on her cheeks.

'Have you been matchmaking too?' Emily demanded. She knew Bea had been sticking her oar in, and after the towel incident on the landing when Mac had helped with the shearing, Emily had suspected her mum might also have been trying to set her up.

'No…' Dina's expression was one of wide-eyed innocence that didn't fool Emily in the slightest.

'I wish you and Bea hadn't interfered, Mum,' she said sadly. 'He's the reason I'm going back to Worcester. He's been dating Lucy.'

'Has he been two-timing you?' Her mum was indignant.

'No. He and Lucy were over ages ago – but that's not the point.'

'Lucy tried to warn me. She said that when it came to women, he was just out for what he could get. But I didn't listen. He told me some sob story about breaking up with his ex because he wanted to settle down and she didn't, but I think he was just trying to get me to feel sorry for him, and for me to think that we were in the same boat, so to speak.'

'Did Lucy like him a lot?' her mother asked.

'I think she was in love with him. She still is.'

'And you? Are *you* in love with him too?'

Emily's face said what her lips couldn't, as once again she struggled to hold back tears.

'Oh, my sweet girl.'

Her mother's pity was Emily's undoing, and as the tears fell, she wondered whether she would ever stop crying over Macsen Rogers.

CHAPTER 23

'Bea is asking for you,' Emily's mother announced the following day. 'I went to visit her this afternoon. She wants to see you.'

'Have they discharged her yet?'

'No. She reckons it'll be Monday before she's released. She makes it sound as though she's being held against her will. She calls herself an inmate, not a patient.'

'How is she?'

'Chirpy, cantankerous, weaker than she'd like to admit. Thank God John and Ivy arrived home this morning. I bumped into them on the way in. They intend to stay in Glynafon until she's fully recovered, but the first thing Bea said to me when I saw her was that she didn't need mollycoddling and she wished Mac hadn't bothered them.'

Emily wanted to ask whether Bea had said anything more about him, but she didn't. It was better not to poke that hornet's nest. The less she heard his name mentioned, the more chance she had of keeping a lid on her emotions. In public, at least. Alone, especially at night, her thoughts turned to him, stealing her breath and crushing her heart, until sleep was a distant memory. Last night, she had crept downstairs to watch TV and knit – anything to keep her hands busy so she didn't chew her fingernails to shreds, and keep her mind from picking at the scab of her broken heart.

It hadn't worked. She had no idea what she had watched, although the jumper was coming on a treat.

'I'll go see her tomorrow,' Emily said.

'Can you visit her this evening? I kind of promised you would – and I said you'd take her a pasty and a Welsh cake. She claims the food is inedible.'

Emily shrugged. 'I suppose I can. I've got nothing else to do.'

Dina nodded in satisfaction. 'I'll pick some strawberries and you can take those in too, plus a couple of apples. Oh, and I bought a magazine for her on the way home.' Dina's expression softened. 'She'll be pleased to see you – she thinks the world of you.'

Emily also thought the world of Bea, and she felt guilty for not messaging Mac to ask how she was.

Instead, she had left it up to her mum to find out on the village grapevine.

Two hours later, Emily was clutching a bag of goodies and trying to find her way to the ward Bea was on. The hospital was a rabbit warren of departments and corridors, and there were people everywhere, but she was eventually pointed in the right direction, and she slapped a cheerful smile on her face and attempted to put a spring in her step as she entered the ward.

Then she stopped.

Bea was nowhere in sight.

Emily scanned the seven beds, but none of them contained Bea. However, the furthest bed from the door couldn't be seen because the curtains had been pulled around it, and she suspected Bea might be behind them.

Reluctant to go charging in, in case the old lady was being examined by a doctor, or having a bed bath, or something, she went back into the corridor and walked up to the nurses' station to ask.

'That's fine, you can go see her,' the nurse said. 'She just asked for the curtains to be drawn so she could have some privacy.'

Privacy for what, Emily wondered, but considering her mother had said that Bea wasn't coping well with her 'incarceration' maybe she didn't want to interact with the other patients on the ward.

Her cheery smile back in place, Emily drew the curtain to one side, and halted.

Her smile faded and her tummy somersaulted. 'Mac!'

'Emily!'

What was he doing here? *I mean, I know what he's doing here,* she thought, *but why was he doing it now?* Surely he could have visited his grandmother at some other time?

Mac looked equally surprised. And displeased.

He was sitting by Bea's bedside, but as soon as he clapped eyes on Emily he got to his feet.

'Stay there, Macsen Rogers,' Bea commanded, in a voice more suited to a sergeant on a parade ground than a frail old lady who had just suffered a heart attack. 'You too, Emily. I want a word with you both. Why have you two fallen out? And don't try telling me you haven't, because it's as obvious as a snout on a pig that you're not speaking.'

Mac glowered at his grandmother. Emily glowered at Mac.

When he felt her gaze on him, he turned to glower at Emily instead, so Emily hastily rearranged her features and stared at Bea.

'Well?' Bea demanded. 'Are you going to stand there like a couple of goldfish in a bowl, or are you going to tell me what's going on?'

'Ask her,' Mac growled, at the same time Emily muttered, 'Ask him.'

'I'm asking both of you. Mac, you go first.'

Mac's glower deepened into a scowl. 'She led me on,' he began.

'I did no such thing!' Emily interjected before he could say anything more.

Mac waved a hand in the air. 'Whatever.' He said to Bea, 'Did she tell you that the only reason she didn't go back to her precious Worcester, is because she had no choice – that her parents would lose the farm if she didn't?'

'Yes, she did.' Bea's reply was mild.

'And you're OK with that?'

'Why wouldn't I be? She was doing her best to help her parents out – I'd say that was an admirable thing to do.'

'But if that book had been worth anything, she would have given them the money and buggered off.'

'She might have done, and that would have been a shame because she wouldn't have had time to realise that she loves you.'

'I do not!' Emily protested hotly.

Bea snorted. 'Pull the other one, my girl. I didn't fall out of last year's Christmas cracker.'

Emily scowled. 'Even if I do – and I'm not admitting to anything – *he* doesn't love *me*, so I don't know what he's getting all high and mighty about.'

'He does love you,' Bea said.

Mac made a strangled sound and Emily shot him a look. He was staring intently at the floor, a muscle in his jaw twitching.

'He does not,' she retorted. 'He slept with Lucy.'

Bea chuckled. 'So? You slept with Cole.'

Emily's mouth dropped open and she gasped. 'I was *living* with him. He was my *boyfriend*, so *of course* I slept with him.' She was aware that the noise level in the ward had dimmed significantly, and she guessed everyone could hear exactly what was being said.

'But he wasn't your boyfriend when you spent the night with Mac, was he?'

'No, but—'

'And Lucy wasn't Mac's girlfriend when he took you to bed?'

Emily cringed. She had never been so embarrassed in her life. She sneaked a glance at Mac out of the corner of her eye. He was positively squirming and his cheeks were an interesting shade of pink. As were her own, she suspected.

'So, what's the problem?' Bea persisted. 'You were both single. You weren't hurting anyone.'

337

'We were hurting Lucy,' Emily protested. 'She loves him.'

Mac barked out a bitter laugh. 'She hates me. For your information—' his voice was loaded with sarcasm '—when I moved back to the village, she threw herself at me, despite me telling her I wasn't interested.'

'You slept with her. I heard her say so, and you didn't deny it!' Emily was flabbergasted.

'To my shame, I did. I'd just heard that Verity was pregnant and had got engaged to the baby's father. The baby she refused to have with me. I know it's no excuse, but Lucy caught me at a weak moment. One minute she was sympathising with me, the next she was kissing me. I never should have let it go that far, and I apologised to her straight away. She wasn't pleased.'

'Poor Lucy, I bet she wasn't,' Emily snapped back.

'She's been stalking him for months,' Bea said, and Mac flinched. 'Mac hasn't said a word about it, but I've got eyes in my head. She's forever walking that dog up and down my road and Mac's, spying on him. She's bad-mouthed him all over the village, yet despite that, she keeps trying to get him to go out with her. If you ask me, she's unhinged.'

'Or in love,' Emily countered.

'You don't treat people you love like that. She's just cheesed off that Mac turned her down.'

'I don't believe it. She—' Emily stopped. Suddenly, Lucy's expression when she informed Mac that all he was to Emily was rebound sex, swam into her mind. She had looked smug, self-satisfied, triumphant even. She had enjoyed taking him down.

Emily realised that Bea was right… Lucy didn't love Mac. She had been out for revenge, and she had got it.

And not only that… she had stuck the knife into Emily, too. Lucy must have overheard Emily tell Bea about the book, when she was walking past Bea's house the other day.

Emily swallowed – what had happened to her friend to make her so vindictive?

Mac and Bea were watching her. Bea's face was expectant. Mac's was blank.

'Lucy doesn't love you,' Emily said to him.

His expression didn't change, but there was a hint of acknowledgement in his eyes, that could have been relief that she believed him.

She drew in a long, deep breath, and added, 'But *I* do.'

The silence beyond those hideously patterned curtains was grave-like. Not even a machine beeped.

Bea raised her eyebrows at Mac.

He didn't make a sound, and was preternaturally still. Then slowly, so slowly he dipped his head in a nod, and said, 'And I love you.'

Almost before Mac had finished speaking, the ward erupted in a cacophony of cheering, clapping and whistles.

Emily couldn't hear herself think. But she could *feel*. And what she felt was a rush of love so strong it made her dizzy with the enormity of it. Her heart thudded and she trembled from head to toe, her mouth was dry and she couldn't catch her breath.

'Oh, for God's sake kiss the girl,' she heard Bea say, and then she was in Mac's arms, and he was kissing her so thoroughly that the world around her faded, until they were the only two people in it.

Then a voice from the bed piped up, 'Good. Glad that's sorted. Now bugger off – some of us haven't been well, you know…'

CHAPTER 24

Three months later

Emily teased the wool fibres apart so she only had a few strands in her hand, caught hold of the end of the spun yarn and firmly held the two pieces together, then she set the wheel to spinning, her foot working the treadle to keep it turning.

It was immensely satisfying to watch the clump of washed and carded fleece, transform into yarn. It was soothing too, and she was able to let her mind roam, while her hands and her feet got on with the business of spinning.

She was just wondering what colour she should dye the resulting yarn, when she heard Mac's foot on the step leading to her workroom and her face broke into a smile.

In two strides he was at her side and bending to kiss her.

Emily stopped the wheel, and tilted her head back so he could kiss her properly.

'Mmm,' she murmured. 'You taste nice.'

'You don't taste too bad yourself. Are you done for the day?'

'What time is it?' When she was in her workroom, created out of one of the outbuildings that sat to the rear of her parents' bungalow, Emily often lost track of time, especially when she was spinning or felting. In it, she was cocooned from the outside world: it was just her, the wool, and a soft playlist to fill the empty air with soothing music.

'Four-thirty,' he said.

'I suppose I'd better stop. I want to give my old boss a call and see if they are ready for the next delivery of wool.'

Emily had sounded out the company she used to work for about using fleece as insulation – something they had been considering before she'd left, but hadn't got further than that. In the past three months, Emily had convinced them to trial it, using the wool she had taken from the farm before it had changed hands, and she had been working hard to present a business model that would earn her a modest income from the wool she would supply them with.

The company was now conducting the initial production phase, and so far everything was going swimmingly. Not only that, but she had also used her love of yarn and felt to begin a cottage industry, with the emphasis on sustainable, locally sourced wool, that was both environmentally friendly and biodegradable, especially since she only used natural plant-based dyes.

The demand for her products was growing, and she could see a time in the not-too-distant future when she would need to scale up operations.

Emily got to her feet and stretched, and Mac took the opportunity to catch her around the waist and draw her towards him.

'Do you know how much I love you?' he murmured into her hair.

'Nope, not got a clue,' she teased.

'In that case, can I show you?' He ran his hands down her back to cup her bottom.

'Later,' she giggled. 'I've got a phone call to make, remember?'

'Can't it wait?'

'I suppose five minutes won't matter…'

'What I've got in mind will take a lot longer than five minutes.' His voice was low, and she could feel the sexy rumble of it go through her chest, to penetrate deep into her heart.

She tingled with anticipation. Maybe that phone call could wait, after all…?

Locking up the workroom, Emily knew how lucky she was. She had a man who loved her, her family nearby (when they were in the country, that is) and a thriving business. And as she stepped into Lilian's house, which she now shared with Mac, she caught sight of something that had pride of place on the shelf in the living room.

Lilian's little black book.

She owed that little black book a lot – because without it she might never have realised that she had been in love with Mac all along. And although it mightn't be worth the thousands she had originally hoped, to her it was absolutely priceless.

ABOUT THE AUTHOR

Liz Davies writes feel-good, light-hearted stories with a hefty dose of romance, a smattering of humour, and a great deal of love.

She's married to her best friend, has one grown-up daughter, and when she isn't scribbling away in the notepad she carries with her everywhere (just in case inspiration strikes), you'll find her searching for that perfect pair of shoes. She loves to cook but isn't very good at it, and loves to eat - she's much better at that! Liz also enjoys walking (preferably on the flat), cycling (also on the flat), and lots of sitting around in the garden on warm, sunny days.

She currently lives with her family in Wales, but would ideally love to buy a camper van and travel the world in it.

If you'd like to see what else she's written, then head on over to her website elizabethdaviesauthor.co.uk

Or you can find her on
Twitter: lizdaviesauthor
Facebook: LizDaviesAuthor1

Printed in Great Britain
by Amazon